ACCLAIM FOR

*A Splinter in the Heart:*

"A sensitive treatment of the ubiquitous coming-of-age theme, with the descriptive power of Purdy the poet lending vivid, at times beautiful, images to the narrative of Purdy the prose writer."
— Saskatoon *StarPhoenix*

"Purdy creates a number of scenes and images that carry conviction and power."
— *Books in Canada*

"A touching, semi-autobiographical coming-of-age novel. . . . At times it is brilliant. . . . "
— *Alberta Report*

"We should be grateful for this book. It is a solid addition to Canadian literature. . . ."
— *Brantford Expositor*

"This is a sensual and poetic novel that has all the verve and humour of Purdy's verse combined with some splendid story-telling."
— *East Toronto Weekly*

[Purdy] creates vivid images in a crisp and clear style. . . . Once I began reading it [I] found it difficult to put down. . . . Highly recommended."
— Fredricton *Daily Gleaner*

# BOOKS BY AL PURDY

## POETRY

*The Enchanted Echo* (1944)
*Pressed on Sand* (1955)
*Emu, Remember!* (1956)
*The Crafte So Long to Lerne* (1959)
*The Blur in Between: Poems 1960-61* (1962)
*Poems for All the Annettes* (1962; revised ed. 1968; 3rd ed. 1973)
*The Cariboo Horses* (1965)
*North of Summer: Poems from Baffin Island* (1967)
*Wild Grape Wine* (1968)
*Love in a Burning Building* (1970)
*The Quest for Ouzo* (1971)
*Hiroshima Poems* (1972)
*Selected Poems* (1972)
*On the Bearpaw Sea* (1973; expanded and revised ed. 1994)
*Sex & Death* (1973)
*In Search of Owen Roblin* (1974)
*The Poems of Al Purdy: A New Canadian Library Selection* (1976)
*Sundance at Dusk* (1976)
*A Handful of Earth* (1977)
*At Marsport Drugstore* (1977)
*Moths in the Iron Curtain* (1977)
*No Second Spring* (1977)
*Being Alive: Poems 1958-78* (1978)
*The Stone Bird* (1981)
*Birdwatching at the Equator: The Galapagos Islands Poems* (1982)
*Bursting into Song: An Al Purdy Omnibus* (1982)
*Piling Blood* (1984)
*The Collected Poems of Al Purdy* (1986)
*The Woman on the Shore* (1990)
*Naked With Summer in Your Mouth* (1994)
*Rooms for Rent in the Outer Planets* (1996)
*To Paris Never Again* (1997)
*Beyond Remembering: The Collected Poems of Al Purdy* (2000)

## OTHER

*No Other Country* (prose, 1977)
*The Bukowski/Purdy Letters 1964-1974: A Decade of Dialogue*,
edited by Seamus Cooney (1983)
*Morning and It's Summer: A Memoir* (1983)
*The Purdy – Woodcock Letters: Selected Correspondence, 1964-1984*,
edited by George Galt (1988)
*A Splinter in the Heart* (fiction, 1990)
*Cougar Hunter* (essay on Roderick Haig-Brown, 1993)
*Margaret Laurence – Al Purdy: A Friendship in Letters*, edited by John Lennox (1993)
*Reaching for the Beaufort Sea: An Autobiography* (1993)
*Starting from Ameliasburgh: The Collected Prose of Al Purdy* (1995)
*No One Else Is Lawrence!: A Dozen of D. H. Lawrence's Best Poems* (a critical work,
with Doug Beardsley, 1998)
*The Man Who Outlived Himself: An Appreciation of John Donne* (poetry and prose,
in collaboration with Doug Beardsley, 2000)

# A SPLINTER IN THE HEART

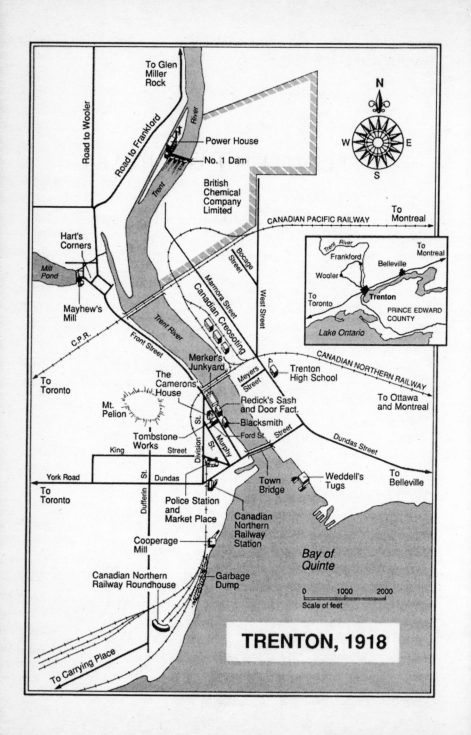

TRENTON, 1918

# A SPLINTER IN THE HEART

# AL PURDY

M&S

Cloth edition published 1990
This trade paperback edition published 2000

**Canadian Cataloguing in Publication Data**

Purdy, Al, 1918–
A splinter in the heart : a novel

ISBN 0-7710-7195-7

I. Title.

PS8531.U8S68 2000     C813'.54     C90-094813-2 rev
PR9199.3.P87S68 2000

We acknowledge the financial support of the Government of Canada
through the Book Publishing Industry Development Program for our
publishing activities. We further acknowledge the support of the
Canada Council for the Arts and the Ontario Arts Council for our
publishing program.

Cover design: Ingrid Paulson
Cover image: C.J. Boyle/Photonica
Map by James Loates

Printed and bound in Canada

McClelland & Stewart Ltd.
*The Canadian Publishers*
481 University Avenue
Toronto, Ontario
M5G 2E9
www.mcclelland.com

1 2 3 4 5    04 03 02 01 00

# AUTHOR'S NOTE

Although parts of the narrative are based on historical events, this is a work of fiction. There are certain instances where I have compressed time, and taken a few liberties with the year 1918, with regard to particular facts and locales.

Some of the people mentioned were alive on October 14, 1918, the date of the Trenton disaster. Several of these have written letters, narratives, or have been interviewed about their experiences. Those mentioned by name include Roy Morrow, Ralph Bonter, Winnifred Gauthier, Ian and Emma McMaster, Gordon Coughlin, British Chemical Company foreman Hayden, Company general manager C.N. Barclay, Alan Dempsey, Joe Barry, Eva Curtis, Mrs. Susan Campney (who was born on the day the munitions factory exploded), Dr. W. Johnson, Corporal Ernest Cunnell, Mr. and Mrs. William Pickell, and Mr. and Mrs. Wesley Hyatt. I have based certain parts of my own narrative on their written memoirs and reminiscences, but in a heightened and dramatized form.

Passages containing information about the cholera epidemics of 1832 and later years were based on historical fact. In 1832, immigrant ships bound for Montreal were stopped and inspected for cholera and typhus at Grosse Isle, a quarantine island in the St. Lawrence River thirty miles downstream from Quebec City. Many victims of the plague were buried on this island.

Sources for information about early Ontario and Quebec lumbering were *Hurling Down the Pine*, by John W. Hughson & Courtney C.J. Bond, Gatineau Historical Society, 1965; *The Upper Ottawa Valley*, by Clyde C. Kennedy, Renfrew County Council, 1970; *A Hundred Years A-Fellin'* by Charlotte Whitton, Gillies Brothers Limited, 1942; and certain issues of the Ontario Historical Society's publications.

I owe special thanks to John Melady for information from his book, *Explosion, Trenton Disaster*, Mika Publishing Co., 1980 (the only book on the subject); and to Dorothy Davies, Chief Librarian, Trenton Public Library and her staff. Thanks are also due to the municipal offices of Trenton. Their map served as a basis for the map that appears in this book. The telegram which appears in this book is an actual message sent during the Trenton emergency, as it was reproduced in *Explosion, Trenton Disaster* by John Melady.

And to Dennis Lee for seven pages of suggestions, many of which were adopted; and Bill Percy, for taking an interest in a neophyte, even if an aged one. But most of all to my wife: for reading, criticizing, and supporting my book during and after periods of discouragement after its two-year gestation period. Often I fled to the bathroom or simply vanished at the mere mention that more revision might be needed. I'm sure I tested this noble woman's nature to its farthest limits.

*Al Purdy*
*Ameliasburg*

# A SPLINTER IN THE HEART

# ONE

# The Runner

# 1

HE WAS GOING INTO THE HOUSE through the woodshed when he heard his name mentioned. He stopped, thinking he might be interrupting something he wasn't meant to hear.

It was Mrs. Morris from next door. "Kevin was first in his class again last month," Mrs. Morris said to Patrick's mother. "He seems to do best in mathematics and languages." She paused and said complacently, "We're very proud of him, John and I."

"And so you should be," Mrs. Cameron said.

Was there a slight intonation of strain in his mother's voice, he wondered. And at what point in the discussion had his own name been mentioned? Uneasily he decided this wasn't a good time to make his presence known. Rather stealthily he withdrew into the bright morning outside.

Gyp, who was half Airedale and the rest unknown, thumped his four-inch tail twice from under the woodshed, then followed Patrick across the road to the river. Patrick stood on Corson's dock, chewing over the fragment of talk he had overheard. There had been a meaningful note in Mrs. Morris's voice, as if she were implying that since Kevin was doing very well, why wasn't he, Patrick, doing just as well.

Kevin was clever, of course. Patrick admired him, even wanted to be like him in some respects. But it was unfair of Mrs. Morris to force a comparison down his mother's throat. He felt a slight surge of resentment, a useless emotion that was nevertheless pleasurable.

He picked up a stone and flung it into the water, about fifty yards or so. Would Kevin have thrown it farther? Go ahead, Kevin, he said to himself, throw the stone a mile! And chuckled. It wouldn't be surprising, since Mrs. Morris's admirable son had outstripped all his Grade 10 classmates at French and Latin, and was a champion athlete as well.

Kevin had been a long-distance runner since public school, and was now brushing aside all opposition at high school field days. A model and exemplar for other boys, especially those living next door. Patrick both admired and resented him, wanted to be like him and hated the thought of it.

He gazed at the blue-black water and consciously let his mind go blank. The late-spring sun dulled his senses and allowed his muscles to slacken. A tall youngster at age sixteen, he looked gawky and raw-boned in movement but curiously graceful in stillness. As if the projecting edges of his limbs and personality had withdrawn to smoothness in repose. His face had the look of pale marble with a few almost unnoticeable freckles across his nose. An ordinary face, one rarely looked at twice by other people. But with a hint of stubbornness around his mouth, mixed with a slight bewilderment in the eyes that gave him an odd expression. Patrick was young enough to be still rather shy and naive at times; and old enough to be almost mature physically.

The Trent River is wide and sluggish as it approaches the town bridge. A half-mile upriver, beyond the Canadian Northern Railway footbridge, creosote works squat near the shore; many acres of black railway ties, piled high by sun-darkened men with bulging muscles. Patrick had watched them work, marching down narrow aisles in tandem between the wooden towers, balancing two hundred pounds and more on their shoulders. They made him feel lazy and excessively grateful that he didn't have to lift such enormous weights, and a little mournful that he probably wasn't strong enough anyway. And he fantasized another sixteen-year-old with huge muscles, his own face hovering above the muscles. He chuckled, and allowed the other boy to escape into nothingness . . . .

Two miles northeast of the river above the creosote works, a thick soup of smoke and smelly garbage spewed upward into the sky from the British Chemical Company's chimneys. Patrick could see a faint blue haze hovering over the giant factory. It occupied a full three hundred acres of countryside, producing sulphuric and nitric acids, guncotton, and T.N.T. in this wartime year of 1918.

Among the townspeople there was some apprehension about their proximity to dangerous explosives. Patrick had heard two or three regulars who occupied chairs at Keddy's Barbershop on Front Street sometimes discussing the munitions plant. These were very old men who used the barbershop as a convivial meeting place rather than for tonsorial purposes. They gossiped.

"That dynamite place," one of the ancients was grumbling. "It'll blow Trenton sky-high and us with it! You mark my words now."

"Yer a scared old woman, Jim Ketcheson," another voice mocked. "Should stay home and hide under the bed."

And the argument continued. Then it was interrupted by a customer, a man of about forty-five, wanting a haircut. Keddy gestured toward the leather and nickel-plated barber's chair as if it were a king's throne. He tucked a cloth under the newcomer's chin.

The old men had fallen silent, appearing not to notice the new arrival, but all the time observing everything about him. "Where ya from?" one of them chirped.

The man eyed them humorously. "Same place as you. Trenton, I guess you'd say. Needed a haircut before leaving town."

Then he relented, realizing that for these old men he was the morning's diversion. "Halifax before that. Name of Hildebrand," he added with a smile.

His interlocutors were silent, curiosity squirming beneath wrinkled foreheads. Then a thought struck all three of them at the same time.

"Halifax," Ketcheson repeated, as if the city's name was dangerous and he was holding it at arm's length like a dead snake. "Halifax!"

Hildebrand knew what they were thinking about. "Yeah, those two ships that ran into each other and blew up the town. I wasn't there at the time."

Ketcheson had elected himself spokesman. "You mind tellin us about it?"

"Nothing much to tell," Hildebrand said, voice muffled by the barber's arm in front of his mouth. "I was stevedorin on the docks, loading ships. Freighters mostly, waiting for their convoys, cargoes of food and arms, whatever it was . . ."

As if he had saved up the question, Ketcheson said, "Why'd you leave Halifax?"

"I don't know exactly," Hildebrand said thoughtfully. "I'd come down from Barrington Street to the harbour that morning, and just stood there before work lookin out at the water. Sea gulls flyin back and forth, a nice day. I stood there a while, nothing in my head. And I thought, better get out of here. Just a hunch about things."

His eyes passed over the old men sitting alertly as crows on a farmer's fence, all three with identical expressions of curiosity and a certain wariness.

"Why'd you come here?" Ketcheson demanded.

"That ought to be obvious," Hildebrand said, a little stiffly now. "I got a job at British Chemical, a good job."

"But you're leaving again?"

"Yes. Time to move on. I get restless."

"How long after you left Halifax before the place got blown up?"

"Not long. I'd been gone only a few days by December 6 when it happened. I was in Trenton for Christmas."

Hildebrand stood up while Keddy brushed him off ceremoniously, the barber's manner somewhere between obsequious and slightly arrogant.

Old Ketcheson stood up, too, determined to ask one more question, mouth working from the effort to speak quickly. "You didn't say why you're leavin Trenton...."

"No reason. Maybe just a hunch."

Hildebrand smiled at them pleasantly from the doorway and left.

Ketcheson glanced at the other regulars significantly. "Just a hunch," he repeated, turning the words into ciphers that meant something different from what they said.

The town of Trenton seemed inhabited mostly by old men, Patrick thought. The young had either gone to war or were working at British Chemical. Every week the local newspaper published melancholy statistics of their deaths in Europe, or reported others as missing in action. Bob Weir's brother's name was posted as missing in France, and Bob himself didn't show up at school for a couple of days. When he did there was a rigid look about his face, and his eyes didn't focus when they looked at you.

Trenton's population was about five thousand, the town divided in two by the river and connected again by an iron bridge between east and west. It was an industrial town, with cooperage mills, the Canadian Northern Railway shops, silver-plating works, Mayhew's gristmill, and a sawmill at the north end. Mount Pelion, a fancy-named molehill of a mountain, dominated the northwest near Dufferin public school. It had a nineteenth-century Crimean cannon on the summit, pointing east across the river.

7

Once a year on Victoria Day boys stuffed the cannon with fireworks, skyrockets, powerful Buster Brown firecrackers that would blow a tin can a hundred feet high.

The Gilbert Hotel in Trenton always had two or three men leaning against it indolently. On Saturday market days this number increased to half a dozen. They were "the leaners," and they leaned. There was no upper or lower age limit, but the leaners were no longer youthful. Some had a few days' growth of whiskers, and chewed tobacco. A little brown trickle of it decorated their mouths. Some wore overalls, behind which their bellies bulged, uncaring. Others wore work pants and flannel shirts.

Once the leaners leaned, their old characters changed. They became indifferent to the passing show. Their eyes lost focus. They saw you and yet they did not see you. It was the generalized and non-specific scene which they absorbed, as the human skin absorbs moisture. They were philosophers, monuments of indifference. Their identity as individuals was lost the moment they began to prop up the town hostelry. They were the leaners.

If you stood across the road from them at the post office and watched them as they watched passersby, you realized another species had been added to zoological listings. They spoke from the sides of their mouths if anything reached the periphery of their attention. A woman of notable physical attributes evoked no obvious reaction. But a stir passed over them the moment she went by. A chemical and molecular change. They were appreciators; they were enjoyers without being participants.

Across from Patrick's mother's house on Front Street was Redick's Sash and Door Factory, just north of Corson's dock. Pine and cedar lumber was piled in sheds close to the river, where giant willow trees trailed their leaves in the water. Sometimes Patrick went there with Gyp to do nothing, the dog's brown body wedged against his leg, the

8

sweet scent of new-cut boards in his nostrils, and red willow roots waving gently underwater.

He'd tried to imagine once how you'd describe the colour red if you were forbidden to use the word itself. And what about green, blue, and orange? There are some words you can't explain, except with themselves for examples; and there must be feelings inside you that you can't use words for, that nobody else ever had. . . .

A block away was Yourex's blacksmith shop. Standing at the door with his friends Jack Corson and Billy Coons was like watching something magic. Mr. Yourex, a jut-jawed man with horn-rimmed glasses and leather apron, had been an awesome giant when Patrick was six years old. And the horses, clomping nervously on wooden planks, their eyes rolling and wild, as if waiting for the dentist to go to work; shadows moving among cobwebs, horseshoes festooned on nails . . . .

And that sick sweet smell of burning hooves. How could the horses stand it? The bellows blowing air into a volcanic fire; iron shoes radiant with light and hissing, doused in cold water. Iron shoes nailed to feet, like Christ to the Cross in Sunday school. The horses, those poor horses!

When the blacksmith had an idle moment, Jack Corson once asked him how horses could stand the pain.

"They know they need shoes, and a good smith don't hurt 'em. Why, the shoes I give'm, they could run all the way to France and back and never need new shoes."

"How could they run over water?" Jack Corson said. "Isn't there a lot of water before you get to France?"

"Um, well," Mr. Yourex said, "they move their feet so fast and run so hard they never touch the water."

His eyes twinkled behind horn-rimmed glasses at the silly expressions that came over the boys' faces. "Don't you believe me?"

But, since the boys had entered high school, (with the lofty educational status conferred by Grade 10), the smithy was left unvisited. As was old tobacco-faced Maclean at the nearby pump works where he held forth among his lathes and pulleys, with cedar shavings spreading incense in the air. Maclean's wooden pumps were destined to decorate farmyards and do useful work providing water for colonial farmhouses.

Billy Coons said the wooden pumps looked like small men. And you could see the resemblance if you allowed your mind some leeway. Four feet long and six or eight inches square or round, they had black iron bands encircling them to prevent splitting. There was an almost-face where the handle would be installed. It was easy to imagine that the pumps held converse with springs deep inside earth, with underground rivers and waters whose source was unknown to even the best water witches.

Old Maclean's temper was notably uncertain. Patrick could remember him asking such pointed questions as: "Didn't I hear your mother calling you?" Or: "I'll take my belt to your hide if I catch you here again." This fierce impossibility passed without notice among his hearers. But the warning had to be taken seriously, since the pump-maker had been known to use his belt for just such ungentle purposes in past years.

Patrick's mother was a short woman with a broad face and sometimes a wondering expression. A pleasant face, but it often appeared to be pondering about something that puzzled her.

His father had died of cancer on the family farm ten years before. Afterwards, Mrs. Cameron moved to town with her small son. There was money – when you say money and limit it to a relatively small amount. Or enough, if you weren't extravagant. Eleanor Cameron was not. The farm was sold a few years later, after an irresolute week in which she couldn't decide whether she was being cheated or not by the purchaser. And before it was sold, there were apples, apples, apples. She hired men to pick them. They filled the backyard of the old brick house on Front Street. Apples! She hated apples!

When Patrick was seven he sold quarts and baskets, bushels and pecks of apples from the lost farm he could scarcely remember now. He pedalled his small wagon door-to-door – collecting dimes, quarters, shinplasters, and the rare dollar from housewives – rushing home with the loot, wanting to see his mother smile before the brown smell of rot in the backyard twitched her nostrils. And ever after the names of those apples, Northern Spies, Russets, Tolman Sweets, McIntosh, and Snows, brought saliva to his mouth, burst on his tongue in a memory of childhood.

Fred Cameron had been an educated farmer, attending Guelph Agricultural College to learn the latest word on how to make things grow faster and better. There was a small vineyard on the Wooler Road farm. There were horses and cows, there were diversified crops – and prosperity of a kind. When Patrick was three, cancer came. It crawled all over his father's face, so that he became a horror even to himself.

Surgery was impossible. The new radium treatments did nothing for him. And there were no drugs or medication at the time to lessen pain that screamed into his mind and body. He died at age fifty-six. And even memory of his father in Patrick's mind disappeared with the spring snow; only a few snapshots remained when the child asked his mother, "Who's that man?"

Religion saved her. Or perhaps it did. She attended King Street Church every Sunday in a slow passion for God. It was a low-key love affair for something she didn't completely understand, but which could be relied on for comfort. The Saviour, the Redeemer, He with nail marks scarring his wrists and feet, who poured glory into the minds of His children. His children? Patrick, who was an enigma to her as he grew older, a boy who lived on a different level of being, his strangeness or hers unable to meet on common ground. But he was a good boy, a *good* boy. She was sure of that.

When they moved to town after her husband's death, it was like being lost in a crowd of people. On the farm there had been silence, except for the waking birds every morning, except for the cattle bawling at night and a dog three farms away howling with moonlight discontent. But Trenton was like a giant factory, with noisy automobiles on the dirt road outside the house; Fords and Chevys, and some of the more exotic cars like the Stanley Steamer with its dull *chuff-chuff* and loud whistle. And the people – they passed on the street going nowhere continually, at least it seemed that way.

She had taken years to become acquainted with the neighbours; then some had moved away after friendly relations had been established. She had to buy groceries at downtown stores, being careful crossing a street lest a bad-smelling automobile try to rid the town of one more pedestrian. Ada Kemp and God had been her salvation? She giggled at the thought of Ada and salvation.

They had met at King Street Church, spinster Ada and widow Eleanor, listening to the Reverend Hartwell's full-bodied, slightly fruity voice. Ada was a talker herself, hatchet-faced and "mature" rather than any more flattering description. But she was warm-hearted, liked Patrick, and was a news source for the entire neighbourhood and beyond.

The Reverend Hartwell was an intermittent subject between the two women. "Ever since his wife passed away – bless her soul – Mr. Hartwell has had his eye on you," Ada would say to her friend. "I've seen it every Sunday at church, and he preaches his sermons partly for you. I'm sure of that. When he talks of Susanna and the Elders, there's a glint in his eye, and he looks your way . . . ."

Eleanor Cameron hadn't noticed the slightly predatory glances the reverend had directed at her, having closed her eyes to allow the holy words to join with her conception of God. With eyes closed, she thought of Mr. Hartwell as an intermediary of heaven, rather than a beefy human being with thick lips and four chins, the father of a rather odious boy named Chester. On warm days in church, with her eyes open, she noticed beads of sweat on the minister's upper lip and forehead, which gave him a greasy look.

She gasped and thought, I'm not being fair. Mr. Hartwell is a good man, and that's the end of it. She placed the last stitch in her sewing and bit off the thread. Removing her thimble she thought of the farm. Memory of it returned to her – the wind rippling a wheat field into waves of gold; crickets singing in late afternoon; and Fred looking at her sometimes as if she were beautiful, whether that was true or not. She had hoped it was, and sighed and laughed. The farm and the town. . . . To live in so many places and times and never be completely at home anywhere. But perhaps the Heavenly Kingdom . . . .

At school, often Patrick dreamed the classroom time away. He was sometimes startled to find Mr. Splore's eyes staring into his own, the French teacher's question gone beyond hearing. And he'd stammer, his face turning red. The class would laugh.

Now, at the end of another long winter of watching the teachers, they had become much more than names; there were faces and personalities attached to the names. Mr. Clubb, gaunt and thin, coughing a little, completely bald in his mid-fifties. It was said that Mr. Clubb had been an

13

officer in the British army during the Boer War in South Africa.

Mr. Clubb was a man who never talked about himself. He taught mathematics. Occasionally while explaining something at the blackboard his eyes would lose focus, he'd stand there with chalk in hand, waver dizzily on his feet, and grab the ledge in front of him. Then he'd shake himself, the dead men that he may have been remembering lying down in their graves again. Patrick shivered.

Mr. McIver taught Latin, a dead language that was chanted in church and made animal names sound like Roman citizens. When Mr. McIver said something to him in Latin, he stiffened and came instantly alert, not wanting to admit he hadn't been paying attention. But hadn't Caesar been mentioned?

He took a chance and guessed, "*Veni, vidi, vici*; I came, I saw, I conquered," mispronouncing the Latin and stuttering over the English. He looked at McIver with apprehension, finally with relief, hoping none of this feeling had left the inside of his face and showed on the outside.

Mr. McIver smiled, a brown-faced man of thirty with a dark moustache, and a stern expression behind the smile. Patrick sat back and relaxed.

English literature was Miss Darley. Tall, with skin stretched tight over a hawk-nosed face. She was fifty-two, a mover and shaker in the community. Miss Darley did things for charity, started funding drives, raised money for good causes, took over, took charge of people, and evoked a certain amount of fear in her English students. She knew poems by heart, recited Shakespeare and Christopher Marlowe. And stared challengingly at youngsters in their mid-teens, daring them to criticize her textbook diction and compelling obeisance to the Gods of Literature.

Worst of all was listening to Lampman's "The City of the End of Things," and being required to memorize the poem. Then having to memorize "The Burial of Sir John

Moore." Worse than worst of all was Hastings Doyle, a name for future generations of students to avoid. He wrote "The Private of the Buffs," in praise of a young British soldier who died, but most of all praise of the English by the English. Patrick thought it the worst poem ever written anywhere. It aroused in him a distaste for the English he never quite outgrew, however unreasonable.

But Kipling, who also praised the English – that was different. The difference between bad poetry and good?

Miss Gothard, the geography teacher, was best of all. Her personal travel stories melted into foreign landscapes and dreams of far places.

She would go off on a rambling reminiscence of the Parthenon in Athens; how it was built with the money from a silver mine after Athens and the other Greek city-states defeated Persia at the battles of Marathon and Salamis. For Lydia Gothard's special and passionate interest was Greece of the classical era. It took very little prompting for her to forget the amount of precipitation in the Canadian Arctic (hardly any) in favour of Sparta's three hundred warriors holding Xerxes' million-man polyglot army in fear of their lives at Thermopylae – the "Hot Gates."

"And the entire western world was saved by Leonidas and his three hundred. . . . " Her voice always broken with emotion; a small woman with blonde-grey hair that seemed to crackle with electricity.

Patrick knew he wasn't learning very much about geography during some of the study periods presided over by Miss Gothard. But the teacher herself fascinated him, the way her voice changed and her back stiffened as if she, too, had joined Leonidas's small army near the shore-sea-green Aegean. . . . Xerxes, the Persian king and army general, was also someone he wanted to know more about. A man who scourged the Hellespont Straits with whips to punish the water when it wouldn't calm down to permit his

15

army's transit to the other shore – that man was a fool, but an interesting fool.

And if she was completely carried away by the book memories that seemed to her much more personal than that, she quoted poetry. And when they were calibrating the inches of rainfall in British Columbia, or talking about monsoons and the distance above sea level of Mount Everest, Patrick would find reason to deposit wastepaper in the basket beside Miss Gothard's desk. From his place at the rear of the classroom among the taller and larger boys, he'd walk briskly to the front and deposit a deliberately crumpled ball of paper, then return. On the way back he'd slow his steps, having noticed then and before an enchanting view. The completely new and previously unnoticed panorama of girls' breasts.

During study periods, Patrick's female classmates often leaned forward, chewing their pencils, cogitating about boys or isotherms, the relation of Fahrenheit to Celsius. Their dresses or blouses would fall slightly down and open. And since public school it seemed a wonderful transformation had taken place. Whatever the difference between girl children and budding women, the balance was now definitely tipped toward women in most instances. Evidence for that was directly under his eyes.

Patrick feasted, in a manner of speaking. Whatever had been flat-chested and stringy and not worth noticing in public school had become more than it was, changed in such a way that he felt a corresponding change inside himself. In more than one instance, globular shapes enticed more than his eyes, and made his fingers tremble. With one per cent of his mind he knew that this feeling was part of the great engine of the world, a feeling that produced children and was one of the prime reasons for existence.

Dizzily he'd regain his desk, face slightly red. Kevin Morris's eyes would be on him inscrutably, Billy Coons's eyes knowingly. And the girls, demurely working away at

16

Miss Gothard's class assignment, would have their own eyes modestly lowered. Harold Wannamaker, star football player, once winked at him delightedly from the corner of the room.

One day, after four o'clock, Patrick stood on the school steps with the crowd around him beginning to scatter and dwindle. On the cinder track behind the red-brick building someone was jogging – no, not jogging, running. At a time when everyone else had taken their homework and themselves home, Kevin Morris was running.

Wearing shorts, undershirt, and running shoes from his locker in the basement, Kevin circled the track with easy stride, not pushing himself anywhere near the limit, running almost mechanically with minimum effort. But after every two laps of the track he speeded up, stride lengthening, arms pumping faster, but face remaining impassive, mouth slightly open. He slowed down again at the end of the circuit, mouth closing, legs flashing, changed into an almost lackadaisical lazy runner, with the rhythm of a slowly trotting horse.

For five minutes Patrick watched. Then he shucked off his sweater and started after Kevin, fifty feet behind. Wearing light wool pants, cotton shirt, and rubber-soled running shoes, his clothes were small hindrance. At sixteen he was six feet tall and weighed 170 pounds, perhaps five of those pounds excess baggage.

His elbows flapped wildly as he ran, trying to push the air behind him, succeeding only in making himself pant for more oxygen, chest burning after a few minutes, sweat running down his forehead into the corners of his eyes. But he kept going, although the distance behind his classmate increased to more than a hundred feet.

Kevin didn't notice at first that he had company on the school cinder track. Starting his run to the right (the way runners always do – did ancient Greek marathoners also run to their right?), he made the turn farthest from the school, and noticed the flapping arms and laboured stride of his pursuer, now much farther behind.

A scarecrow. Kevin's impulse was to laugh, until he recognized the other boy. Patrick almost ran into him, head down and panting, pulling up hurriedly, red-faced and with his extremities seeming tangled.

"What's the idea?" Kevin said, keeping his face still, irritation held inside.

Patrick didn't know what to say, how to answer that embarrassing question. Besides, he wasn't sure he knew the answer himself.

"Uh, I – I –" he stammered.

Kevin turned into a stern accuser. "You're making fun of me," he said, missing the point that it was the other way around, since Patrick's running resembled the gyrations of a mad windmill.

Kevin's face remained still, but there was no mistaking the anger that gave his voice a sharp edge. "Why?" he said.

Patrick was angry himself, as much because he couldn't think of an answer as at the other boy's demanding attitude.

"I didn't know it was your track," he said lamely.

"It isn't," Kevin said. "But I think you're trying to irritate me, make fun of me, throw me off my running – "

"I'm not, I'm not!" Patrick almost screamed.

And he searched in his mind for a reason to follow this clever young man – probably far beyond himself in intelligence – around the school track, when he could be doing his homework, could be romping with his half-Airedale playmate, could be . . . could be. . . .

And an answer came to him. "I wanted to do something different. You were, you *are* doing that. Why can't I be a runner, too?"

18

His reasons seemed inadequate, even to himself. He felt panicky, because tears were forming behind his eyes, voice growing hoarse.

Kevin studied him, pale grey eyes uncanny in slanting late-afternoon sunshine. The neighbour boy, always near the lowest in classroom work, not unfriendly but never friend. And not a rival in any sense.

Do something different? Kevin thought. If your studies are easy, why not do something different? That was one reason for his own running. He shrugged mentally and dismissed the thought.

"You want me to help you?" he said.

The offer threw Patrick into confusion. And perhaps there was pity in the other boy's eyes, the consciousness of superiority. He felt a flooding shame, seeing himself standing there talking to Kevin Morris, a beggar in front of a superior being. He turned and ran off the track without a word. Without stopping, he snatched up his sweater at the school doors. On the footbridge over the river he was still running, thoughts in his head chaotic, scarcely aware of where he was, a splinter of glass in his heart.


After supper, when Mrs. Cameron wanted to know about her son's homework, Patrick said he was caught up. And crossed the road to Redick's lumber sheds by the river, Gyp behind like a doggy shadow, sniffing at his hand.

Overhead in high willow leaves, the sun was trapped a million times on three-inch strips of green. And a rainbow island drifted atop the water – red, blue, and green colours from the creosote works upriver. He threw a sudden stone, and the rainbow broke into fragments.

Lounging on the sweet-smelling boards he thought about himself; about Mrs. Morris and her bragging words about Kevin. Was he envious of Kevin's abilities as both student and athlete? The answer was yes and no. Yes, he wanted to do some running. But no, he didn't want to be like Kevin. He visualized himself as he must have appeared to the other boy – a flapping scarecrow on the track, a figure of fun, something to be ridiculed – and winced inwardly. But did it matter how you looked to someone else? And was the separate world in your own head changed and altered by someone attempting to peer in from the outside? There wasn't any answer.

A bird called overhead in the willow tree. "Yes," said the bird. "Yes, yes, yes." Patrick grinned, called the dog, and went home.

He woke early next morning – 7:10 a.m. His mother was still asleep. He located a lightweight pair of pants in the closet with some difficulty, an undershirt, and his ordinary rubber-soled running shoes. Sluicing water on his face, he cleaned his teeth and was out on the road.

On the sidewalk, Patrick took a deep breath, glanced back and forth on the dirt road, and started running. He turned right on Front Street, right again at Ford Street to Division, and on around the triangular block of houses back to Front Street.

How far was that? Suppose each of the three sides was around 500 feet, that would make the circuit 1,500, and getting close to a mile if you circled the block three times. But after one go-round his legs felt like wood.

The dog joined him after the first go-round. Patrick looked at Gyp closely. His mother had told him neighbourhood chickens were being harried, worried, and sometimes killed. His dog was suspected. Gyp panted, with a more-or-less innocent doggy expression, hairy face and lolling tongue betraying no secret thought of poultry.

Patrick stopped suddenly, kneeling down and grabbing Gyp by the ears. He lifted the smelly face close to his own. "Good dog!" Then, thinking that Gyp's goodness was not the point: "Bad dog? Are you a bad dog, killing chickens?"

Gyp smiled at him, or seemed to. Patrick threw his arms around the dog's body and pulled him close. "I can talk to you better than to anyone. . . . You understand even if you don't understand." The dog licked his face. Patrick got up and started running.

He passed Kevin Morris's father's tombstone works next door: memorials to the dead, and even sometimes to the living. Buyers of the red, blueish, black, and grey granite markers often had their birth dates carved in the stone; the place for their death dates left blank but anticipated soon. Patrick shivered, despite the sweat running down his back and soaking his face. The small transitory graveyard of John Randolph Morris, memorial craftsman, wavered past in a sweltering haze.

Then he started around the block again. He was sweaty, tired, a little discouraged. A fire was spreading to arms and legs and feet. He had to count them off, and say to himself, My feet are okay, my legs are fine, my arms as well. . . . Then he gasped with the pain and sweat ran into his eyes despite the restraining headband, improvised from one of his mother's dishtowels.

On Ford Street, the McMaster house. It looked like a bungalow, even if it wasn't, with sort of hunchback bricks and veranda; big barns at the side with horseshoes nailed to the doors. When Ian McMaster reached sixty years, he and his wife had moved to town. And the horses had to come as well. Dandy and Donny and Emmy; they were friends, they had names, they liked sugar. Patrick remembered old Ian and Emma talking about these horses as if they were the children they never had.

"We have no children," Ian had said to his wife.

"But Een," his wife said, pronouncing his name like food and adding salt. "But Een – "

"I know, I know," he said.

Patrick glanced at the barns in passing, glimpsing horses inside. Ian McMaster, coming out of the house to feed

21

them, stared at the boy in surprise. He waved his hand. Patrick waved back from the pain in his gut and chest and head, then stopped thinking about anything at all. His feet hurt. His head hurt. Everything hurt.

Will it always be like this, running? Yes, his worst enemy in his head replied, it will always be like this. "Shit!" he said, and looked around to see if anyone heard but himself. And collapsed beside the road.

"What about a nice drink of water, Patrick?" It was Mrs. McMaster standing above him, holding a glass of water. "Come into the house and have a cookie."

He followed her into the kitchen, accepting a ginger cookie and some lemonade after finishing the water. Mrs. McMaster was a small lumpy woman with shrewd eyes, a little over sixty.

"Een is out talkin to his horses," she said indulgently. "I swear he talks to them more'n he does to me. That's why I asked you in here, for someone to talk to me. Now you just sit there and eat your cookie and tell me how your mother is. I saw her at the market last week and she . . . ."

Patrick almost fell asleep listening. He said he had to go after a few more minutes. She watched him as he picked up speed again on the road. And began watering the young pansies in her garden, watching the eyes in the centre of blue velvet petals. Mrs. Cameron, all alone in that big house except for Patrick, she thought. A pity. . . . She shrugged her shoulders.

Gyp appeared from nowhere and frisked sedately at Patrick's heels. Probably been doing something illegal, Patrick decided. A tiny white dog ran from a house on Division Street, barking at Gyp. The larger dog stopped and looked at the small one. Patrick watched.

The big dog did nothing, just stood there, which seemed to annoy the little white shrimp. It ran around in circles, practically biting its tail with rage at this monolithic stranger invading private territory. The white dog dashed within a few inches of the silent Gyp, swaying its muzzle close to the ground in a parody of ferocity. Then it darted about, yapping excitedly.

Gyp looked quite dignified, entirely still, feet planted four-square. Then his head swerved suddenly toward his tormentor, lips pulled back over big yellow teeth in solemn menace, but not moving otherwise. Little Whitey went "yipe-yipe-yipe" and skittered toward home.

Patrick collapsed in laughter. Gyp came to him and licked his face with something much like human concern. Patrick grabbed the dog's ears. "Bluff," he said, "pure bluff. You wouldn't lay a finger on him, hey? – I mean, lay a paw."

The dog grinned at him.

# 2

A NEW STUDENT HAD TRANSFERRED to the high school from Toronto. Her name was Jean Tomkins. The seating arrangement was altered, and she was placed beside Patrick by chance. He had had some experience with a previous Jean at public school, a Jean who looked like red geraniums. He couldn't remember why that had been so. This present Jean had blue eyes and blonde hair. There were various other colours about her person, and he reeled those off in the spectrum to describe her. None of them did.

He kept glancing sideways, as if to imprint the shape of her on his retina. His classmates noticed first, then the teachers. "Patrick," Mr. McIver said, "if you're feeling ill, you have permission to get a drink of water."

Miss Gothard said, "Is there something wrong with your neck? You keep turning your head sideways."

Patrick looked straight ahead after that, neck muscles so rigid it hurt when he did try to move his head. And Jean, he could see, was even more embarrassed. A delicate pink stole up from beneath her dress and stained her face like a pale watercolour.

Even though he stopped looking at her entirely, he felt in his bones every movement she made, her every expression made an echo behind his skin. Her thoughts, he decided, caused little electrical impulses that made his fingers twitch, his arms jump suddenly. As if an umbilical cord had sprouted between them, with reciprocal current flowing back and forth.

After school, he noticed some of his classmates grinning at him, whispering to those in other grades. And wondered if he was imagining it. Finally someone, who couldn't

24

resist, made that finger-crossing gesture which means "shame on you!" Patrick glanced at the boy with irritation, then barked like a dog, very loudly, and chuckled at the sound. Someone else laughed, and the ordeal was over.

He ran onto the street with a great flapping of limbs. Remembering Kevin Morris's running form, he drew his elbows in close to his sides, opening the throttle full out for ten seconds. Thinking of Jean. "Yowee, Yowee!" he said to the wind, smelling the purple smell of lilacs in somebody's garden.

Patrick didn't try to analyze his own feelings. But he wanted to see more of this girl who'd appeared from nowhere. Someone at recess said the girl's father was a chemical engineer, and probably worked at the munitions factory.

He circled the track a couple of times after school was out the following afternoon. He kept an eye on the girls' exit where Jean must emerge sooner or later. She did, a small figure in a blue dress, walking west. Leaving the track, he saw her turn down Myers Street less than a block away. The house was an ordinary brick one, but large. He stood there watching it intently for five minutes, then turned toward the footbridge, on his way home.

Next morning Patrick went into the classroom before anyone else, having looked around carefully beforehand. He located Jean's desk and left a white geranium floret in the open inkwell. She noticed it after classes began. Without looking at him she smiled slightly, pulling the flower through a buttonhole in the blue dress.

And that was probably the end of it, he thought, since he lacked courage to ever speak to her. It was the end of it, except for this curious sensation of sinking and floating and drifting in the air, all at the same time. It was something he didn't completely understand. And even for boys

25

with more nerve than Patrick, it was thought to be daring and unusual to speak to a girl at recess. Girls stayed at their end of the school ground during the break; boys kept to the other end.

Even among adults, relations between male and female were often awkward and self-conscious at this time. There was no sexual instruction in schools. And unless parents were unusually free-thinking, children had no idea where babies came from. Sexual gossip among teenagers was prurient, but generally inaccurate. Cursing and swearing amounted to direct evidence that the devil had you in his fiery grip. The Reverend Hartwell at King Street Church described "bad language" as a "mortal sin."

War had loosened things up only slightly. The skirts of women's clothes very nearly reached their feet. The majority of them wore dark colours only. Bathing dress was similarly restricted.

The two sexes got acquainted anyway, but with difficulty. Patrick had noticed a boy and girl in the grade above his own who had been going steady for several years. He saw them everywhere, riding bicycles together, walking about with linked arms downtown, even wearing the same colour and pattern of clothes. They were beatifically indifferent to everything outside their own orbit. And that was rarely more than two or three feet in circumference. Two of them made a cluster. And their expressions were often the same. They had a dazed, bemused look, a kind of vacancy in their eyes.

He marvelled that their parents allowed it, this abstracted condition whereby everything outside the enthralled pair was unreal. If schoolmates of the besotted duo made fun of them, they smiled indulgently, with pity, even. Because of them, Patrick had looked up "love" in the dictionary: "A strong, usually passionate affection for a person of the opposite sex." Until very recently, he had considered such persons as foolish, not all there.

He sighed deeply, a little tragically, then began to wonder how and in what circumstances he could speak to her. Could it be done naturally, without his throat seizing up and words choking him? Stand outside her house, as he had done several times in the last week, and wait for her to appear? Then he'd stroll up to her casually with big-city sophistication and say: "Hello, Jean, I've been waiting for you. Would you walk with me?" But strangulation must ensue before the words came out. He turned red just thinking about it. On the way home from school, his legs settling into a hypnotic rhythm, her image danced before him along the cinder path beside the railway tracks.

How could he meet her? But somewhere in a remote part of his mind was the feeling that they had already met. And how could that be? He sent his thoughts sweeping backward over the past few years – school and summer holidays – back to being a small child. It was amazingly difficult. His brain felt numb from the attempt, refusing to register anything at all; there had to be an anchor point in time. There had to be one strong memory that other memories could cluster around: the year I had measles, the year I broke through the ice at the sewer outlet on the river and nearly drowned. . . .

Jean – and not the red-geranium Jean, but she of the pink tinge at the roots of her hair, of the slightly bent shoulders. In a strange rush of future memory he saw her very old and stooped into a gnarled knot from which vivid blue eyes peered out. His thoughts swooped backward again, to public school and the fat face of Mr. Fairman, a teacher he had detested. Looking for Jean back there, feeling desolate now because of her absence then.

But perhaps his memory of her was only a dream? Was he wishing her into being in his mind? Because it was important to him? Did the flesh-and-blood Jean appear in obedience to what his thoughts imagined? The idea that he could do that made him uneasy. He touched the wooden railing uprights of the bridge as he ran, making a pop-pop-pop noise. The sound of reality comforted him.

He decided that he had brought a phantom into being, a shimmer in his mind, and this gave him a feeling of power. He smiled to himself, stopping on the footbridge, climbing down to a wooden platform near the swing-bridge mechanism. Twenty feet above river water he let his legs dangle, watching a three-foot-wide misshapen oily rainbow from the creosote works float past. And a smaller rainbow like a dying flower, its petals suddenly shattered by river current.

He let his mind drift backward again, to 1917, the summer of – nothing of Jean. To 1916 – the roar of battles in the two weekly newspapers, a newsprint sound far from reality. Farther: 1915, the year British Chemical came to Trenton, when fear only a little less than terror twitched behind faces on the street. Because of T.N.T., the genie raging inside a bottle, and Trenton was the bottle.

1915, early spring, he was thirteen. Standing up in the school classroom, the geography teacher asking him to tell the other students all he knew about mountains. And the sound of his own voice, confident, and much deeper. He was sure of himself, remembering what the geography textbook said about mountains, repeating it almost verbatim. Then a high girlish squeak interrupted him, the sound of someone nervous and frightened. He looked around trying to find its source, then realized that he, Patrick, was responsible. And all knowledge of anything fled out of his head. Everyone was laughing.

The teacher said, "That will be all, class." But she was laughing, too.

Patrick sat down, his face red. He was being taken over by someone else, he thought; or else several people inside him trying to speak at once, in a squeak, a whisper, an unexpected baritone shout. Even bass, when some other self inside him tried to imitate Mr. Yourex in the church choir singing "Throw Out the Lifeline."

1915. The year hair sprouted under his arms; the year of the pubic jungle. A dark, luxuriant growth, much darker and wilder than the hair on his head, it sometimes accidentally and embarrassingly stayed outside his pants and got tangled in buttons. As if the heavy rains that made the world turn green and roadside flowers spring to life, as if all this was related to the strange forest between his legs.

And the sudden arrival of testicles – balls, family jewels, so-called by older boys. They had been present before, of course, a part of himself he had noticed no more than little toe or tailbone. Now they had acquired personality and character, swung low during leisure time, nestled close to his body while swimming. And one seemed to droop below the other, perhaps aware of its inferior station in life.

Everything was different that year, the season that girls changed from playmates to alien creatures, who smirked derisively if he spoke to them. They weren't children any longer. And the dreams came.

The usual pursuit fantasies that he knew were unreal, and he was always on the verge of yelling into his dream: "Go away! I don't believe in you!" Then the familiar faces of his teachers appeared, silent and accusing, about to denounce him for something he hadn't done yet, but about which his guilt was inevitable. That unsettled him, made his hands tremble under the blankets when he woke up, avoiding the genitals, then inadvertently shifting them into a less cramped position.

He felt persecuted, and speculated on the reasons for this. Once, awake in the night, cream-coloured moonlight visible on the black river, he heard noises outside the window. Peering out he saw a male and female figure clasped together into almost one, and heard little moans of pleasure. This was something he had not read about in books, and was very thoughtful getting back into bed.

At church and Sunday school there was much talk of Original Sin, as if everyone except God had committed something evil in the past and had to be reminded about it continually. Religion was to remind you, make everyone a little uncomfortable. And when Patrick felt very good about himself, jumping and kicking up his heels in sheer good health, grinning at his image in the bathroom mirror, then something was bound to remind him of Original Sin.

In one dream he was pushing a wheelbarrow down the main street of Trenton, the wheelbarrow heavily burdened with his own enormous penis. He started to laugh at himself, then woke up. Another dream was of looking through somebody's window at night, watching glued-together lovers. And peering through a keyhole, turning to see the whole population of Trenton watching him and laughing.

Another dream, someone smiled at him, someone he wanted to know. He couldn't see who it was, only a bright spot in the midst of darkness. He said to the brightness, "Who are you?" No reply, only that shining. And an itch of curiosity worked in him.

After heavy springtime rains, the summer of 1915 had no rain at all for most of the season. But the air was sultry; people gasped for breath. The August nights were steam baths; Patrick slept without pyjamas and tossed restlessly. But the dreams were like an exciting serial, with a perceptible sequence for each instalment.

He awoke once to find the late moon shining in on flannelette sheets; his hands spread out on both sides of the bed were silvered by moonlight shadows that moved when the smallest of breezes blew the curtains. Still half asleep, he saw a face turn inward from the window and smile, a shining face. His body felt weightless, as if it didn't really exist, and yet he had never felt more aware of himself. Whatever birds in the sky must feel, Patrick felt lying in bed; whatever fish knew, floating in their water-air, he felt the same awareness.

He cried out for the girl – for the visitor was a girl – to come back. And heard his voice grow very loud, a falsetto scream.

Mrs. Cameron rushed into the bedroom gasping, "What's the matter? Are you all right, Patrick?"

"Yes, yes," he muttered. "I was just dreaming."

"Here, let me fix the bedclothes for you. They're all over the place. I'll turn on the light."

"No, no, Mom," he said in alarm. "I'm okay, perfectly all right. Leave the light off."

Half an hour later he got back to sleep, thinking of the night visitor, wanting to see her face, which had been obscure among the curtain shadows. Wanting to again experience the sensation of leaping over Niagara Falls, visiting the outer planets; his body weightless and able to pass directly through walls, enter solid objects and emerge from them renewed and reconstituted as Patrick.

He was not alone. And kept turning his head quickly on the feather pillow, hoping to see the face clearly. Her face. She had no name except "her." During the day he searched faces on the street, peering at girls intently sometimes, causing them to turn away in real or feigned alarm, avoiding his eyes.

And Patrick grew. Between April and July he had shot up three inches closer to the sky, an inch a month. "My lands," Mrs. Cameron said, "you're like a weed. It must be the sulphur and molasses I'm giving you for what ails you."

"Nothing ails me," Patrick said.

He haunted the river all that hot summer. The Trent, after draining most of four counties, was nearly a quarter-mile wide before plunging into the Bay of Quinte. The water was deep at Corson's dock and generally thronged with summer bathers. Patrick avoided them, swimming to the navigation buoy three hundred feet out, or paddling around in an old rowboat.

31

An awkward swimmer, he had developed his own version of the sidestroke, certainly not for racing competition. It occurred to him that a tortoise on land or a hare in water would both be swifter than he was. But lying on his left side, attempting to embrace the entire river with left arm, his face dipping under with each stroke, he felt like a world explorer. Sometimes, forgetting all about the river, he thought his own thoughts and daydreamed of the girl who wandered through the night and sometimes came to his bed. By chance, or perhaps design?

Her features were now imprinted on his mind by long repetition. She was pale, as should be expected in moonlight, or even in the darker light of his brain's interior. Blonde, of course; eyes probably blue, although he couldn't be sure of that. She was what occurred to him every time female thoughts came. And the explosion of self that occurred was such that furiously churning arms and legs seemed to propel his body upright: and he raced over the crests of waves like a skimming sea gull.

The sun hung overhead while he dozed in the water, mind empty, body idle as driftwood in the small waves. Near the navigation buoy he turned upstream to push lazily against the river's current. Half asleep, or nearly awake, he became aware of a face, a face that was regarding him calmly as if this happened all the time: a girl meeting a boy in mid-river as if prearranged.

A dream? No, not this time. Her eyes were brown and awake. Face narrow and brown from the sun, so that her freckles blended and perhaps weren't there at all. He felt a completely unexpected gladness. From a distance of fifteen inches, they looked at each other. She not more than his own age – or even younger. Like something from the woods, he thought, slipping between the trees until she was nearly one of them.

Long moments of realizing each other, then they turned and moved out toward the central river; he on his left side and she on her right, so that their faces dipped down and then reappeared in a series of solemn glances, each one slightly different. Two brown faces rising and falling among the small waves of summer.

Beyond each of them a procession of foam-tipped waves, curling and breaking, white as a wedding cake, with blue beneath. Beyond them the town. But mostly they saw only each other, rising and falling, never more than two feet distant; until their eyes grew large with each other, brown velvet and hazel intermingling, a slow dance of vision. Bubbles formed and fled behind them as the river erased their passage.

The strangeness of it kept him silent, and yet it was entirely natural. He saw there was the beginning of an expression on her face: not a smile, but the look from which a smile is born. And wondered what his own face said. Because she was exploring him, entering through his eyes, her mind wandering over his face and body.

On the east shore was an unpainted wooden boathouse, its water-doors open wide. They heard the altered sound of the waves lapping against its sides, turned briefly away from each other, and clambered onto a wide wooden shelf six inches above the water. They crouched there, Patrick keeping his legs close together because the crotch of his wool bathing suit was rotted from urinating while swimming.

In the semi-darkness of the boathouse, they balanced precariously, dripping water that ran back into the river. Neither looked at the other. But Patrick was stiffly aware of the female presence, a very small girl, beginning breasts outlined by the cheap cotton bathing suit.

They had not touched each other, and their seeing was peripheral now, changed from the direct regard of their eyes while swimming. As if they had learned enough during that prolonged marine exchange to allow the other a relative privacy inside their dual aloneness. As if there were no more unasked questions. Balanced on their toes, arms braced against rough, slivery boards.

In the distance, horse and motor traffic drummed over the town bridge; waves made small lapping sounds at their feet. From directly west the sun entered the boathouse, turning their bodies a brown-amber shade. Patrick's legs and feet were beginning to get numb, but his mind refused movement. Scrotum and penis were a softly compressed bundle between his legs; goose pimples had sprouted on their arms and shoulders.

They slipped into the water again, simultaneously, swimming straight out into the river. In the middle they turned, allowed their bodies to sink at right angles to the river. They looked at each other then, as if each of them wanted to remember the other's face. Hers was like a brown triangular heart, Patrick thought. Her mouth opened over small uneven teeth, as if to say goodbye, but she made no sound. The luminous brown of her eyes seemed enormous to him. Looking into them he forgot to paddle, and swallowed a mouthful of water and choked on it.

When he recovered she was gone.

He wanted to shout the name he did not know from the top of the mountain. He wanted to pour words from his mouth, ask questions, talk about himself, tell her he liked her, wanted to know her.... And yet, Patrick realized later, he had already known her longer and better than anyone else in his life until that moment.

The weather turned warmer late that evening. A smothering blanket of moist air overlaid the earth. Workmen sat on their verandas in undershirts, reluctant to go to bed, dogs panted. An obdurate Gyp refused to move from under the woodshed; soldiers in heavy wool uniforms avoided the hot streets. The touch of hand on hand became loathsome to people; they avoided each other's eyes – a great lethargy had overtaken the world.

At midnight it rained. There had been no announcement of thunder or scimitar of lightning in the sky. Water fell in gusting sheets; the dry earth seemed to breathe and sigh with it. When the rain subsided to a low murmur of sound on roofs and gutters, the air was cooler and more tolerable. Patrick slept.

He had expected to dream, and even in sleep was impatient to begin dreaming, as if his mind could summon the brown girl or pale blonde one to his bed, and he could speak to them for the first time. But it was not so. Those night wanderers of the mind clung to a vestige of independence, refusing to make themselves known. Patrick awoke frustrated in the rain-cooled morning, gulped his breakfast without enjoyment, and returned to the river.

On succeeding nights, though, they did come. Singly, then in swift alternation, the sun girl and the moon one. The brown girl in his dream had become visibly older; budding breasts under the thin cotton bathing suit were larger and more shapely. A flood of sensation poured through him. In exaltation he raced through his own dream, cherry-red horseshoes from the blacksmith shop on his feet. Maclean's wooden pumps frantically geysering water from the earth as he worked the pump handle.

The pale blonde girl's features were now clear and precise: slender, delicate nose all that a nose should be, eyes a concentrated and overwhelming blue, an invitation of a mouth. But she was something his mind had created, imagined and shaped; she was insubstantial as moonlight mist, whereas the brown girl was a sky full of sun. He felt nothing for the pale one any longer except remembrance. He did remember.

And it came about, years later, that she emerged from his mind and became flesh.

# 3

EVERY EVENING MRS. CAMERON trimmed the coal oil lamps as possible supplements to the newly installed electric lights which she didn't trust. The new lights flickered on a framed living-room motto, "Christ is the Master of this House, the Unseen Listener of Every Conversation."

Over the past weeks Patrick's schoolwork had improved. French, Latin, geography, mathematics, all showed noticeable improvement. He had allotted a certain amount of time to each of them, rather than the desultory moments snatched from whatever he was doing previously.

It was a time of concentration, study time, work time, with Kevin Morris's face often peering over the top of a Latin text: *"Would you like me to help you?"* Patrick gritted his teeth and went "urrhh" under his breath. And once he noticed Kevin watching him from an upstairs window over the tombstone works. The grey eyes met his own hazel ones, and Patrick knew there was nothing for him to say. He felt sadness, as if a door had been closed.

Patrick was running. For the first few days he ran around the block three times before school, and four times after school. Once he found the school track empty on a Friday afternoon. He was just into his second lap when he saw Kevin Morris standing on the school steps in running togs, watching him. A speculative look on Kevin's face. Patrick turned off at the far end of the track, continuing down Marmora Street and over the bridge to home, leaving the track to Kevin.

During the first days, he could think of little but his own body. His legs hurt, his chest hurt, his arms hurt from the pumping motion of progress, sweat ran down his forehead and into his eyes. Luckily there were no blisters on his feet. He wore an old white housepainter's cap against the sun, tying a cotton rag around his forehead to soak up sweat. And stopped wearing an undershirt, running stripped to the waist. Several times he noticed curtains of neighbourhood houses twitch as someone looked out to decide whether this partial nudity was entirely decent.

After a month of running, at the beginning of June, Patrick had lost ten pounds, down to 160. His upper body was browned from sun, blood circulating a little faster, face thinned into a narrow sound, a short word that could cleave the wind. He was becoming an athlete.

His friends Billy Coons and Jack Corson came in search of him on weekends. They said: Stop that silly running and come fishing; or, Come play ball; or, Just wander over Mount Pelion with us looking for girls.

"I'm afraid of girls," Patrick said. That was true, although he knew they wouldn't believe him.

Billy Coons said, "Who was that I saw looking down the front of girls' dresses two weeks back. Miss Gothard said you couldn't have near that much wastepaper . . . ."

"It was me," Patrick admitted. "But I've reformed. And I'm gonna run in the next Olympics and win a gold medal for Canada."

"Haw," Jack Corson said. "There ain't no Olympics, not when there's a war on."

The two boys left. Patrick called after them, "I'll come next week, just wait for me then . . ."

And he did, but it wasn't the same. They caught sunfish and rock bass in the river on hooks and worms. "What are you doin with yourself?" Billy Coons said. "This running, I mean?" And the lightly freckled face was serious. "It don't get you nowhere. And you know, we kinda miss you."

They did, he knew they did, and felt guilt, but couldn't say exactly why he was running. He grabbed Billy's hand and caught Jack Corson's eye. "I don't know," Patrick said. "I don't know."

The question bothered him. Why does anybody do anything? Sitting on a pile of fresh pine lumber behind Redick's Sash and Door Factory, he thought about that, and also about the puzzle of having an entire world inside your head, one that shut out the so-called real world outside yourself. His mind stumbled over it, trying to explain why this private world was so different from the one other people saw and talked about and lived in.

The minister's red face flashed into his mind. Everyone seemed to respect Mr. Hartwell – because he's a preacher, or because he's himself? What a silly lump of lard he really is, Patrick thought, and wondered if that was sacrilege.

He felt like two different people. At least two. The first one looked out behind his eyes, saying and doing things the adult world would approve of, might even give him prizes for. Or, best of all, would forget he even existed and allow him to go his own way in forgetfulness. The other world was his alone, no outsider permitted there; a world in which he made up his own mind, made mistakes that were his own mistakes, not someone else's.

But apart from the outside world, there was the sheer glory and excitement of having an inner one; the mystery of himself, the part he couldn't predict, in which there was a "soul" that sat in judgement over himself and everything else. His mind veered off from remembering that framed motto in the living room, "Christ is the Master of this House," and its spying religious connotations.

He thought of Kevin Morris. Not just the idea of Kevin Morris, but Kevin's face as well, complete with a rather superior expression. He asked himself the old questions: Am I jealous of Kevin? Do I want to hurt him somehow? And what is there about the guy?

None of these questions had a yes or no answer. Kevin's expression was remote and supercilious; it was scornful and disdainful. Worst of all, it knew it was all those things and didn't always try to keep them from showing on the outside.

Patrick chuckled. He, too, tried to keep his feelings from showing on his face. If feelings showed, everyone would be punching everyone else on the nose. Or killing them, even. But he couldn't escape the niggling suspicion that he might be imposing some of these qualities and aspects on Kevin Morris, that his own imagination was working overtime.

Now it was his grandfather who appeared in his mind. Patrick hadn't seen him in weeks, not since he'd started running.

Marshall Portugal Cameron was ninety years old. He had been born in 1828, almost fully adult and sexually equipped. That was the legend among his poker-playing cronies anyway. "Portugee," as he was called, was six feet tall and weighed 260 pounds. The reason for that odd middle name was lost in time.

Of uncertain temper and eccentric tastes, he was now living over a dry-goods store in downtown Trenton. Previously he had been staying with Patrick and his mother, and had moved there after his son, Patrick's father, died. No one could have ever plumbed the courage Mrs. Cameron finally summoned up to throw him out of her house several years before. He had invented some new and quite pungent cusswords. He had expressed some old but decidedly atheistic opinions about the very existence of Patrick's mother's Redeemer. Besides, she couldn't stand the way he slopped food all over his vest, and left his dirt-coloured underwear lying on the bathroom floor like a dead animal. And he was a bad influence on her young son, Mrs. Cameron decided.

Portugee was a force of nature, a movement of earth's interior bowels. As a boy of fourteen and fifteen, he had worked for the Gilmour Lumber Company just northeast

39

of Trenton. Later, come to full growth and maturity, he was a handfaller with double-bladed axe, his fifty-inch chest bursting buttons off homespun shirt. Vitality and ferocity screamed silently from his eyes. When the logs floating down cold Ontario rivers got snagged on stones or themselves, he would pry them loose for the sawmill journey, with peavey and oaken arms.

For a small Patrick there were tales of those times, tales that repeated and overlapped themselves. In the logging shanties at night, a legendary mouse peered over the bowl of applesauce. Portugee lifted his rifle again and again, and shot the mouse again and again. When the smoke lifted and he finished the story, the mouse revived, came to life and waited for its doom once again. And again.

"Never touched that applesauce atall, atall," Portugee would brag.

There were battles in the green forest. Caulked boots caressed unfriendly faces. There was whisky and plug tobacco and snoose, and shrill song of sawmill steel, steel that is eternal and flesh that's mortal.

Portugee, grown unexpectedly old, vented the remains of his chewing tobacco somewhere. A sharp *spl-aa-aat!* indicated that most of it had disappeared in the spittoon, but a few lost drops made the greasy floor very dangerous.

Portugee's life was a story for his grandson. He told of following a girl onto a ferry boat in San Francisco Bay. "I wanted her," he said, parrot nose and ancient face gone from the shabby rented room to sunny California.

His grandfather went on and on while Patrick shivered with discomfort, the story becoming repetitious and obscene. But he worshipped the storyteller. He had the feeling of just being tolerated by the old man. Not loved or respected or wanted in any affectionate way.

Portugee's face had the remnant of youth, despite the scars of ancient combat. Not an innocent youth, but the bull moose time of being a lumberjack, backwoods wrestler, and don't-give-a-damn-about-anything indoors-or-out stud and hellraiser that he was.

Something burned and smouldered inside him, out of the far past. He was seventy-four years back of Patrick in time, and seemed less a relative than a queer, aging animal from forests where other animals had avoided him in fear. Patrick's father had been fifty at the birth of his son; his mother forty. His own connection with these people seemed many generations distant. All the world was old, this very world that was closest to Patrick.

His grandfather's ferocity, that burning, smouldering self, concealed or half-concealed in rotting flesh. His talk about wrestling the "bully of the woods." No doubt he'd been a bully himself. Barn raisings and booze, descriptions of the anatomy of women that omitted nothing. And nothing softened or euphemized for a boy. He said what he thought and what he said was Death: "I'll turn up my toes," and "You don't dast stop." Or everything would fall down. Everything fall down.

Patrick had a picture in his mind of a much younger Portugee, long before Confederation in 1867. When Portugee was sleek and trim as a wolf, the first ancestor of wolves, but even then having weird foretraces of being an old man living above a dry-goods store in Trenton. He had the stench of stale food around him now, dirty dishes in the sink, and most of his friends were dead – yet he exuded power! And Patrick knew he was not mistaken about that.

In memory Patrick became five years old again, holding on to his grandfather's hand, walking to Tripp's Poolroom on Dundas Street, the old man's great flat feet beating onto the concrete sidewalk toward earth beneath, a signal for dead seeds and crushed flowers to revive and blossom.

He'd glanced at the old man, his heavy walking stick, the scarcely waning strength on its journey from darkness to darkness, and felt a jolt of pride. An aura of rightness from being there. A kind of gift that is not tangible, passing from

41

one person to another without volition, or even intention, but a rare thing of value received from another person.

In mid-June there came a spell of hot weather to blister the pants off a statue. All wind died, washings hung limp on their lines without a stir, leaves of trees were visibly tired of being leaves. Humidity was such that there seemed as much water in the air as in the river. In the evenings men sat on verandas in undershirts; women were bare-armed in light cotton dresses, some of them languidly waving fans. Dogs lay panting in the dust.

In the midst of the heat wave came word that a local high school athlete had died in France. A boy of twenty-one, whom everyone had liked and some had even loved. His photograph in the Trenton weekly newspaper made him look like a girl. The accompanying story exaggerated his good qualities, but the grief of people who knew him was genuine. During that same week an eight-year-old youngster drowned while he was learning to swim at a nearby beach. Gloom encompassed the town.

Patrick's running had settled into routine. Three to five circuits of his home-block in the morning; a hundred yards of speed, nearly full throttle at the end. After school, forty-five minutes more. Sometimes north along the river road, or over the footbridge to the creosote works on Marmora Street. He ran facing oncoming traffic, meeting a few Fords and Chevys, sometimes a buggy or horse and wagon. His body hadn't so much slimmed down as filled out, as if some kind of disguise for what he actually was had dropped away, leaving the genuine Patrick unmistakably there.

He thought back to the day, after his first week of running, when he'd asked the part-time football coach, Bob Prebble, for advice. There was no track coach at Trenton High.

Prebble had told him to stay within himself, "Don't wear yourself out. Make sure your socks don't have holes so you get blisters. Do like you said you're doin, take it fast every so often and try to keep something left inside you for the end. That's what wins races, a big kick at the end."

Prebble was about thirty, available for consultation only on Saturdays. That was because he worked the night shift at British Chemical. Indoor heat there drained much of his strength. A greyhound-looking man with a small belly and two days' beard, he stared at Patrick curiously. "I could ask you why you're doin it," he said, and waited.

When there was no answer: "It might be a good idea to get yourself looked over by a doctor."

Patrick was silent. After a moment: "When I was sick last year, Dr. Johnson said there was nothing wrong with me."

Patrick was embarrassed. It sounded as though he'd only pretended to be sick last year, and that was close to the truth. But he didn't intend to reveal any more about himself. Not much anyway. "Dr. Johnson said my heart and lungs were sound. As a bell." And wondered, How sound is a bell?

"You're outrunning your competition because there isn't any competition," Prebble said. "No marathons around here, even on field days; no other long-distance runners either. Except Kevin Morris." He grinned. "You got some kind of thing goin with Morris? What I mean is, you got to be running for the sake of running, unless it's young Morris?"

Patrick squirmed. Bob Prebble was coming much too close, almost looking inside his head and squinting at something shameful there. He turned his face, sun-browned and bony, away from the ex-football player.

"Look," Prebble said, "I know I'm not helping you much, but listen to what I'm sayin. If you get hot and sweat too much, if you get dizzy, then stop and rest. Sit down, lie down beside the road until you feel better. It's nothing to be ashamed of. Hot-weather running like this takes water; if you're near a house, ask for a drink of water. You could get sunstroke if you don't. And wear a shirt when it's bright like this; that sun is too hard on your back.

"And take care of your feet. Wash them every time you come back from a run. If your heels blacken up a little, don't worry. Just give it a rest." His voice turned rough and a little harsh, "You hear me?"

But there was kindness here. After their brief fragment of talk, Prebble knew much about him. "Go on, enjoy yourself," the man said. "Maybe that's not exactly it, but you hafta get something out of it. You give something and take something, spend and receive.

"I'm not bein nutty, you know," he said, pale blueish eyes like stones underwater. "And whatever your reasons are, you'll find there are others. Reasons, I mean."

Prebble turned away, then said, "Come back and see me when you feel like it." He grinned again, with a very likable expression. "I useta do a little running myself, like I needed something to get outa myself, something to get away from" – his voice changed – "I don't know from what exactly. A hobby, maybe that's what it is. No, I can't say it. But maybe you know what I'm gettin at."

He slapped Patrick lightly on the shoulder, and said again, "Come back and see me. I mean it."

Patrick was astonished. Blank face and lowered eyes could shut out teachers and neighbours and friends from his innermost thoughts, but Prebble could reach inside those defences. It mystified him.

Now he slipped back into his habitual running pace, so automatic by now that he could let his mind reach somewhere else. And remembered what he'd said to Prebble those weeks ago: "When I was sick last year, Dr. Johnson said there was nothing wrong with me."

He stopped in the middle of the road. Now what on earth possessed me to say that? he asked himself. It had been several years since Dr. Johnson had expressed an opinion about Patrick's health, some time before the war. And reminding himself of that time now was a little embarrassing.

His mind skipped back over those years until he remembered Mrs. Shaw. With a concentrated effort of mind he caused her to materialize in his thoughts. She was about forty then, her face like a crumpled brown grocery bag when she smiled, which was often. The Shaws were neighbours, and Mrs. Shaw, having no children of her own, had been fond of Patrick.

When she and her husband were moving to another town, she offered him some books. "My sister's boy had them before we came here," she said. "I can't think why I haven't thrown them out before now. But I guess I saved them for you, Patrick."

The books were paperbacks, about a hundred of them. Their author was Burt L. Standish; the publisher, Street & Smith of New York. Their titles all contained the name Frank Merriwell, or his brother, Dick Merriwell. Patrick dipped into one to find out more about this fellow Merriwell, who turned out to be not so merry after all, and was absorbed immediately.

Frank Merriwell was a student at Yale University in the United States. He played all the sports there: baseball, hockey, football, you name it. And Frank nearly always won at whatever it was. If he didn't win, there was something crooked afoot or underfoot. His enemy, black-browed Bart Hodge, had slipped him a Mickey, poured molasses in his underwear, cut holes in his baseball mitt, whatever. Something crooked, underhanded, completely unfair. But Frank rose above everything. Or else, if there was a setback, it didn't last long; virtue always triumphed in the end.

Frank's girlfriend was Inza Burriage, very beautiful, as was to be expected. She was always up there in the stands cheering for him wildly. That is, she was there if she wasn't kidnapped or being carried away down a raging river in a canoe or run away with on a horse – waiting to be rescued by Frank, wherever she was.

The American virtues were often mentioned in these books: winning was extremely important. Honour was also mentioned; and the good guys, Frank and his friends, always had more of it than anyone else. American honour was also at stake in most of these athletic contests, but that could never be really permanently lost, because just living there in the healthful American geography and climate made everyone permanently virtuous and superior to people who lived anywhere else.

On the day he said goodbye to Mrs. Shaw next door, Patrick became inexplicably ill. His mother was much concerned. She put him to bed, the Merriwell books beside him on a table and overflowing to the floor.

"Would you like some ice cream?"

Patrick would.

She called Dr. Johnson.

Knowing the doctor was coming, Patrick shoved most of his books under the bed, just in case the doctor should be keener of mind than of medicine.

The medico, a corpulent man with red face, thumped Patrick on the chest and back with fingers, listened to his heart with a stethoscope, counted his pulse beat, then declared he could find nothing wrong.

"But Patrick is sick," Mrs. Cameron began.

46

Dr. Johnson held up his hand. "I know, I know. It's just that these things are not always immediately detectable. Even the best diagnosticians don't always know right away."

He assumed that practised look of thoughtfulness that doctors have, and said, "Make sure he has a good bowel movement every morning, feed him up well – that I always recommend – and call me if there's any change."

There had been no change in Patrick's condition. Autumn leaves fell and the weather became noticeably colder outside. Patrick immersed himself in Frank Merriwell at the rate of three a day. Sometimes he skipped a little, but not much. After two weeks Billy Coons and Jack Corson came to see him, both with plaintive expressions.

"How long you gonna stay in bed?" Billy wanted to know.

"Not much longer," Patrick assured them.

"Where are you sick?" Jack said.

"Just kinda sick all over. . . ."

Patrick lengthened his stride over the footbridge, then varied it so the drumming sound pleased his ears. On land again he skimmed over the gravel with elbows pumping, until a runnel of sweat escaped the headband and ran down his forehead. Remembering now, it could be said that Frank Merriwell had taught him something about the great republic to the south: How to be in love with yourself.

In this hot, unseasonable June weather, Patrick had reached an upper level of fitness. He ran without thinking about it any longer. If there were any bad habits in his stride and running posture, they were very minor. Charley horse, the athletic word for a pulled muscle, was foreign to him as well. And an incipient blister on his right foot disappeared when he gave it considered attention.

Capable now of five or six miles of sustained running, the time for such lavish outpouring of his energies was available only on weekends. There was a kind of wild joy in running, he realized. Much different from sitting in a car if you were old enough to be driving, pressing down on a pedal in the steel bug, and going faster and faster. The bug responded to what your mind said to your feet, relayed to the accelerator and motor and wheels, and zip went your mechanical servant. But all that was two or three times removed from your body doing the same thing by itself.

Thinking of this comparison, he pressed down on his own accelerator. And everything worked well. The legs responded, the heart-pump thumped a little faster, elbows brushed his side rhythmically. Like a greyhound, like a rabbit, like western movie star William S. Hart on his horse at Weller's Theatre, Patrick opened up. For sixty seconds of a multi-trillion-second lifetime, he stretched himself into as much as he was or could be.

The grey-brown gravel beneath him blurred. Green on either side of him blurred. The Trent River on its blue road north became a twisty, moving watercolour river in his mind. Those heavy parts of himself, yawning mouth and dopey cabbage head when he climbed from morning sleep, the cumbersome weight of himself – his very Patrickness – these were gone. For sixty seconds. A window into somewhere else, opening and closing.

A robin said something nearby. He slowed, turning his head toward the sound. The bird said two things, and sometimes three things. You had to listen hard to select the robin's voice from a continual slight hum in his ears, remove it from sound of sluffing feet on the gravel road. He glimpsed the bird, marching like a one-robin parade on the road's grassy shoulder; then two more robins appeared. The first had a smouldering copper breast, the other with grey-speckled breast, and seemingly uncertain of itself. Mother and either daughter or son?

He slowed and stopped to watch. The robins marched and counter-marched. The mother, leading, drove her beak into the ground like a yellow jackhammer. She wrestled with whatever it was, Patrick couldn't see. She lost the worm; no; she hadn't. She'd triumphed; yes.

And the sound came to him, the triumph sound, an *ee* sound, with an *ur* on the end of it. He tried to say the same thing with his own tongue. "Eerily, eerily," he said, then raised his voice louder and said it again. But it was a human voice, and the robins flew away. "Eerily," he said, trying to coax them back.

# 4

THE WAR IN EUROPE WAS ONLY real to Patrick when someone he knew died, or someone's brother or father was killed. A schoolmate would sometimes appear with pale face and red eyes. The other boys and girls stayed away from the bereaved youngster, unless they were close friends. But after four years of fighting, the war seemed a permanent condition, almost normal. It had been going on ever since he could remember. Patrick had been twelve when it started, but the war made little impression on him, despite serious faces of other people. Stories in the Trenton newspaper seemed to him just that – stories.

Ever since he could remember, the world outside himself had seemed strange and unfriendly, adults monstrous creatures when you're small yourself; he had withdrawn into the depths of his own mind. Even at sixteen and six feet tall, body lean and muscular, Patrick's expression was still overly serious. Unless reading something he thought funny or off by himself thinking, he rarely smiled.

Children's games he played with solemnity, a grave look that caused Billy Coons to yell at him in exasperation, "Don't you enjoy anything?" Patrick's expression grew even more solemn. "I enjoy the look on your face right now," he said, a twitch of humour on his mouth. Then both of them laughed, as if they had been storing it up for months. And perhaps Patrick had.

In 1915, the British Chemical Company took over Trenton. When their factory was built, just northeast of the town, most of the construction was contracted to the Gaylord Company of Scranton, Pennsylvania. Two years before entering the war, the United States was already involved in many aspects of the conflict. Engineers, executives, and workmen poured into Trenton from all across Ontario, Quebec, the Maritimes, some from as far away as the Prairies and British Columbia. And, of course, the United States.

Men the army didn't want. Men the army did want, but who had somehow evaded the net of military recruiters, changed the names and descriptions on their documents. Old men, with grey hair and a prideful look, who wanted to work and needed the money. As well as these, a few drunks or useless ne'er-do-wells. Those last were weeded out quickly, and vanished into nowhere. In a world at war – and nearly every nation took one side or the other – the weak, feeble, lazy, and simply unwilling-to-work, these disappeared into geographic and social crevices.

East of the Trent River, at the north end of Bocage Street, Gaylord had set up its construction camps. The site occupied more than three hundred acres, some of it heavily forested. Ex-lumberjacks, in the old of their age, from the failed Gilmour Lumber Company, scythed down the trees with axes and rusty crosscut saws. Other men dug footings and made forms. Cement was poured, wheelbarrows trundled back and forth on planks above omnipresent mud, and carpenters carpentered. If one had been able to take in the scene from a sufficient distance, it would have seemed that a colony of ants was establishing its new home.

Apart from the Gaylord architects and planners, and certain unmistakable lesser bureaucrats from Ottawa with important looks, everyone was recognizable for what they were. Their clothes and manner of speech labelled them, ordinarily. But some men who pretended to be carpenters were able to make their imposture good if quick enough of hand and cunning of mind. The difference between 25 cents an hour and 35 cents was only 10 cents, but it marked the difference between skill and ignorance. If you could use

51

a handsaw and square with assurance, pound a nail without removing too many fingernails, keep a straight face at the personnel office when the foreman-boss asked what you did for a living, and lie convincingly, then your metal identification tag said you were a carpenter.

The town swelled and boiled and trembled with the influx. Boarding houses filled, hotels were jammed, the largest hotel in town, the Gilbert House, was booked indefinitely. Tents on householders' lawns were available at inflated rentals; garages, attics, church halls, any space anywhere, all became money-makers for the owners. Even empty boxcars at the railway roundhouse on Dufferin Street had paying guests, and money changed hands for information that a boxcar on the siding was at least semi-permanent. Farmhouses in all directions around Trenton acquired tenants, strange boarders.

During the building boom, rumours circulated around poolrooms and the town barbershops that a murderer from the United States had escaped custody and was working at British Chemical. He was said to be a man of indeterminate age, who might be disguised, whose face could be any colour of the genetic rainbow, who carried a big Colt revolver concealed on his person, and was certainly very dangerous.

A German spy was also rumoured to be lurking among the hordes of foreign workmen. When explosives production began, this man would blow up the factory and town with it. Trenton water was poisoned, disease germs of cholera and the Black Death had been introduced into reservoirs. On weekend street corners, members of a foaming-mouthed religious sect proclaimed that the end of the world was at hand.

Barracks to house a thousand workmen were thrown up quickly at British Chemical; an army detachment guarded surrounding fences, patrolling a long periphery. Metal identification tags had to be produced by workers to gain admittance at the site. And three years later, in 1918, with the war winding down to its end, construction was still going on desultorily. By now the plant was producing over a million pounds of T.N.T. a month, as well as less dramatic items on the list of war's consumer goods. Boxcars were loaded with the stuff every few days, and they trundled eastward by rail to waiting ships on the Atlantic coast.

Some of the so-called carpenters had never pounded a nail or previously sawed a board. There were masons who scarcely knew what wet cement looked like, and plumbers who didn't know the meaning of the word. Some workmen showed up in the morning, then left and played pea-pool in town all day, returning before the end of their shift looking bedraggled and worn-out with labour. These were actors of such excellence they could have played the stage at Weller's Theatre if Tom Mix and William S. Hart hadn't already been there in silent movies. A few workmen moonlighted at full-time jobs elsewhere. But that didn't matter to Gaylord. After all, the British government was responsible for every dollar spent, and Gaylord spent British money as if it were water pouring over No. 1 dam.

Colourful posters adorned every vacant space in Trenton. Citizens were adjured not to discuss their work in public places: the war could be lost by careless tongues. Spies were listening. Recruiting posters that featured Lord Kitchener with his fierce moustache screamed silently at the few healthy young men who had escaped the military dragnet.

In the morning, on his runs, Patrick would encounter workmen on their way to and from British Chemical. Many of them carried lunch pails or paper-wrapped packages of sandwiches. In the late afternoon, men on the shift that finished at midnight swarmed in from everywhere. They walked, rode bicycles, and drove autos; two or three even rode horses, pasturing them wherever they could.

The town, of course, became very prosperous. Employment was nearly 100 per cent. Occasionally there was an accident at the munitions plant. Someone died from a fall, or else from causes tactfully suppressed, arms and legs got broken. It was the nature of things. To be expected. You can't make an omelet without cracking some eggs. But doctors were available, nurses on duty. And all through the war, rumours and counter-rumours were heard everywhere in Trenton; the pubs seethed with them. Submarines were suspected to be in the innocent blue river.

And there was fear among the townspeople, expressed as silence or avoided in speech altogether.

At King Street Church the Reverend Eustace Hartwell, speaking of the Blessed Trinity – Father, Son, and Holy Ghost – mentioned another trinity, not quite so blessed. Tri-nitro-toluene, T.N.T., the three-headed monster, short for the compound chemical formula $CH_3C_6H_2(NO_2)_3$. And short for death. The explosive used in artillery shells and bombs. A brownish solid crystal compound, manufactured in large quantities at British Chemical.

After the Reverend Hartwell spoke of this unholy trinity, some people in his congregation dreamed of it. Three-headed monsters with knobby brown faces were glimpsed at garden gates, peering through doorways like peeping Toms, crawling from toilets with dripping faces, oozing out of rotting compost heaps. A thing that had been impersonal and scientifically remote had been endowed with a frightening name.

Those who dreamed monsters might have been accused of drinking if the existence of a genuine three-headed monster at British Chemical hadn't been undeniable. Still, the Reverend Hartwell toned down his sermon a week later in the interests of the war effort. But the T.N.T. monster, once conjured up, was difficult to exorcize. It glowered over the shoulders of Hartwell's congregation, and menaced worshippers at the Anglican and Roman Catholic churches. Hartwell considered mention of this unholy trinity one of his more profitable rhetorical ideas, since afterwards the collection plate shimmered with silver abundance.

Patrick had his own monster to contend with, and decided the monster was himself. Before the June exams, after which Grade 10 students were allowed to sniff the rarified air of upper academia, he dreamed his own dream. In it he failed the examination. Miss Gothard, Miss Darley, Mr. Splore, and Mr. McIver all stood around him with accusing faces and pointing fingers.

Sitting in the living room, his mother wept voluminously as she read the examination results. The room quickly filled with her tears. "Oh, Patrick!" she sobbed unrelentingly. He tried the exams again and failed again.

A scene of the utmost solemnity: Patrick could see himself outside his own body as a twenty-foot monster. His teachers were only three feet high. They surrounded him with commiserating faces. "Come on, Patrick, you'll do it next time," they chorused like cheerleaders. In an aside to Mr. McIver, Miss Darley hissed, "We've got to get him out of here! He'll crush one of the little ones."

They were all watching him, fearfully, shrinking away from the failed monster. Patrick sobbed, his mother sobbed. And he swam to safety through ten-foot waves of his own tears.

Years passed. Billy Coons and Jack Corson, both about the size of Tom Thumb, shook the monster's hand cautiously for fear of getting fingers crushed. "It was nice to have known you," Billy said, wriggling his fingers to restore circulation.

"Sure was," Jack Corson echoed.

"We'll miss you," both of them said.

Tears were shed. The only nice thing about it was Kevin Morris's reaction. He looked scared. Patrick in the guise of monster said "Yah-yah-yah" to Kevin, then woke up.

He felt depressed. He wanted to stay in bed and not go to school. And not run any more – what was the use? Get those old Frank Merriwell books out of the closet; forget exams. Forget Jean, and the way her pale blue eyes made him tingle at both periphery and interior.

During examination week teachers paraded up and down like overseers in front of labouring serfs. They kept both eyes open for cheaters: students who wrote answers to possible questions on wrists and palms with indelible pencils; or secreted scraps of paper with relevant information up their sleeves, inside waistbands of clothes, somewhere, anywhere, desperate for answers their minds failed to provide.

Surprisingly, Patrick found the exams not nearly as difficult as he'd expected. And a couple of weeks later, when it was discovered that the average of his marks placed him sixth in the class, surprise was uppermost among everyone who knew him. Mrs. Morris's dark face was disturbed at the news. She managed to convey to Patrick's mother that his sixth-place finish was an accident, without actually saying it aloud.

"Mistakes are made," Mrs. Morris said. "And you mark my words, things get adjusted later, things get settled, things get – " she stopped in slight embarrassment, but "things" were apparently still on her mind.

"I'm pleased for you that Kevin continues to do so well," Mrs. Cameron said. "I don't suppose he'll follow his father's profession . . . "

That was a rather risky, if not actually catty, thing to say. The sound of Kevin's father's profession was at that moment carrying through the kitchen window; a thin film

56

of dust dirtied the sill and had to be wiped daily. John Morris employed compressed air to power his chisels. The sound of steel attacking granite, incising names and dates of birth and death, was like that of an angry woodpecker trying to break through a plate-glass window. But amplified a thousand times.

"Of course not," Mrs. Morris said grumpily. "Not that it isn't a good and honourable profession . . ."

"Of course it is," Mrs. Cameron went on. "I've always told everyone that."

Mrs. Morris said "Humphh" huffily, beginning to realize it shouldn't be necessary to tell everyone that being a memorial craftsman was an honourable profession – not if it actually was an honourable profession. She glanced sharply at her neighbour, "What do you mean?"

"I'm just getting ready to go out," Mrs. Cameron said smoothly. "I need some things at the grocery. Is there anything you'd like me to pick up for you? Save you the trip?"


Patrick was afflicted sometimes with a non-divine discontent with himself. Dissatisfaction with his face in the bathroom mirror; the gawky raw-boned impression he knew was what others saw when they looked at him. And was there character in the familiar stranger's face that stared back at him?

Talking with an older person sometimes, he would notice that person's eyes change, lose focus, and knew they'd stopped listening to what he was saying. Most older people were like that, on an ascending scale. People of extreme age, say fifty, scarcely paid any attention to him at all. But strangely, after about seventy, people started listening again. Perhaps they had more time in old age.

Portugee, at ninety, fixed him with pale ferocious eyes and gave his entire attention. His Uncle Wilfred – who wasn't an uncle at all, but some kind of cousin – was also a good listener. Uncle Wilfred was seventy-five. He smoked a pipe and prefaced most of his speeches with a guttural *harr-rr*, then paused as if about to announce something important, like the Second Coming of Christ. His bushy grey-and-yellow moustache was tobacco-stained; it managed to bristle even with the ends drooping.

Old people were a puzzle. A few were garrulous and talked all the time. But many of them seemed to have added another hour to the twenty-four, one they used for their friends. As if, when their jobs and other duties had lessened, lives getting shorter, they grew more aware of other people.

He often saw such people next door. They came to look at tombstones, asking Mr. Morris questions about prices and quality. The memorial craftsman talked to them about eternity, and how their names chiselled on granite would last forever – "Well, nearly." And what kind of lettering did they want – "Now this gothic script is nice."

Patrick watched from an upstairs window. Mr. Morris's manner was sometimes brisk and deferential, and Patrick knew the potential customer was wealthy enough to ensure a good profit. If Mr. Morris's demeanour was brusque, though always polite, the financial status of his visitor was invariably low. The only way of judging this Dun & Bradstreet rating was from Mr. Morris's own behaviour. If he danced attendance on someone, that person was assuredly a millionaire.

Old people assessing the value and attractive appearance of tombstones were generally serious about the amount of money they intended to spend. Once Patrick saw an old man with tears in his eyes, but he was sure the reason was not money. More often the memorial shoppers were ensuring that death did not take them totally unawares. Mr. Morris assured them beforehand that their names and dates of death would be incised on eternal granite.

Rarely, an elderly couple would be holding hands. Most of the shoppers of death were calm. He noticed one couple whose fingers touched as if by accident; their expression was of serenity.

"Shoppers of death" was a phrase that had occurred to Patrick early that spring. He savoured it, the dark clothes, faces written on by time, and the talk of money that was a necessity for both the living and the dead. The gentleness of some, the businesslike manner of others; the yearning that even in death their tombstone should do them credit, testify to respectability while they were alive.

For the summer holidays, Patrick set himself a regimen for his running. Five miles a day through the week: ten or twelve miles on Saturdays; rest on Sundays. The reasons for such heroic or foolish exertions were still vague in his mind. Kevin Morris was undoubtedly a factor, something like the irritating bit of sand inside an oyster that might eventually become a pearl. Kevin was irritating, but he wasn't the entire reason.

One Saturday in July, on the road to Frankford – a village several miles from Trenton – Patrick stopped at his Uncle Wilfred's.

"Harr-rr," the old man said in greeting. Then he attempted to clear his throat with a sound like choking. A great cud of chewing tobacco in his mouth impeded speech; he transferred it to his cheek. Uncle Wilfred spat. A stream of brown liquid fully six feet long flashed diagonally toward the silver spittoon, a few drops quivering on the rim. They hesitated there before falling on the clean blue linoleum.

"What ye up to, boy?"

"It's my long-run day, Uncle Wilfred," Patrick said. "I'm going along the river toward Frankford."

"Don't see any use for it," the old man said chidingly. "If the good Lord wanted people to run everywhere they went, He'da given them wheels instead of feet."

"Maybe He did both."

"Harr-rr – what ye mean?"

"Well, those Ford cars have got wheels. So do carts and buggies from farms. The Lord gave people wheels when He saw that feet weren't going to be enough. Isn't that right?"

Uncle Wilfred meditated while tamping tobacco into an ancient pipe that Patrick could smell across the room. The old man was never seen during waking hours without either pipe or chewing tobacco. His worn blue serge suit was pocked with brown spots where burning tobacco had landed. Rooms of the small frame house were permeated with the smell.

"Weather's good," he said surprisingly.

Patrick nodded, not knowing how to reply.

"Lotsa rain. Farmers ain't complainin. . . . " He took the pipe from his mouth, pointing the stem at Patrick. "What'd this country do without farmers?"

The question was accusing, as if Patrick had somehow been responsible for a recent scarcity of farmers.

Uncle Wilfred had been one himself until a few years before. When his wife died the farm was sold, cattle auctioned off, himself removed to the yellow-painted cottage in Trenton. In rare moments, when he mentioned his past life, he'd say to Patrick, "Aunt Em's waitin for me."

Patrick shivered at the thought, pins and needles in his chest, as if the idea took up too much space in his head and made his chest uncomfortable. His eyes wandered around the living room, to the rocking chair and walnut sideboard. The place had an untended, womanless look, despite a cleaning woman who did for it twice a week. He remembered Aunt Em vaguely, an unremarkable woman to anyone but Uncle Wilfred.

60

"Harr-rr!" The sound fell with a splash into silence. "Ye been readin that book I gave ye?"

For a moment Patrick couldn't remember any book. Then it came to him. It had been more than a year ago when the book was given to him.

"The poems of Alfred Lord Tennyson," he said. "Yes. I read 'The Lady of Shalott' – 'On either side the river lie/ Long fields of barley and of rye – '"

The old man held up his hand hastily. "That's all right. I read it myself years back, leastways your Aunt Em read it to me." He struck a kitchen match under the seat of his rocking chair, holding it to the pipe and making *puff-puff-puff* sounds for a few moments. Obscured behind a blue fog, he rocked slowly back and forth.

"The Frankford Road, hey?"

Patrick nodded.

"You hearda the Glen Miller Rock, boy?"

Patrick shook his head.

"Tarnation big rock. Folks come down from Toronto to look at it. I hear tell they measured it, chipped at it with hammers, took pieces away with 'em. They made a great fuss about it."

"Why did they do that, Uncle Wilfred?"

"Seems like that rock's been there near as long as God made the earth. Old Rentee Burling told me what they said about it. It was glaciers did it!"

He leaned back in his rocking chair and allowed a series of smoke rings to float away from his mouth, blue rings in the almost blue air that sunlight could not really penetrate. Almost reaching the ceiling before dissolution, they reminded Patrick of the small spaceships he had seen in magazines.

"Did what, Uncle Wilfred?"

"Took 'em there. It was the glaciers. You know anything about them glaciers, boy?"

"Only that they're ice."

"Glaciers!" Uncle Wilfred said triumphantly. "It was glaciers brought that big rock to Glen Miller. And whaddaya thinka that, boy?"

The question confused Patrick. For a moment he didn't know what to think. "How do I get to see this big rock?"

"It's more'n a mile off'n the road. An' there's a path through the woods leadin in. . . ."

The faded eyes grew distant. "My place was on the way, on the way to Frankford. . . . It had cows, and there was roses, and Em used to water them roses all the time. . . ."

Blue smoke climbed above Uncle Wilfred, his face seemed composed of it. The rocking chair was moving to and fro, to and fro. Then it stopped.

Patrick left without saying goodbye. Uncle Wilfred wasn't noticing anything at all. The smoke around his head was peopled by the dead. He could speak to them, lips moving around the pipe stem, but his visitors said nothing, just stared from the smoke.

Patrick thought the past must be more real to the old man than here and now. When you thought of people who didn't exist any more, and a world that was greatly changed – when you thought of that most of the time, then the past became real again. Here and now had become partly a fantasy.

He left the town behind, feet touching the gravel road in even rhythm, his thoughts growing lighter. Birds were singing – where were the robins he'd seen the other day? He thought of Jean with her yellow hair and blue dress. She was a fairly tall girl, about five feet six inches. Condensing the thought, he made her small enough to enter his mind. She smiled there inside the bone rooms, as if she knew what he was doing.

Along the roadside, he noticed white Queen Anne's lace, and Indian paintbrush, brown-eyed Susans. Wildflowers. And yellow butter-and-eggs, whose other name he didn't know. He scooped up a few of the blossoms as he ran, a varicoloured rainbow. And pressed them against the side of his head so that Jean could see.

He smiled. "A gift for you." She did not refuse them.

The farmer in his wagon, going late to market, stared in disbelief. "Big potatoes and little potatoes!" he said to his wife. "What's that boy doin?"

A warm July wind touched Patrick's face as he ran. And the clouds were fat tubular faces watching him, wondering why he was wasting his time like this. Wasting his time? No, whatever else running was, it was not that. He slipped the gold-plated watch from his pocket to see how long he'd been running. Not that he'd ever timed his actual running speed; the watch was a talisman, a good luck charm. He ran his fingers over the chased gold design on the snap lid covering the watch face. It had been his father's timepiece. He could imagine the stern-faced man standing in the barn or vineyard, looking at it, saying to himself, "Must get back and help Elly move that furniture. . . ."

In all the snapshots of his father scattered in photo albums and desk drawers, Fred Cameron was serious and solemn – noticeably unsmiling. A horse had stepped on his foot when he was a young man, leaving him with a slight limp. What had he been like at Guelph Agricultural College? Thin face, dark brown hair, rather like the picture of Julius Caesar in history books – a limping Caesar? It was not an altogether fantastic thought.

Fred Cameron had left few mementoes of himself behind. The watch, some books in the old drop-leaf desk, scribblers with writing exercises. He had practised writing, whole rows of O's and P's, all the letters of the alphabet. Time after time, he had written individual letters, then he had written words, until finally he had vanished beneath the words, all his own character and personality gone. A machine might have done the same thing.

The word for all this was calligraphy, for which prizes were awarded at business colleges. And his father had attended one of those as well. In old photographs, he was always wearing a business suit with white shirt and tie, never overalls, and holding a pitchfork with cow shit on his clodhopper farm boots. Never smiling.

It wrenched Patrick's heart to think of that serious face. And his own handwriting, like a chicken's feet scrabbling in mud. Despite scolding teachers, the handwriting that was said to be "the mirror of his soul" would never achieve that machine-like perfection.

There was a puzzle and mystery about his father's face that he would never solve. When his own photograph had been taken by a professional photographer at age three, he, too, had been very serious. Dressed in a Little Lord Fauntleroy suit with lace around collar and cuffs, given a toy rabbit on wheels to play with, the serious small boy's face did somewhat resemble the father's implacable look. But those fancy clothes had been valid reason for seriousness, especially if he'd been seen by other boys. And he'd probably had a furtive expression entering and leaving the photographer's building. . . .

A wolfish-looking dog appeared from a nearby farmhouse. It ran toward him with lowered head, growling and baring its teeth. The slavering beast looked part German shepherd, part wolf, and all monster. It wanted his blood. Twenty feet away the growl had become a deep-throated roar.

Patrick was scared. He did what he had done on other occasions, picked up a couple of big stones from the road. And kept his eyes on the dog's every hint of intention. The beast looked ready to leap at him; its performance had now become a whole series of alternating growls and roars.

Patrick's flesh prickled, as if he were very hot or very cold. Fear. It was like nothing but itself. He threw a stone, wound up like a baseball pitcher, a small prayer invisible with the stone.

It struck the dog's shoulder, with lightning effect. The animal turned and skittered off sideways, with a scared, apologetic look. One foot dragged a little. It was lame. Its lameness was poignant to Patrick, for he had just been thinking of his lame father.

Groundhogs on the river road ahead popped up from their burrows, and popped back down again when he got too close. Brown dots on the roadside grass. A man digging in his garden nearby stopped, one foot balanced on his shovel.

"Beg pardon," Patrick said. "Do you know about a big boulder around here they call the Glen Miller Rock?"

The garden man was about fifty with grey hair, and he chewed tobacco. His jaws moved quickly as if he was talking with his mouth closed. While Patrick watched, he expelled a charge of brown juice. It fled his mouth in a nearly straight line, clipping a potato bug.

"Gotcha," the man said.

"Can you do that again?" Patrick wanted to know.

"Gotta sluice up some more nectar first." The chewer's jaws swivelled sideways and up and down, lips puckering a little. There was a *ptui* sound Patrick hadn't noticed before. This time the brown-missile juice travelled about eight feet, describing a slight parabola in the middle of its flight, interrupting the lovemaking of two potato bugs like a chocolate-coloured Armageddon.

"What was that you was sayin?"

"Glen Miller Rock – have you heard of it?"

"I practically grew up on it. Come winter I useta slide down it when there was snow. Clomb up there with Cal Stevens – but Cal, he's dead now. Got cold two winters back, and it come to pneumonia, the doc said. Cal and me, we useta race each other to the top o' that rock. He was king of the castle. I was generally the dirty rascal. You ever play that game?"

The man's eyes were squinted and remembering, his reddish face had what looked like a three-day beard. "Cal was my friend," the man said, and unexpectedly his eyes filled with tears.

Patrick was embarrassed and slightly stunned, but kept the feeling out of his voice. "Could you tell me where this Glen Miller Rock is? I mean – "

A long arm pointed down the road. "There's a sign for Glen Miller village. Ye see it? Well, right past that there sign is a path goin into the woods. Can't see it from here, but it's there."

The man's lips moved and squinched together, as if he was preparing another bug demolition. Instead he said, "You come back and tell me if you can't find that path." The shadow of a grin was visible around brown teeth.

"I will, I will!" Patrick said hurriedly. "I got to go, I guess. . . . "

He turned quickly, a trickle of sweat coursing down between his shoulder blades. Glancing behind, fifty yards down the road, he saw the man still standing in his garden, motionless as before.

Beyond the Glen Miller sign there was no trace of a village. But a path wandered east through the woods and toward a steep hill. Patrick scrabbled up it, clutching shrubs and small trees on either side to keep his balance. He was sweating, and the bugs started to bother him. Deerflies – they took half a pound of you when they bit. And waiting atop the hill, what seemed like an acre of poison ivy, the triple leaves just yearning to embrace his bare ankles.

A grass-bordered brook wandered around on the hill's other side, in no hurry to go anywhere, just fast enough to be on its way. Patrick sat down on the grassy bank, removing shoes, dangling his feet in cool water. A blue jay scolded downstream. It went "*too-wheedle, too-wheedle*," and scolded some more. He saw a perky head with black necklace, then heard an enchanting trill he couldn't translate to words; a song for visitors to the bird's forest kingdom.

After another mile into the forest, he glimpsed the rock. It was well over twenty feet high by Patrick's estimate; steep and impossible to climb at one end, but sloping at the other. It was covered with moss and lichen, slippery even when you tried to climb on hands and knees. At the summit of the small mountain, he still couldn't see above the treetops and felt buried in all that green. A vegetable sea.

Back down again, he scraped at the boulder with a small sharp rock. When lichen and moss were gone, the stone underneath looked to be granite. It was Uncle Wilfred's glacier boulder, but he didn't know what that meant. And resolved to find out.

By now it was late afternoon. He reckoned the running distance to and from the boulder at about eight miles. That was the longest distance he'd covered yet, and rewarded himself by knowing it.

Behind the house, after returning, he noticed Kevin poking his head from an upstairs window of the Morris residence cum factory. Kevin gave him a small wave of the hand and a half-grin. Then the head ducked back out of sight.

Before he rousted Gyp out from under the woodshed, Patrick said, "Mom, how do I find out about glaciers?"

Mrs. Cameron brushed the hair from her forehead and shrugged. "Why, an encyclopaedia, I guess. Why? Did you study glaciers at school?"

"Uh-uh," Patrick said. "I'd just like to know . . ."

On the way to his meditation place under the river willows, he said to the dog, "Gyp, where were you when I needed you this afternoon?"

The dog stopped and looked at him, closed his mouth on the panting tongue for a moment, and cocked his head sideways.

"Don't play innocent," Patrick told him. "I'm on to you. And you know what I'm talking about, that other dog . . ."

Gyp wagged his stubby tail, that was all.

# 5

IT WAS LIKE A GREAT CITY, the British Chemical Company's buildings, as Patrick approached them. But a city darkened by dirty smoke pouring from pipes and chimneys, steam hissing, and the bubbling of mysterious liquids, alchemists' mixtures. The place squatted and brooded, like something out of another time, despite the railway spur line and a parking area for automobiles and wagons.

Within a hundred yards or so of the factory compound, trees and bushes were leafless, apparently dying. A block from the munitions factory grass was brown and desiccated. There was a faint smell of rotten eggs in the air. Shielded behind a low escarpment called Bunker Hill, lights were shining. The light itself was coloured by chemical smoke, orange and pink and yellow.

Early evening. The day had grown dark with heavy black clouds overhead, rain seeming imminent. The air steamy and wet. Patrick's body felt damp and sticky. It was less than two miles from the centre of Trenton, this foul-smelling place he had come to. But it was a foretaste of hell. Not the hell of the Christian Bible, but a man-made hell.

He decided it was no place for him. That thought was in his mind as a vivid bolt of lightning split the sky. Lightning was attractive to Patrick. As a small boy he had often stayed on the house veranda, watching storms from the shelter of canvas awnings. And felt himself shaken and twisted by thunder and lightning, his insides turned upside-down and tied in knots.

It was a vaudeville show, a fireworks display; it was also a discovery of himself. Only once, when the entire sky trembled all around him, flooring the gravel road with silver and bleaching colour from veranda awnings – only once had he cried out and run into the house terrified.

The storm tonight was worse. Trees and bushes all around him turned briefly luminescent, glowing electrically. Shadows vanished. Shadings of things ended. And rain. Rain so heavy that each raindrop felt heavy, part of a continuous stream, a nail of water pounded into the earth. The ground underfoot was sodden in a few moments. Patrick, dressed in shorts, jersey, and running shoes, gasped for breath under the deluge.

He ran. As if by flight he could escape the rain, cross the horizon, and outrun the storm. Ahead of him chain lightning tangled itself around factory chimneys. The entire complex moved up and down in waves before his eyes, as if the earth were shaking.

Patrick blundered ahead. He crashed up against a chain-link fence, then turned right and followed the fence. And found himself at a guardhouse, soldiers visible through rain-smeared windows. He pressed against the door. It opened suddenly; he sprawled ungracefully at the feet of the soldiers.

"How ya doin, kid?" a voice said good-humouredly.

He stared at the man's feet, puttees like brown bandages wound around his legs, and felt bewildered.

"Too wet for ya out there?" the man said. "I guess, I just guess. Now climb offa that floor and onto your hind legs."

The soldier had two stripes on his arm denoting corporal, and wore sidearms buckled around his waist. "My name's Adams, kid. What's yours?"

Patrick's voice choked and quavered before he could say his name. Corporal Adams threw him a towel. "Go ahead, dry yourself."

Patrick shivered uncontrollably. He couldn't speak, his hands trembled and his face was cold.

Adams was concerned. "I'll find you something to wear, an old sweater of mine, maybe? You don't wanna catch cold."

Without warning, the sky cracked open. Lightning stammered across Bunker Hill, appeared to touch buildings delicately, then left them in total darkness. Thunder rattled windows and invaded their brains, replacing all thought. Lights in the guardhouse went out.

"Dammit!" Adams said, appearing in the murk as a giant shadow moving among other shadows.

Patrick bolted. Almost immediately he stumbled so hard against a building it made his ears ring. Behind him, Corporal Adams was shouting, "Come back here. . . ."

After that he could see a little, dark sky lightening into a greyish gunmetal colour. The shapes of buildings brooded above him ominously. And the lights came on. From all directions lights beamed down, wiping out shadows.

A hearty voice behind Patrick said, "Here to see how the war effort is getting along, son? I thought so. Well, now, you just tag along with me, an' I'll show you the stuff we make that'll blow the Germans to smithereens." The voice became a laugh that gurgled in his throat. "Smithereens!"

It was just a little man who made all the noise, half a head shorter than Patrick. The man's nose, eyes, and mouth were squeezed together in the centre of a broad forty-year-old face.

"Name's Jim Pumper. 'Pumper this and Pumper that,' my wife says." He looked puzzled. "I don't know what she means. But come along now."

Patrick followed the little man. He hadn't intended to be a sightseer at British Chemical, but since the chance had offered itself, why not?

Pumper stopped at some twenty-foot-tall vats, with catwalks around them and ladders leading to the narrow walkways. "These here are cypress-wood vats, where we boil the cotton," he said importantly. "That's how we make guncotton to kill Germans with." He leered at Patrick. "Only good German is a dead German. This guncotton keeps 'em dead."

That seemed rather bloodthirsty to Patrick, but he said nothing.

"Now I'm gonna clomb this ladder. You stay right behind me," Pumper told him.

Peering over the vat's wooden rim, into its interior, they could see workmen below in the dim grey light. The workmen were shovelling with wooden paddles at greyish wet masses of something that looked like a strange seaweed.

"That there's the guncotton before it can go bangbang," Pumper said. He looked at Patrick suspiciously. "You got any matches on ya? It'll cost ya ten dollars' fine if ya got matches in yer pockets."

Patrick shook his head, a little frightened. Ten dollars was more money than he'd seen for weeks. His monthly allowance was only five dollars, which he thought very generous. And this odd little man was threatening him. "Mr. Pumper," he said, "maybe I shouldn't see any more. Maybe it's top secret or something."

Pumper looked grim. "You been vouched for. You wouldn't be here if you hadn't. I gotta show you how we do things. That's my job."

He levered his small body over the rim of the vat, onto a ladder that ended below in a bare spot among the grey seaweed. He disappeared, calling back to Patrick, "Come on, come on, don't waste time!"

They stood on an island of the slimy dark wood, like castaways in a sea of guncotton. Pumper yelled at the men shovelling around them, "This here's Patrick. He's the mayor's son, come to see how we do things . . ."

The men glanced up with sweaty faces, four of them, grinning at him. One looked Oriental, maybe Chinese, another was black. He noticed their trousers and shirts were an odd shade of pink.

Pumper saw him staring and guessed what he was thinking. "Acid does that, takes the colour right out. Why, I seen guys with red hair and blue eyes come outa here bleached near white."

He pointed at the black man, whose classically handsome face wrinkled in response. "See Hackett there?"

Patrick nodded.

"He's gonna come outa this cypress-wood vat with pink eyes, pink hair, pink skin, and no prick . . ."

A roar of laughter poured out of the workmen, rebounding from narrow walls and sounding like "ah-ah-ah." It was eerie, this place – and so was Pumper. Besides, he couldn't remember telling the man his name was Patrick, or saying anything about himself at all.

"I'd like to leave," he said stiffly.

They climbed the ladder to outside; it felt like an escape from something. And Pumper introduced him to another man, much older, and without Pumper's own twinkling eyes. A grumpy face – that judgement borne out when the man said, "You come along quick now, I've got no time."

When Pumper left them, Patrick was sure he saw something like pity in the man's eyes. "Goodbye, Pumper," he said, and a blinding searchlight made Pumper disappear in the glare. There had been something lovable about him; he missed Pumper already.

He didn't hear his new guide's name and title. "I'm Mr. Foreman," Mr. Foreman supplied, staring at him with a demented look.

Patrick noticed constricting lines on both sides of Mr. Foreman's mouth and nose that kept his expression prisoner.

They stopped at a barn-like building. "You ain't dressed for no sightseeing," his guide accused. "You sure you got your pass to come here?"

Patrick was confused, then irritated. "Mr. Foreman, if you have any doubts about me, ask Corporal Adams at the guardhouse." He narrowed his eyes the way he had seen Tom Mix do in a western movie. "Otherwise . . . otherwise, you'll answer to the higher-ups. Understand?"

Mr. Foreman did, but wasn't noticeably humbled. He pointed at half a dozen men nailing boxes closed. Patrick thought the hammers they used looked peculiar.

"That there's guncotton." And he recognized the grey seaweed-looking stuff from Mr. Pumper's previous tour.

"We hafta use copper nails and copper hammers to box it. You know why?"

Patrick said "No."

Mr. Foreman gestured impressively. "On accounta we'd blow the world sky-high if we didn't."

No one spoke. The copper hammers kept hitting the copper nails without producing sparks. Patrick felt his face change into the expected expression, mouth open and rather awed. But behind how he looked was a small boredom. These people were doing their best to make him feel impressed, to make him say "Sir!" He was annoyed, as much at himself as anyone.

"Let's go!" he said, with a stern look at Mr. Foreman. "I have just so much time to spend here. Let's get on with it."

Mr. Foreman was unchastened. "Young fella," he said, "you just do like I say. Ain't no use complainin 'cause you're the manager's son. I'm the official shower-arounder here. I got the authority" – and he puffed out his chest – "I got the authority, on accounta you don't do like I say you could get killed. Understand me now?"

Patrick subsided within himself, resolved not to say another word. But he was annoyed. This sour old man acted like all his schoolteachers rolled into one.

They stopped before another large vat, from which came a rumbling gurgle like someone being sick to their stomach. Mr. Foreman climbed the ladder to a catwalk around the vat, gesturing to Patrick, "Come along now."

The disturbed digestion sound proved to be that of a heavy-looking liquid of a dull red colour, rather like porridge, with bubbles surfacing all over it and making a popping noise.

"That there's nitric acid," Mr. Foreman said. "Don't you touch it; the stuff burns your skin. See here." He rolled up his shirtsleeve to reveal an angry red area on his forearm about three inches long.

"I want to see the T.N.T.," Patrick said impatiently. A vision of the three-headed monster the Reverend Hartwell talked about flashed before his eyes. *Tri-nitro-toluene*. It was like a spell, a conjure formula. Three small gods rolled into one large one. And those others: black powder, dynamite, saltpetre, nitric and sulphuric acids, guncotton. . . . And they too were very deadly little gods. Did they bow down and worship the stronger deity T.N.T.? Our Father Who art in Armageddon, unhallowed be Thy Name; Thy Kingdom, which is the Kingdom of Death, Thy Face no man dares look upon. . . .

Patrick shook his head vigorously. His imagination was entirely too vivid. He looked at the gunmetal sky, its focus narrowed by black buildings. The rain had stopped. Mr. Foreman was urging him ahead.

"No, I've seen enough. Don't show me anything more."

Pumper jumped out of the shadows, giggling, rubbing his hands together. "I've got some nice things to show you." He extended his closed fist in front of Patrick. "Guess what?" he challenged. "What've I got in my hand?"

"I've no idea," Patrick said.

"Guess, guess!"

Mr. Foreman, looking on, smiled indulgently. He'd seen this byplay before.

"How can I guess? Give me some kind of hint."

"It begins with a *d*, it begins with a *d*!"

Patrick ran through the *d*'s that came to mind . . . dishes, dasher, damn, diddle . . . but he couldn't think of any more *d*'s. "I'm sorry."

Pumper danced up and down with impatience. "All right, all right, but I think you're pretty stupid." He opened his hand, disclosing a belt buckle and some metal buttons. The kind of buttons you see on overalls and work clothes.

"Is this a joke?" Patrick said indignantly.

"No joke, no joke. The buckle and buttons came from the bottom of the acid tank after it was drained. The gun-cotton shovellers gave them to me for souvenirs." He reached toward Patrick. "Here, I want you to have them."

"No, I don't want them . . ."

"Don't be so hard to please," Pumper said. He reached inside his overalls and produced a round yellowish object, about the size of a football. "Take this then. It came from the bottom of the vat. I want you to have something to remember us."

He thrust it at Patrick. "Its meaning starts with a *d*."

What Pumper had in his hand was a skull, bare of flesh, grinning with the unfailing grin of the dead.

Patrick screamed – or someone did. Lights went out again, and the rain came down hard. His face was wet with rain, or perhaps blood? An image of the yellow skull filled his head. Perhaps his own skull wasn't there any more, and this yellow bone thing had replaced it. He reached up his hand to feel hair, his own hair, fingers exploring for empty eye sockets and fleshless mouth.

"It's all right, dear," his mother said. "You've been dreaming."

"What happened? Where's Pumper, where's Mr. Foreman?"

Mrs. Cameron bathed his forehead with a cool towel, the water running into his eyes. There was difficulty in focusing them because of the wetness.

He shoved her hand away. "What happened to me?"

"He'll be all right," a man's voice said. "There's no concussion, just a bump on the head."

It was Dr. Johnson, now so fat he didn't need suspenders. "Keep him in bed a couple of days, that's all. The guard corporal at British Chemical said he must've stumbled over his own feet and fell – "

Patrick resented the sound of that. He *was* clumsy, but they were accusing him of even greater clumsiness. "I did not stumble over my feet," he said clearly.

"There," Dr. Johnson said, "you see? He's feeling better already. Just a couple of days in bed." And musingly, "I wonder what he was doing at that munitions factory anyway. Nobody's supposed to get in there without a pass."

Patrick felt indignant. "They invited me in. And Pumper showed me around. So did Mr. Foreman."

Dr. Johnson shook his head at Mrs. Cameron and came to Patrick's feet, a large belly taking up most of the space between Patrick and his mother.

"He may be a little mixed-up for a while. Keep that bandage on a few days more while he's getting better. Sleep, let him sleep, that's good medicine. And remember, a bowel movement every day."

He waved one pudgy hand, "I'll see myself out."

And Patrick slept, dreaming of bowel movements.

On the second day in bed, Kevin Morris came to see him. Mrs. Cameron showed the visitor into Patrick's room, her face unreadable. She raised the window blind and adjusted the blankets. "I'll be just downstairs. If you want anything, call me." She glanced briefly at Kevin before leaving.

There was a slightly uncomfortable silence. Then Kevin said, "I've been thinking about that time when you were running behind me on the school track . . ." and he paused, seeming to gather himself to say, "I was rude. I want to apologize."

This was entirely unexpected. Patrick stared at Kevin as if he'd never seen the other boy before. As if by registering his physical appearance, he'd be able to decide what was happening inside.

Kevin was the same age as Patrick, but shorter and slighter in build. He was dark-faced, now slightly flushed, grey eyes embarrassed. "I meant what I said that day. I'd be glad to help you."

To say those words cost Kevin Morris something, of pride perhaps. And Patrick felt confused at this generous attitude. On the other hand, Kevin's little speech meant he thought he was capable of helping, that he was superior enough to help.

"I appreciate the offer," Patrick said. "I did go to Bob Prebble for advice; he gave me a few hints. You mean help with running, don't you? Or maybe Latin?" He grinned at Kevin. "If I were a legionnaire with Caesar's army in Gaul, he'd never be able to understand my Latin."

Kevin grinned back. "If you even spoke to the commanding general, if he didn't speak to you first, they'd have you crucified. Did you ever think that our mathematics teacher looks a little like Julius Caesar? I mean like the pictures of Caesar taken from old Roman coins . . . ?"

It hadn't occurred to Patrick, but the idea delighted him. "Mr. Clubb, on entering Cleopatra's bedroom: *Veni*, *vidi*, *vici* – I came, I saw, I ran like hell."

That eased the situation, after some laughter. Patrick chose his words carefully, realizing as he said them that the carefulness showed. "I owe you something," he said, and it surprised him to be saying it. "Yes, I did get the idea of my running from your running . . ."

Kevin nodded, "I thought so."

And there was that superior look again.

"But only that, just the idea," Patrick said hastily.

It was awful to be saying these things, leaving himself open for anything Kevin might think about him. He realized he did care about Kevin's opinion of him. "I still haven't figured out all my reasons yet. There are some in a corner of my mind that I haven't been able to separate from other things . . ."

"Yeah, I know," Kevin said. And after silence, "What happened to you at British Chemical?"

"I nearly drowned in the rain when I was running near there. Then hit my head on something. It knocked me out." He touched the white bandage on his head. "Just a little cut, six stitches."

"How did you get in there in the first place?" Kevin said.

"You remember the big storm? Well, I was running on the town side of Bunker Hill. When it began to rain hard, I was under some trees and getting very wet. I looked around for some other kind of shelter. The guardhouse was close. Corporal Adams was there, and he said it was okay. So I waited for the rain to stop, but it didn't stop . . ."

Kevin's eyes were alight with curiosity. "I mean, how did you get into the plant itself? You hafta get a pass to do that!"

"I'm coming to it. Like I said, there I was in the guardhouse, about as wet as can be. . . . Corporal Adams was getting me a towel to dry myself with . . ."

And it was almost like being back there, to talk about it. The words brought back pictures in his mind. Pumper and Mr. Foreman spoke to him sternly; imaginary people becoming more interesting than real people.

"I could see the lights across the river," he went on with some effort. "You could see them through the rain, past No. 1 dam and the powerhouse. Then a big crack of lightning, and all the lights went out." He glanced at Kevin. "I guess they went out in the town as well."

"Yeah," Kevin said, stifling impatience.

"Well, I was in the guardhouse, out of the rain . . ."

"Yes?"

"And there's a door in the guardhouse leading outside; and there's another door leading into the building area. I took the wrong one."

"Whaddaya mean, the wrong one?"

"My sense of direction got mixed-up somehow. I couldn't see much of anything . . ."

"You ran inside instead of out?"

"Yes. It was a dark day anyway, and nearly night. All I could see in there was shadows."

"I guess you were scared?"

"Of course. Wouldn't you be? But that wasn't the worst of it." Patrick took a deap breath, wondering how vulnerable he was becoming. "Being scared wasn't the worst. I met some people in there, but they weren't real people. They seemed strange to me. Maybe I made them happen."

Kevin was now intensely interested, hanging onto the words. "You mean you invented them?"

"I hit my head when I fell. And must've passed out."

"What about those people? Tell me about what happened at British Chemical. Were you hallucinating?"

That was a nice word. Patrick felt a slight dizziness from talking, but savoured the word: I hallucinate, you hallucinate, we hallucinate.

Patrick began to relish his lead role in the retelling of his little drama. "Yeah, I guess I hallucinated. There was a little man named Pumper. A tiny little guy. Pumper thought I was the mayor's son, so he showed me around the place."

"Jean's father works at British Chemical," Kevin informed irrelevantly. "I wonder what he does there."

"Chemical engineer," Patrick said, then regretted saying it. For him to possess that knowledge meant he had some interest in Jean's father.

"So what happened?"

"I climbed up on the nitric acid vats. And saw how they shovelled the guncotton."

"Did you see any T.N.T.? Of course it wasn't real." Kevin's tone was disparaging.

"I don't think so. What does it look like?"

"I don't know either."

"And they use copper nails and copper hammers."

"Why do they do that?"

"When they box the guncotton. If they used steel nails and hammer, there'd be sparks, and the whole place would blow up. Pumper said so."

"But this is all in your head. Nothing really happened – I mean after you got hurt."

"Sure, but it seemed real. There was another man called Mr. Foreman. I didn't like him at all."

After a long silence Kevin said, "Do you ever think of the war?"

"Not much. 'Buy bonds.' 'Don't talk, Germans may be listening.' Or when somebody's father or brother is listed missing or killed in action. Is that the way you are, too?"

"I guess so. It's gonna be over soon anyway. It says in the paper the Germans are retreating, from Cambrai to Verdun – "

"Where's that?"

"I'm not sure. Anyway, seems to me British Chemical is our war right here in town. . . . I mean, in case anything happens . . ."

Some cordiality, or at least goodwill, had seeped into the room. They were both aware that neither was as each had imagined the other. Mrs. Cameron brought some lemonade and left quietly.

The conversation came back to running. "There are no marathons run around here," Kevin remarked thoughtfully. "That's twenty-six miles, and too long for me. But the mile run on field day is too short. I don't have much of a finishing kick," he said ruefully.

"I never thought of racing," Patrick said. "But running seemed necessary, and not just to fill in time. It does something for me. Sure, I saw you running, and that was one reason. But not the only one. Maybe I don't know why." He smiled at Kevin. "Do you ever lose yourself, forget where you are on the road? As if there was some barrier you broke through? And when you did that, you left the town, the road, everyone you knew, as if you were ... I don't know...."

"Yes," Kevin said.

"Like flying, being weightless, swimming without water..."

"Yes."

Then there was a silence, which lasted a long time. Patrick may have snoozed a little. When he looked up again, the room was empty.

Patrick stayed in bed for three days. He looked at the old Frank Merriwell books again, but without much interest. Edgar Rice Burroughs's *A Princess of Mars* was a little better. The books he'd read when he was a few years younger – Doctor Dolittle, the Oz books, Horatio Alger – they seemed rather silly now. In some ways he felt very much adult; in others, as if he were still getting used to a strange planet.

Most of the adults he encountered seemed very sure of themselves. Whether they actually felt that way or not. They looked comfortable with themselves, at ease in what they were doing. A storekeeper's identity was that of a storekeeper; a doctor a doctor, more than just a human being. Patrick supposed they, too, had a lighted universe inside their heads, a similar one to his own. There was a public world and all these private ones, but you caught a glimpse inside the private worlds only rarely.

Gyp was allowed in the house during Patrick's convalescence. The dog leaned a black muzzle on the quilts, button eyes staring at him soulfully. He wondered if the dog also possessed this lighted place in his head, where pictures were forming and fading.

"Gyp!" he said loudly. The dog made an *ur-r-r* noise in response. "Now what does that mean?" Patrick wanted to know, and ruffled the dog's ears.

"Tell me now," he said to Gyp urgently, "have you got a soul in there, like Hartwell is always talking about? Will you go to heaven, even if you do steal chickens? Is there a heaven for dogs?"

This prolonged scrutiny and urgent words had gotten Gyp excited. He leaped onto the bed, lifted his muzzle, and howled. An ear-breaking sound so close to Patrick's head; the sound of puzzlement and dog frustration. Patrick howled, too, but with laughter. His mother burst into the room, ready for anything. She took in the scene and smiled. "I guess you can get up."

After two more days, he was running again. Only a mile at first, then stretching it into two miles. Once or twice he saw Kevin, who had taken a different route. They waved to each other.

# 6

TRENTON WAS A WARTIME TOWN, but far from the scene of battle, where life went on as if nothing had changed.

A few soldiers could be seen in the streets, especially during evenings. The shopkeepers kept their shops, bankers handled money; on Sundays the various religious denominations worshipped their slightly dissimilar gods. But it was noticeable that fewer young people attended services. Fewer men between the ages of eighteen and thirty-five were on the streets. Young women seemed as plentiful as ever, but their escorts on Saturday nights were much older.

At the shipyard on the bay, a frenzied roar of multiple activity. Wooden mallets slammed down, oakum was pounded into seams of half-built ships; the smell of pine, cedar, and oak shavings – the repetition of a repetition. At British Chemical, northeast of town on the far side of Bunker Hill, noxious fumes poured at the sky. Creosote made coloured islands in the river. The fearsome cannon atop Mount Pelion – said to stem from the Crimean War – overlooked the town, its muzzle empty and meaningless. Another repetition, of an earlier war; and one might speculate that everything human beings do has been done and said before.

1918. Perhaps a year of disillusionment. In France, young Canadians died. English, Americans, Australians, South Africans, and soldiers of several other nations were killed as well. The solemnity of a funeral service repeated and repeated to the ears of the last man left alive – that solemnity must finally begin to seem different. How different? Well, maybe comic, if you're the last man left alive. If that last man should be religious, does he have a vision of God up there in the beautiful blue sky? God laughing like hell? And laughs himself, the sound frightening in its uselessness. . . .

Below the town bridge, on the north shore of Quinte, a half-dozen tugs leaned into silence. They lay in shallow water, resting on the muddy bottom, only their decks and upper cabins showing: sunken relics of the town's lumbering heyday.

Their builder was Robert Weddell, a Scotsman from Edinburgh. Weddell arrived at Trenton in 1873. He built a machine shop and foundry in that year. This enterprise blossomed into a large-scale industry by contemporary standards. Weddell manufactured iron bridges, marine engines, dredges, tugs, and steamboats. In 1894, he organized the Weddell Water Company, to supply the town. Later, and appropriately, he became fire chief.

Weddell's tugs eventually became sunken hulks, brass fittings tarnished, railings broken, black water in their holds. Once there had been a night watchman, dating from the time when the tugs first anchored on Quinte's north shore. His wooden shack nearby had tumbled down long ago. The tugs, once used for dredging and towing log booms, now had a mysticism attached to them. They spoke of a slightly earlier era; their silent bells atop slanting wheelhouses seemed vaguely glamorous. Smelly water of rotting interiors was thought to be dangerous, infested with water snakes perhaps. They were nevertheless lures for adventurous boys.

One day, Patrick was out on the river with Jack Corson and Billy Coons. A hot afternoon, but not exceptionally so for midsummer. The river danced in sunlight. A breeze clipped a few drops from the crests of waves. Two sailboats tacked beyond the new town bridge, before the Trent River became the Bay of Quinte.

"This running stuff," Billy said, "what does it do for you?" Billy was not introspective, but his mind was sharp and alert.

Patrick didn't know how to answer. "Why are people so curious?" he said. "If I played football, would you want to know why? Or basketball? If I dug around for reasons to give you, they'd be phoney reasons. I don't know why. Not exactly."

Billy assessed this for a few moments, looking at him intently. "Well, it's making you . . . different."

"Different from what?"

"You useta kinda flop around," Jack Corson contributed. "As if your arms weren't going where the rest of you was. I could've picked you out in a crowd right away, just how you looked."

"And now I look like everyone else . . ."

"No, that isn't it either. It's as if you're not standing with the rest of the crowd any more. A little to one side."

Patrick was astonished by both the opinion and its source. "Then you'd recommend running for whatever ails anyone? Place it on the school curriculum instead of Latin?"

But he knew that wasn't an answer.

"I never did understand why they teach Latin," Jack Corson said. "It hasn't been spoken by ordinary working people for hundreds of years. I read that somewhere."

"I vote we take the boat down to Weddell's tugs on the bay," Patrick said. "Anybody in favour?"


The three boys tied their skiff to a railing and stripped down to woollen bathing suits.

"How about exploring inside?" Billy said, pointing to the tug's dark and flooded interior.

"You're nuts," Jack Corson said. "Liable to hit your head on something down there and never come back up."

They contemplated this sodden fate a moment.

"Remember the time you dared me to jump off the top of the bridge?" Patrick said. "That was you, Billy. You claimed you'd done it yourself, and said I didn't have the nerve. Well, I never saw *you* jump off that bridge, but if you dive into the tug here, I'll be watching." He stared at Billy challengingly.

Last summer it had been. He remembered being perched atop the town bridge's steel framework, a flat place where two girders joined. Sixty or seventy feet above the river water, maybe more. The boardwalk for pedestrians was directly below his feet; the leap outward to avoid crashing down on that boardwalk and breaking his neck would have to be at least six feet. Sitting there above the bridge, sweating, waiting for something to take the decision to jump or not jump out of his hands.

Below him, the bridge traffic, autos, horses and wagons, flowed by sedately. Pedestrians passed on the board sidewalk and never once looked up. All the other boys had gone home, sure he'd never jump. As Patrick himself was sure. Because it had to be done just right, holding legs tight together during the outward leap, arms hugging his body, lungs filled with summer air.

He was afraid – in fact, nearly scared to death. Patrick admitted it to himself both then and now. But then, Billy Coons's "I dare you!" had soaked into his mind. The loathsome, unendurable thought of being a coward, making his hands tremble in sun heat, turning his leg muscles to wood. He crouched on the highest girder, half standing, then sank back, despising himself. "I'll never do it," he muttered.

Then he did it.

The leap outward was nearly perfect, in retrospect. Arms and legs clamped close to body. The river felt thick as he entered it, neither liquid nor solid. There was no lapse of time. He went down like a slow bullet; his lungs a precious bag outside himself. His feet were thick with mud, a slimy touch that made him wriggle inside. Then he kicked vigorously upward, letting bubbles of air trickle from the side of his mouth. The roar in his ears stopped. Traffic was passing, voices again, afternoon sun seeming to fill the sky white after the dark river. He clambered ashore, shaking his head violently to expel the river from his ears. Even now he could feel the terrible pain in his groin, remembering a thing he'd forgotten before the high-falling: keep your testicles tucked between legs to protect them from the water's impact. His balls had ached like twin coals of fire. Hopping up and down in agony, he'd felt a little silly and a little proud. And resolved never to do such a stupid thing again.

Now, sitting on the Weddell tug a year later, Jack Corson said, "Did you ever jump from that bridge?"

Patrick thought for a few seconds before answering. If he admitted he'd jumped, then Billy Coons might be forced to leap into the tug's black, water-filled hold, with its unknown perils. Billy might think of it as a dare he couldn't refuse to meet, since Patrick had faced his own challenge last year.

"No," Patrick said, "I was too scared."

He felt relieved and a little virtuous over what he had said, and thought Billy looked relieved, too.

"Let's go swimming," Jack Corson said.

"Last one in is a horse's ass!" Billy Coons yelled.

But they were all first.

Thinking about it later, lying on the tug's slanting deck, Patrick was surprised at his own duplicity. And the power of words to manipulate other people was interesting. Also dangerous. The incident remained in his mind a few moments, until the sun bleached out everything in its white blaze.

There were times when Patrick felt lonely. He didn't know exactly why, but friends were not enough to alleviate the feeling. Nor were his mother, grandfather, and Uncle Wilfred. The books he read didn't say much about such feelings. And anyway, the long hot days of summer, along with running, left small time for reading books.

Only rarely did the dog accompany him on his runs. And when he did, Gyp's interest was easily distracted from running. He'd stop to urinate, sniff at other dogs, growl at them sometimes, and look menacing. Then Patrick would grab him by the collar and haul him away.

Once a black-ruffed German shepherd in someone's front yard planted both front feet atop a picket fence, glaring outward at them with the sound of doom in its throat. Gyp stopped to investigate this phenomenon, his own hackles rising, his own special doom-sound sandpapering the air. And incongruously, his tail wagged at the same time.

Patrick wondered: Could the German shepherd possibly be female, and this the prelude to courtship? But no, the other dog leaped the barrier onto the road. They circled each other warily, neither in doubt as to the other's intentions. Teeth bared, lips curled back from yellow fangs.

Patrick didn't know what to do. How does one halt the seemingly inevitable? Interposing his own body between those two dogs, one could be slashed and mangled. He was just about to take that chance, grab Gyp's collar, and haul him bodily down the road.

Then a thin middle-aged woman came out of the house. She chattered at him, "He won't hurt you, he won't hurt you. Just ignore him, don't look at him!"

Patrick almost grinned. Ignore a beast that seemed about to kill you, then disinter your body from its grave to bite off an arm or leg. "How do we do that?" he wanted to know.

The dogs were now making short dashes at each other and veering off at the last instant. The German shepherd was taller and rangier than Gyp, but not as heavy bodied. Both dogs were cautious, their doggy brains retaining memories of similar encounters, but a gradual hysteria was beginning to take over.

"We've got to stop this!" Patrick shouted to the woman. "Listen. I'm going to count one, two, three. On the count of three, you grab your dog by the collar and pull him away. I'll do the same with mine. Your dog *has* got a collar, hasn't he?"

"He won't hurt you – he won't hurt you," the woman stuttered, unable to say anything else. She looked scared, with hair curlers peeking out under a kerchief.

Patrick ignored that. "One," he said portentously. "Two," he said, with a tension in his voice like the starter with blank cartridge pistol at a track meet. "Three!" he screamed, like a man in extremis and near drowning. And snatched at Gyp's collar.

Down the road he found a grassy spot and pulled the dog into his arms. "Good dog, good dog," he moaned in the hairy ears, rolling into the grass. Then, "No, I guess not so good; you're just too damn quarrelsome," whispering that "damn" word so that no one but the dog could hear.

He pulled the Airedale ears and scratched the unidentified pooch species of body. Gyp licked his face as if trying to placate a master who acted so oddly.

Lying in the grass with the dog on earlier mornings stole into Patrick's mind. Mornings of waking early, stealing downstairs softly in order not to wake his mother. The dog as silently joining him from his doggy couch under the woodshed. Screen door closing without a bang. The dog's feet and his own *scuff-scuffing* across Front Street to the river. You couldn't see any water; it was covered with white mist, cotton wool, a cold blanket from the night. Downriver from Corson's dock the black-painted steel bridge arose, shadowy as a cobweb. Patrick, as a spider waiting in the silence, was not visible.

A rainbow patch of creosote drifted in to shore. The mist's white lace made it resemble a strange volcanic island, its cone upside-down underwater. There was a bird, too, somewhere. And the mist made silence out of itself. This was peace, in which nothing more was needed, sufficient unto itself.

Patrick's mind skipped suddenly. He projected a future when there was no dog, no mother asleep across the road, when there was no memory of now. He shuddered.

After several months of running, the question was beginning to seep into his mind again – Why? Not just Kevin Morris, or the need to change and move in some new direction (although that was part of it), but the quiet scream inside himself he heard sometimes in sleep. If there's a river, cross it. If there's a mountain, climb it. And "Who am I?" he whispered to the memory of mist on the river.

But the loneliness? You could think about that when there was a long space before and after you, the sky above and earth beneath. When his mind became disengaged from the actual, he could float and ramble, visit things and leave without saying goodbye.

"Who am I?" he said to the wind.

He sometimes felt a simple happiness, without it seeming to come from anywhere. Like a piano tuner arriving to change tensions in steel wires, tones subtly changing from near-dissonance to near-harmony under the man's plonking fingers. And made a list of them for his own satisfaction, these occasions of harmony, these times when he glimpsed something close by, something that never stayed.

Running. It was aloneness intensified. It was a speeding up and a slowing down of the neighbourhood universe. Someone had scraped his whole body with sandpaper; the epidermis of inattention was scrubbed off. He was awake. And knew things and couldn't say what they were. He kept asking himself questions, more and more questions. . . .

Over the summer he had compiled a list of places that interested him. One of these was the Glen Miller Rock. (An encyclopaedia would have to be found with information about the Ice Age.) Mayhew's Mill was another such place. It was an old gristmill at Hart's Corners, north of the town. The pond feeding the mill wheel was so shallow it froze all the way down to its weedy bottom in winter. Patrick had skated there in cold December and January, a plumed scarf of breath flung behind, exploring the network of streams leading into the pond.

An image entered his mind: the millpond as a huge living body, composed of vegetable matter, earth and water. That widespread network of streams carried lifeblood to the liquid centre. A sleeping hugeness, over which winds blew back and forth; and little scampering feet of humans scratched its frozen face with steel runners in winter . . .

Running north toward the footbridge, he passed Merker's junkyard. A place of tangled steel and iron, a jungle of waste that was not wasted. Walking there was traversing tangled roads into the secondhand past, meandering paths beside looming rusty hills of metal. . . . Spiderwebs of rails and girders and poles and plates and wire. . . . Caves of steel, hidden compartments of shadow inside the tangle. A place of worn-out clothes and ragged ends of nothingness; of newspapers inside a screw press that would have filled a small room outside the press, condensed into a paper monster.

On summer Sundays, four years ago, Patrick used to sneak into that junkyard, the strangest place in town. It gave him the oddest feeling of displacement, of being there and not being there. Junk was both the past and future; old iron was melted down to make new iron. Old newspapers made new ones. And the bodies of animals were fed into the bodies of people. All old things changed into something else.

But the screw press inside a small open-sided frame building was the biggest attraction for Patrick. Many thousands of newspapers were condensed by the press into six-foot bundles encircled by metal strapping. And these bundles often concealed treasure – old pulp magazines: *Argosy*, *Blue Book*, and *All-Story*. The magazines became, briefly, his favourite reading matter.

The river side of Merker's establishment provided easiest access. You followed the weed-grown shoreline stealthily, keeping one eye open for the skull-faced owner, or anyone else who might be watching. And explored the compressed bundles with questing fingers, searching their edges for stiff spines of magazines, the telltale feeling of smooth covers. The magazines could be tugged back and forth and worried at, a bit like pulling angleworms from wet lawns after rain.

Rider Haggard's *Ayesha* was hidden in *Popular Magazine*. So was H.G. Wells's *The First Men in the Moon*. The most fascinating of all was a man of blood and romance, John Carter, whose interplanetary adventures were told in *Under the Moons of Mars*. The author of John Carter and his beautiful Martian princess was one Norman Bean. Later on this same Bean turned out to be Edgar Rice Burroughs, who gave birth to *Tarzan of the Apes* in *All-Story*.

Over a period of several weeks, Patrick was plentifully supplied with dozens of pulp magazines. He feasted on them. Tarzan, Lord of the Jungle, became a personal exemplar. He practised the Tarzan yell on the Trent River waterfront late at night; the yell went off-key because his voice broke in the midst of it. All the town dogs howled happily back at him, their masters screaming at them in turn. And Patrick sneaked back to bed, hoping he hadn't been seen.

For a few weeks that summer Patrick's clothes had been covered with little flakes of paper. The pulp magazine paper, recycled from old newspapers, which was brittle and had edges that broke off when handled, became a kind of literary dandruff on the clothes of readers. Mrs. Cameron grumbled.

Retrieving this paper treasure was both scary and exciting. Patrick well knew that he had no business in Mr. Merker's domain, on Sundays or any other day. Mentally, the shadows of blue-uniformed policemen hovered over him. Mr. Merker hovered there, too. Entering the precincts of the Kingdom of Junk, he stopped and listened every two or three steps; the keenness of his ears able to detect the small sound of John Carter's sword rattling in its scabbard on Mars. Tars Tarkas, friend of John Carter, loomed over him; and giant shadows of the green-skinned warriors of Mars.

But it wasn't Tars Tarkas. Blood rushing to his face, lips sputtering saliva, Mr. Merker grabbed him by the ear. "You!" he said. Said it like the voice of doom – *you* – and John Carter fled back ignominiously to his home state of Virginia.

"Young man, do you have any idea of the time and money you've wasted here? My time and money."

Patrick hadn't. But he suspected and wasn't anxious for more precise information.

"We've had to do the same work twice because of you. . . . I'd like you to think about that sometimes . . ."

Mr. Merker frog-marched him to the entrance, with a final tweak of the ear. "If I catch you," he said in measured tones, repeating it for emphasis, "if I catch you. . . ." After a pause, while the word's isolation made it even more terrible – "*Again!*"

Sin, in the words of the Reverend Eustace Hartwell, carries its own penalty. Running past Merker's junkyard years later, Patrick remembered that word "*again.*" But seemingly, Mr. Merker had never reported the incident to Mrs. Cameron. Nevertheless Patrick wondered if he sometimes saw a faint smile on his mother's face when she mentioned the paper dandruff on her son's clothes: "And those trashy magazines! I can't think what you see in them."

When he thought of Jean, there was a reciprocating current between his head and groin. As if his total self was occupied by remembering. It was near the end of July, and he hadn't seen her since school closed. But her image danced in his mind – sometimes in passing Merker's junkyard, sometimes atop Glen Miller Rock high above the surrounding forest, or hovering over British Chemical, her father calling and calling for her to come down and act like a lady. Sometimes at breakfast or dinner he remembered, and his reality became memory of her. The reality of fantasy.

The father's name was James Eagle Tomkins. He'd found that out from discreet investigations at the post office. The Tomkins bit jarred in his mind; it didn't sound like an engineer, the bravura sound of an engineer. A grocer maybe. But it was Jean he thought about most often, memory of her face visiting him at the most unexpected times.

Jean, the pale girl with yellow hair and pale blue eyes – that girl was invading him while his legs splatted in the gravel and his mind groped for her image. Of course she was fantasy. He knew that he was imagining her as she most probably was not, that he had invented and manufactured a young female – and was annoyed with himself for having done so.

It made no difference. Running provided no escape.

Once he had read the Christian Bible for its dirty passages, dirty being sexual in an unknown sense. Somebody begat somebody, but that was alien and much different to this marvellous pale face that floated before him – on the street, while eating, in the bathroom, anywhere and everywhere. It was not dirty: this he knew. It was the chain drive and mystic dream source of power turbines at the world's roots. This he knew and couldn't say.

He began to look again at the basic spectrum of colours, the earth colours he had thought so marvellous as a child. Questions he had asked: Why do shadows remain flat and two-dimensional? Why do coloured things leap into the mind? Yellow hair, yellow hair: Is the colour the thing, or thing the colour? I close my eyes and there is another related world inside. How is it possible for anyone else to also possess their own private lighted world? Mine, and only mine, is the Kingdom.

The waving pink hair of willow roots in river mud was the same. Billy Coons's carrot hair was still uncookable in the furnace mind. Bricks, boards, siding of houses, grey limestone of the clock-tower post office, these remained. And he, Patrick Cameron, was he still the same? But she, who had once been a seed, a foetus, a gilled climbing creature in the womb, a small girl and then a delicate, pale semi-adult – how had she changed? Or was it he, Patrick, who had become so different?

A kind of terror came over him. He was being taken away from himself, changed from what he was. The decision-making will had nothing to do with it. His body did. Patrick was just along for the ride, an involved observer of himself.

Running. Several times his route had passed her house, as if he or his feet were magnetically drawn there. He wanted to see her and didn't want to see her. Fear clogged the little spaces in his brain, became a heaviness in his chest.

In the last few years, in fact, since puberty, Patrick had never talked to girls his own age. But since age thirteen, he had felt their strong biological attraction. In school they were giggly and conspiratorial, whispering together, with sidelong glances at boys. Much more clubby and prone to cluster in gossipy groups than boys.

Male conversation either dismissed them or ascribed to them sexual qualities of a wondrous nature. Older boys whistled at them, catcalled after them sometimes. Their physical attributes were often exaggerated to monstrous size: breasts became huge as pillows, buttocks were cumulus clouds in myth-making young minds.

Women. For the most part, they were regarded as alien. The reward for being male. But there was more than a hint of fear in this attitude, something the masculine gender did not understand: their delicacy and difference.


One day, near the high school, Patrick came face to face with Jean. She was pushing a wicker baby carriage. He stopped, she stopped. Patrick, with bony, lean face, sunburned and sweating. The girl, cool in a white dress, her face pale.

She remembered him well, Patrick knew that. Their classmates had mocked them with crossed forefingers that signalled: We know you're sweet on each other. We know.

But the sweetness was on Patrick's side only, no hint of reciprocal unbending.

Despair seized him. "Hi," he said, and was about to turn away and continue running. But she said, "Hello," the word different on her lips in a way he could not interpret.

Patrick noticed her hands trembling slightly on the baby carriage handle. He knew then she was just as nervous as he was. If he moved suddenly toward her, would she skitter off down the street in terror? If she said something sarcastic, would he turn away himself?

He hadn't warned himself he was going to speak, he just blurted it out. And held his breath. The die was cast, Caesar was about to cross the Rubicon into Gaul – or whatever that damned river's name was.

The silence became too long. If he didn't say some very ordinary things about the weather, about school, about the war, anything – if he didn't do that, their little dialogue would die. At least it seemed that way to him.

"Is that your baby?" he said desperately.

"No," she said, "it's a neighbour's."

Jean smiled. Jean smiled. Jean smiled.

"And you know," he said.

"Know what?"

Then Patrick's mind went blank. He couldn't think of anything to say.

"My name is Patrick," he finally said, and knew she must know that already. "I live across the river. I run for exercise, I run because it's something to do – "

He stopped, foolishly aware that he was burbling, then went on determinedly. "I wanted to talk to you. . . ."

"I can see that," she smiled.

"And I'm talking, but it isn't getting me anywhere."

"Where do you want to go?"

That brought him up short. He hadn't looked beyond his own fear of her.

"I want to see you – "

"Well, here I am."

"I mean, I want to see you again."

"Mom and Dad have taken a cottage on the road to Frankford, north of Glen Miller. . . ."

"West side of the river?"

"Yes. We go there weekends. Tomorrow."

"I do some running on that road."

"I've seen you." And she smiled again.

"Um," he said, rather like an idiot.

"Come Sunday. Maybe around noon."

"How do I know what the place looks like?"

"White house, green roof. Just north of Glen Miller village. I'll be on the lawn. Bring your bathing suit."

And there was a secret between them. Not the secret of where the river cottage was, nor the projected meeting the next day. But there was a knowing between them, and both admitted it to themselves. Something of each of them had flowed into the other, a romantic something that was retained.

"You look a little peaked, Patrick," his mother said to him Sunday morning. She measured him with a long look. "You're not eating enough. And this running..." She shook her head.

"I've never felt better in my life," Patrick said.

He ducked his head, covered the breakfast oatmeal porridge with brown sugar, and began to eat it hurriedly. When his mother was in this mood, you never knew –

She said, "I want you to take two teaspoons of sulphur and molasses every morning. My mother used to give it to me on the farm. And greens, you should be getting more greens."

He glanced up from his cereal, smiling. "Just look at me. Don't I look healthy?"

"Perhaps. But thin. And you don't stay home any more, always off somewhere. My lands, it's an itch you have, the seven years' itch."

"Has Mrs. Morris been over lately to mention how well Kevin is doing?" he said, interjecting a known irritant to change his mother's direction.

"You were listening, were you? Well, she's proud of Kevin – that's natural." Mrs. Cameron stopped, considering. "As I'm proud of you." She touched his hair, and Patrick writhed uncomfortably.

"Mom, where can I find an encyclopaedia?"

"Well," Mrs. Cameron said thoughtfully, "I think the Reverend Hartwell has one. Now that school is over, you can look at his. What do you want to find out about?"

"There was an Ice Age that lasted hundreds of years, maybe thousands. I want to know more about it."

"An Ice Age. . . . That means there was ice all across Canada, where we're standing now? It doesn't seem possible."

"I guess it was here," Patrick said. "But I don't really know very much about it. Miss Gothard in geography has hardly mentioned it. Maybe she will next term. It seems there was ice over Ottawa, over Toronto and Montreal. There was ice on the prairies and in British Columbia – "

"It must have been cold."

"I don't think there were any people. It was long, long ago . . ."

"And there was no Canada then?" she prompted, watching the wonderment on her son's face.

"Maybe there were Indians. But I don't know."

"Or Eskimos?"

And both their faces went far away, while Indians and Eskimos skied and snowshoed over the North Pole, and snow began to fall in their minds for the next two or three seconds of their lives . . .

"I'll ask Mr. Hartwell about it at church," Mrs. Cameron said finally. "Maybe you'll go see him later. And this Ice Age you're talking about, I want you to remember one thing: even if there were no Indians and Eskimos, there was God. There was always God!"

Mrs. Cameron's voice was intense. Her hair was beginning to grey; steel-rimmed glasses gave her a stern look. She was fifty-six years old, and sometimes lonely. But there was a sweetness about her, even when her face was most severe, as if she didn't believe her own expression or any admonitory thing she might say to Patrick.

She went to the cupboard, pulled out a pint milk bottle filled with something dark and thick. She poured out a spoonful of the stuff. "I want you to take this."

"Sulphur and molasses," Patrick said disgustedly. "It tastes awful. You know they use sulphur to make T.N.T. at the munitions factory?" He wasn't really sure of that, but someone had said so.

"My mother took it," Mrs. Cameron said, pointing her forefinger at him. "And her mother took it before that. So did their menfolks. They all grew up to be big and strong, the children did. Don't you want to be big and strong?"

Patrick grimaced comically. He stretched his arms akimbo, making the biceps swell into quite respectable mounds of muscle. "There," he said.

They laughed. It was a companionable laughter.

# 7

RUNNING. ON THE FRANKFORD ROAD, called the "river road" by local people, its margins coloured with flowers. Devil's paintbrush crimson, wild snapdragon yellow, blue chicory, and cornflowers, which Patrick knew as bachelor's button. Fat groundhogs stood like brown guardsmen with busbys in front of their burrows, eyeing him curiously but without alarm. They dived into the earth when he got too close. And there were daisies, whole fields of them. Their white petals looked like the fringes on a wedding dress; with a yellow centre, they were called "the day's eye" in an earlier England.

And birds. They moved like streaks of coloured light across his vision. Domestic birds, their houses built every spring. Orioles, robins, sparrows, so many! And goldfinches, their small breasts like dozens of buttercups held under his chin. From faraway childhood, he remembered the sun-yellow buttercups reflected under his chin. There had been a meaning to it, something he had now forgotten. Appearing from nowhere, more goldfinches. They flew in thirty-foot swoops, sinking and rising, little ski-jumpers over invisible molehills in the air.

But Patrick saw little of the kaleidoscope today. His thoughts were mostly Jean-thoughts, the world outside himself blurred.

When he came to the cottage, it wasn't rose-covered, in fact it was slightly dilapidated and shabby. The siding, white-painted shiplap, noticeably needed more paint.

Jean met him at the front door – having been waiting there? – and allowed him to take her hand in his own. It was a cool hand with long white fingers, and felt very different from anyone else's hand. She let it stay there a moment. Someone had once told him that the custom of handshaking came about because people didn't trust each other; they couldn't strike an unfriendly blow when their hands were captives of the other person. It would be difficult anyway. Patrick smiled.

She asked him why, and he told her.

"Why didn't they use the hand that wasn't being held?" she said.

"Maybe each of them shook both hands – I mean, all four hands were held, arms kinda crossed over and tangled. And they just stood there, neither daring to let go of the other."

The picture this conjured up broke the ice of strangeness between them. They laughed.

Later, sitting on warm grass beside the river, Jean said, "Mom and Dad will be here soon."

She was wearing a blue wool bathing suit, the skirts coming nearly to her knees; a delicate film of sweat shone on her upper lip; tiny hairs like gold wires at her temples. At sixteen, she had fully formed breasts, shapely under the shapeless bathing costume. Patrick was self-conscious; he tried to keep his eyes away from them. He fidgeted.

"What's wrong?" she said. But saying it brought a pink tinge to her face, as if she knew.

"Nothing," Patrick said, then amended it. "Well, I'm not used to talking with girls. Didn't I say that before?"

"I guess so. I don't remember."

He thought: I'd better not say I've never been out with a girl before.

She said, "Haven't you ever been out with a girl before?"

"Are you reading my mind?" he said, astonished.

They laughed, which made them still more at ease.

The river, north of the creosote works, was shore-green with blue farther out. The glittery sun seemed composed of countless white needles in their eyes. Beyond the cottage's wooden dock, a white sailboat tacked back and forth, trying to move upriver against the current. A silence, with crickets or cicadas whose singing seemed the same as silence. Or maybe it was his nerves, wondering what to say.

She said, "You're an only." It was a statement of fact.

"What?"

"I mean, you have no brothers and sisters. Neither have I."

"Yes. But I had a brother before me, before I was born. He died."

The blue eyes considered him. "What does it do to you? I mean, how does it make you feel?"

"I don't know. How could I ever know? Maybe" – and he hesitated – "as if there was a choice made back then . . ."

"What kind of choice?"

"I don't know that either. But maybe a choice that he should go one way and I another . . ."

Jean wrinkled her brows, "This is too much for me. I don't know what you mean."

"There had to be some effect. Suppose you'd had a sister, and she died. Wouldn't everything now be different for you?"

"I guess it would be, but how?"

"It would have to have happened for you to find out."

"You're crazy," she decided.

"Why? Didn't you ever play the game of 'what if'?"

"Yes, but you make it sound important, this brother of yours. You make it sound as if you are because of what he was. . . . Besides, you weren't there when your brother died."

"No, but my ghost was."

They sat there, saying nothing, thinking about the dead brother.

"How old would he be if he were alive?" she said.

"Eighteen or nineteen, I guess. She never told me, my mother didn't – how long ago it was . . ."

104

"You can't keep thinking about it," she said, reaching for his hand. "But you've got me doing it, too. Would he have been large or small, dark or light, when he grew up?"

"I don't know anything at all about him, what he was like. Just that he once existed. And my mind keeps going back to him."

"He was just like you," Jean decided. "Or he would have been. You are your dead brother. But you're alive."

Her hand moved in his hand; his fingers tightened over hers.

When Jean's parents arrived, their Model T coughed, seemed to exhort itself to continue, emitted some blue smoke, and stopped. Emerging from the car, James Eagle Tomkins said to his daughter, "This your young man?"

Patrick squirmed.

"Have you had anything to eat, you two?" Mrs. Tomkins said. "Jean, what are you thinking of?" Her eyes were on the kitchen table, bare of crumbs and dishes. "Did he run all the way out here without you offering him something? You did say he was a runner?"

She looked a little like his own mother, but younger, Patrick thought.

"I'm not very hungry," he said.

"Nonsense," Mrs. Tomkins told him. "Of course you're hungry!"

She bustled them all inside the cottage, her manner and intonation of voice making things commonplace. She very nearly shoved them into chairs beside the kitchen table. And busied herself at the icebox.

"Now, Patrick, tell me about yourself." It was an order.

"Oh, Mother!" Jean said.

"Don't you 'Oh, Mother' me," Mrs. Tomkins told her daughter. "Everyone likes to talk about themselves. Even my Eagle does. Don't you, dear?"

Mr. Tomkins looked uncomfortable, shaking his head, a lock of grey hair falling down on the side. "Ellen," he said, "I know you – "

"Of course you do, after twenty years," she interrupted him. "And you ought to know me. Patrick!" – and the name plunged into emphasis – "I'd like to get acquainted. My daughter says she likes you and – "

"Oh, Mother," Jean said.

Mrs. Tomkins was slicing cold roast beef onto brown bread for sandwiches. The tea water was beginning to boil. Her eyes twinkled, nearly as blue as her daughter's. "I like you, too, so tell me about yourself."

Patrick did. Laboriously. While he said the few things that seemed to matter to anyone but himself, he felt astonished. There were so few of them. The facts are these, he said to himself and to the Tomkins family: My mother is – My father was – My full name and age are – But who am I? And in the midst of relaying these small bits of information, he noticed the eyes of James E. Tomkins. The cold, considering chemical eyes of an engineer. Wanting to know "Who am I?" Patrick thought. And realized he had said it aloud.

"The universal question," Mrs. Tomkins smiled at him. She passed sandwiches around, poured tea, and sat down herself. "I know. We're putting you on the spot. But don't think of it. You're among friends." And turned to her daughter. "Jean, why don't you and Patrick take your sandwiches onto the lawn? I'll call you later when it's time. . . . "

They took out a blanket, and sat facing the river. Patrick reached for her hand, amazed at himself that he should be so daring.

"I like the way you look," he said, and was again amazed.

After a while she asked, "When did you start running?"

Patrick tried to explain. He stumbled over things: he mentioned Kevin Morris next door; he said he was dissatisfied with himself. Things poured out that had baffled him about himself, and there were no words to say some of them. He tried to make the look on his face tell her what it was like inside him. And perhaps he did. In any event, she knew what an effort it was for him to try.

Neither of them was glib; all the things so hard to say remained that way. Which teacher do you like best? How about music? And the European war? Anybody you know who was killed? What will you be or do when you grow up? (I *am* grown-up – well, almost.) Questions skirting the outside edge of importance.

They talked about nothing all afternoon, nothing of much importance to their personal selves. They also talked about everything. Tingling silent nerves revealed each to the other. Projected the future, foretold the past. In that previous time it was fantasized they had known each other as well. Their heads swayed together in the past that was almost upon them in this future; their bodies swayed and touched and drew apart; their hands held.

"I have to go," he said.

"Yes."

"I really do."

"Yes."

"Close your eyes, Jean."

She did, but that large-as-the-sky blue disappeared.

He said hurriedly, "Open them again." And watched himself reflected there.

"Tell me, why does your mother call your father 'Eagle'?"

"It's his name."

"Jean," he said wonderingly, "Jean. That's your name."

Another faint tide of pink flowed into her face.

He said, "You know what you look like?"

She shook her head.

"Sunrise and sunset, pink."

And more pink flowed. "That's kind of unfair, isn't it? You doing that when you see my face – "

107

"Want me to stop?"

"Doesn't what we're saying sound kind of silly to you?"

Patrick felt delighted with her. "Of course it does, but who's listening except us?"

No one was.

And then the question he had been waiting to ask: "Will I be seeing you again?"

"Yes."

"When?"

He didn't remember anything about the run home: farm wagons returning from market; the river's blue-silver in the sun; sometimes a rare automobile. He ran as if her face were suspended a couple of feet in front of his own, and he ran continually toward that face. Sometimes her mouth was slightly open and one of her teeth was crooked; there was a mole on her left temple. It was comforting about that tooth, that she wasn't perfect.

Jean's face was much clearer and brighter than other faces that sometimes appeared in his mind. He thought of Mr. Hartwell, and made the King Street Church minister's face into a larger-than-life cartoon with rubber lips like auto tires. But Hartwell's picture was vague by comparison to hers. And he wondered if everyone could do that, conjure up faces of people they knew, cause friends to appear from nowhere, like pictures in a book you didn't have to buy.

He imagined Jean and himself in situations where he would appear heroic or rescue her from some danger. And laughed at the idea. He began to add years to her face: suddenly she was twenty years old, then twenty-five, then thirty. And then he made her old. A very tall old lady, five feet nine or ten, the blonde hair grey, wrinkles around her eyes, body slightly stooped, her expression vacant – as if she wondered what world was this, the place she had come to in the future. And yet she was still recognizably Jean; the old woman was the girl and the girl lived still.

He tried to reach his hand into the place where this older Jean was, and couldn't. That's another time and place, his mind told him. You can't go there, at least not yet. But I can't stay here for very long either, he told himself. It was uncanny, this way of thinking. It was like being separate from yourself, trying to watch where this earth-self was going on the road to Trenton. And at the same time, you could project yourself high into the clouds, the big cumulus ones with faces he'd watched lying on his back in summer grass. . . .

He ran easily over the smooth gravel, elbows like featherless wings, heel and toe, heel and toe, everything working the way it was supposed to work. With the feeling that he was in charge of things here, in complete command of his own body. His blood rushed and churned. He felt exaltation and a fierce joy.

Then, for a hundred yards or so, he poured everything he was into his legs and arms. The world went into slow motion, everything still, every leaf and blade of grass like a painting, unable to move and sway until he had passed by. And white-capped waves on the river defied gravity, hung there until his flashing body was gone.

He felt as if he could run around the turning world in space, arrive where the world was going before it did. Which way did the world turn, left to right or east to west? There was no knowing. He saw Jean's face in front of him again. Then a whole succession of Jeans, all with different expressions.

Mr. Hartwell blew out his flabby cheeks at the door of the manse. Patrick decided the man's eyes were mud-coloured, with red mud around their edges. The mud-red eyes focused on him sharply.

"Your mother said you were coming. I told her I'd be glad to help your curiosity, though I think it might be employed to better purpose."

His voice developed a little hoarse burr, a mannerism that lengthened the last syllables of words. Patrick thought it sounded as if he, Patrick, was being addressed from the pulpit.

"It's about glaciers, isn't it? That's what you want to know?"

"Yes," Patrick said, feeling that the less he said the better. If he went on talking, it would give Mr. Hartwell a handle to hold on to him, supply information about himself he didn't want to give.

"Chester's in the garden. He'll be wanting to see you when you're finished."

Patrick shuddered. The ten-year-old Chester was a horror of a child. If his forefinger wasn't in his nose, it was up his ass. He crawled over people. As they drew away from him in disgust, their bodies off-balance on chair or sofa, the child-horror would push against them until they fell stiffly backward. Then it climbed on them, dribbling on their clothes, rubbing its face all the way to their summit, as if they were a human Kanchenjunga.

"Yes," Patrick said, gritting his teeth.

"Come along now," Mr. Hartwell said briskly.

The house was dark, wallpaper in the hall dark; leaded-glass windows in a room lined with books he was ushered into allowing small light, and that shadowed by the church next door.

"This is my study, where I write my sermons. You can use the same desk. I'll leave you for a while then."

The muddy eyes grew less dull. "I've told your mother I'm coming to see her some time soon."

"That will be . . . nice," Patrick said, and knew he lied.

"The encyclopaedia is here. And perhaps you would like to peruse other volumes. I have Hurlburt's *Story of the Bible* as well. And I have the narratives of our missionaries in Africa and the Far East. They are very edifying for young minds . . ."

He made a sort of "urrr" sound in his throat. "I will leave you, I will leave you." He made his leave-taking become a grandiose departure.

Patrick said "Gah-h-h!" to the closed door.

Mr. Hartwell's encyclopaedia was a Britannica, published in Cambridge, England, 1910; the eleventh edition. Patrick ran his fingertips over the smooth green leather, which felt like velvet, holding all those jagged bits of knowledge in the width of a single inch. Printed on India paper, the books occupied no more than a total space of three feet on Mr. Hartwell's shelves.

The glacial period. Page fifty-six, volume XII, more than three double-column pages on the subject. Patrick's mind flew directly from this green leather book to the twenty-five-foot-tall boulder called Glen Miller Rock, four miles north of Mr. Hartwell's study. And what was the connection between the encyclopaedia and boulder?

Somebody named John Allen Howe, B.Sc., had written the Britannica entry. This man said there had been half a dozen glacial periods. These periods were called "epochs," meaning a very long time. How long? Professor Howe seemed not to know how long. But probably each epoch had lasted for thousands of years. Glacial periods and the time between them were discussed in terms of "peat deposits, forest beds, and boulder clays."

The last glacial period in North America was the Wisconsin, ending ten thousand years ago. A map showed the ice had covered present-day Canada, reached south of the Great Lakes, probing deep into Michigan, Ohio, and New York State. It had once inundated northern parts of the United States.

In Mr. Hartwell's study, Patrick dreamed. Weather grew unseasonably colder. Even in summer a raw wind blew over the place where Trenton was later to be. And snow fell. A few flakes at first, a flurry of no great matter, playful, fluttering like confetti at a wedding, Patrick imagined. Then a roaring blizzard drowned all other noise; a wind like the scream of a world gone insane.

The tiny molecule that was Patrick crouched in the storm. Under his feet, a mile of ice. The ice shuddered and moved, a bobsled for the mind. Riding the ice the same way he rode the earth – on his own two feet. Running.

And somewhere in all this madness would be other human beings, shivering in the sub-zero furnace of cold. Somewhere, too, there was a twenty-five-foot child's marble being nudged along, slowly, quickly – how fast? Mister Doctor Howe didn't say how long it took.

Who's pushing who? Patrick said to himself. How did that boulder get shoved from where it was and arrive at Glen Miller? Not just a glacier doing it. Was God responsible? A big soiled hand with dirty fingernails, playing marbles with itself, forefinger snapping out at the rock like it was dice, and "Snake-eyes," He shouted, "snake-eyes forever!" God playing with all the other kids?

Patrick shook his head violently, and the printed page stopped being blurred.

But it didn't seem that Mister Doctor Howe, called a Bachelor of Science, really knew very much. And I know no more than he knows, Patrick said to himself. And I don't know who to ask questions about it.

Then his mind went back again. He crawled over the mile-thick ice where Trenton was not, laid his cheek against a snowbank, and called down into the blue depths: "How the hell am I gonna get outa here without running into his son Chester? Or God?" God!

Mr. Hartwell, the Reverend Mister Hartwell, carried a Bible in his left hand when he knocked on the Cameron door two weeks later. He carried it like a pair of kid gloves. It was 8 p.m. Patrick sneaked upstairs, feet scarcely touching the stair treads, when his mother ushered the reverend in parlour directions. He heard them murmur together. And thank heavens, no Chester!

"Tea?"

"Thank you, I will."

After short silence, a chink of cups. The woman's voice sounded coy; a put-on insincere voice. Patrick hardly recognized it as that of his mother.

It occurred to him that his mother had anticipated just such an evening as this one, and wasn't very pleased about it. He heard a brief apology from her, then a flurry into another room, perhaps to regain composure.

Mr. Hartwell sat on the edge of the big mahogany rocking chair, stiff and straight. Only a couple of inches of his ample posterior connected with the rocker. It looked as if he were afraid to move, either because of nerves or because he distrusted the rocker. When Mrs. Cameron fluttered back into the parlour with tea and cookies on the tray, he gave her a glancing smile. A smile that tried to disguise his own discomfort, and didn't.

"Are you comfortable?" Mrs. Cameron said. "You don't look it."

She took his arm and hurried him to the well-stuffed sofa. "There now. Just sit there and relax. Have some tea and my nice cookies."

Mr. Hartwell tried. His thick figure and short stature left his legs hanging a little above the carpet, a badly fashioned doll. He was sweating. He wore the hard clergyman's round collar even for social calls; it seemed to dam the blood passing from his body to head and back again, at least to slow it down.

113

At age fifty-eight, Mr. Hartwell's skin had subsided into thick folds on the bones of his face, blood beneath concentrated at the rounded edge of the folds. The commanding figure he presented in the church pulpit was much changed. Nor was it possible for him to walk back and forth to relieve his obvious discomfort.

Mrs. Cameron did her best to help, out of good nature and perhaps Christian charity. She said, "How is your boy, Chester?"

"I need help with him," Mr. Hartwell said eagerly and gratefully. "Chester is too much for me in some ways. When his mother died four years ago" – and Mr. Hartwell's eyes rolled piously – "rest her soul, I hadn't realized the burden would be so heavy. But it has been cumulative."

Mrs. Cameron looked apprehensive, as she realized where this subject might lead. "But Chester is such a good boy," she said hurriedly.

"That's true. But he has so much energy. He never stops getting into something." Mr. Hartwell mopped his brow with a handkerchief, gazing at Mrs. Cameron imploringly.

"But it isn't for me . . ." she muttered.

"What?"

"Nothing, nothing," Mrs. Cameron said distractedly.

"I've devoted my life to the service of God and our Lord and Saviour, Jesus Christ. And it has been very hard for me in these last few trying months to compose my sermons, visit my flock, and console those with heavy burdens in their hour of need, and to do my duty to God and man – " He stopped, lips purple with the effort that had seemed so effortless at King Street Church.

"I know, I know," Mrs. Cameron said desperately but sympathetically.

By this time, Patrick had sneaked out of his bedroom onto the staircase, avoiding the third tread from the top, which creaked loudly. He leaned across the banister, listening hard, wondering how Dejah Thoris, Princess of Mars, might feel in *All-Story* magazine, if proposed to by the Reverend Mister Hartwell. For that was coming, he could feel it just in the offing. So could Mrs. Cameron.

"More tea, Mr. Hartwell?"

"It is a heavy burden for me without help, my dear. But I take consolation that we here on earth are always bountifully aided when we pray to Him in the Heavenly Kingdom for help."

Mrs. Cameron was startled when she heard "my dear" leave Mr. Hartwell's lips. Those words had an implication of intimacy. Matters were getting out of hand.

Mr. Hartwell stared at her fixedly. "I think of thee as Jacob did of Rachel in the land of Shinar. When he laboured seven years for Rachel and another seven years for the hand of Leah." His face changed, growing paler. Uncertainty seemed to enter his words. "But I am not a handsome man, I am not young – "

"What are you saying, Mr. Hartwell?" Mrs. Cameron was very worried by now. "What are you saying?" And then thought, I don't really want to know.

On the stairs Patrick rocked back and forth, arms around his knees. It was the caricature of a marriage proposal going on in the parlour. And it was not a bit funny when you realized the torture in Mr. Hartwell's voice. He wondered if he should rush down and interrupt proceedings, come to his mother's aid.

Mrs. Cameron was thinking exactly the same thing. Shall I call Patrick, she wondered? But he might be asleep. And anyway, that would be rude. . . .

Mr. Hartwell was having difficulty. "I am not young," he repeated, making youth a requisite in the eyes of the Lord. "And I am not handsome." His lips quivered with the effort of speech. "But I would lay my devotion at your feet; as I worship the Lord, so, too, would I love the wife of my bosom."

115

What can I say, what can I possibly say? Mrs. Cameron wondered frantically. But he is a good man, I must not be unkind to him.

"You were telling me about your son."

"Ah yes, Chester. He is so active. . . ." And Mr. Hartwell seemed to dream for a moment. "He goes and goes from morning to night. And lately he has been taken with a love of music."

"How is that, Mr. Hartwell?"

"You must call me Eustace. It is not right that we should be kept apart by polite words."

"I will try," Mrs. Cameron hesitated. "And you may call me Eleanor if you like. But perhaps not right away. It will take a little time for me to get used to Eustace."

"Of course, of course, my dear," Mr. Hartwell said more smoothly.

"And Chester has become a music lover?" she said, hoping to get Mr. Hartwell's mind off marriage.

"He has taken to singing hymns," the minister said thoughtfully. "In the bathroom, and late at night when he is abed. And there is a certain high but raucous quality to his voice that disturbs me. "Onward Christian Soldiers" seems to be especially favoured. It is distracting, when my thoughts are on higher things."

On the sixth step down, Patrick was now rocking back and forth trying to suppress laughter. He remembered that Chester had a notably high and somewhat unpleasant voice, penetrating and whiny. Poor Mr. Hartwell! That the son of his loins should have produced –

"Your housekeeper, does she – ?"

"Mrs. Oates? She comes to the manse only twice a week. But Mrs. Oates and Chester are not especially well suited. Perhaps it is a matter of temperament. Nor is Mrs. Oates musical. Chester's singing has been mentioned by her occasionally. She has expressed regret for the possible necessity, but has threatened to leave."

116

"I can see the difficulty. . . ."

"The boy needs a mother," Mr. Hartwell said decisively.

Mrs. Cameron's alarm was renewed. Was Mr. Hartwell considering her in the unromantic light as Chester's stepmother and his own housekeeper?

"Mr. Hartwell," she said.

"Yes, my dear?"

"It's not that you aren't handsome, or a good man – "

Mr. Hartwell's face changed, fell into deep lines of melancholy.

"We need time to think about this," she said quickly.

"Look before you leap," Patrick chortled to himself on the stairs.

"I am conscious indeed of the honour you wish to bestow," Mrs. Cameron said.

Mr. Hartwell managed a bow, while sitting, inclining his head toward her.

"We need to think about this a little longer. It is very serious."

"Marriage is an honourable estate in the eyes of the Lord," Reverend Hartwell said.

"Yes, and a very serious step indeed," Mrs. Cameron said. I do need more time." She looked at him appealingly. "Perhaps we should talk about it again in six months' time. You would not wish me to rush unprepared into such a union." And thought: My Lord, he's got me talking the same way he does.

"No indeed. And in the church, when I am speaking the Lord's word in obedience to His commands, I shall sometimes look down where you are sitting, and pray for you, as I pray for all of us. . . ."

When the minister had gone, she went upstairs to Patrick's room. The light was out. "I *know* you aren't asleep," she said in the darkness. "You were listening, weren't you?"

"I ain't sayin I wasn't," Patrick said in a muffled voice. "That third step creaks, doesn't it?"

"Well, what do you think?" she said, turning on the light.

"About what, Mom?"

"You know very well what I'm talking about, Patrick!"

"Well, there's Chester . . ."

"I can't say I'm exactly fond of Mr. Hartwell, but it might be the best thing – "

"Do you really think so, Mom? If you do, well – "

"In just a few more years you'll be gone."

"That's true, I guess," and he felt a small shiver thinking of it. "But you should be talking to yourself, shouldn't you? Not me. It would be your decision, your life," he said.

Patrick felt stunned. He had never talked to his mother on this level before. Life and death, marriage and remarriage, these were very intimate subjects. It was the next thing to talking about sex, and she had never mentioned that either.

A couple of years previously, Patrick had gotten hold of a medical book that supplied authoritative answers to these questions. And certain passages in the Bible were also enlightening. He grinned thinking about it.

"What is it you find so funny?" Mrs. Cameron said coldly. "I was under the impression that we were discussing something important. Your own life would be changed if I married Mr. Hartwell."

There, it was out, she had said it, and felt relieved at hearing the words in her own mouth. "It does concern you, Patrick," she said more softly. "How would you feel about it?"

"You really want me to tell you, Mom?" he said apprehensively. "How can I tell you that?"

Patrick felt ashamed of himself, but also irritated at his mother. She shouldn't ask questions like that. It was placing him in the position of being responsible for her life. If the wrong decision was made, it would be partly his fault, depending on what he said now. And she might blame him. . . . No, of course not; she wouldn't do that.

"Mom," he said plaintively, "you know what you're doin to me . . ."

"Yes, I have some idea. But you're more important to me than Mr. Hartwell."

Patrick felt out of his depth, gasping in deep water. And a wave of warmth was coming from his mother, an affection he knew existed but didn't appear on the surface very often. Just the same, it was wrong, these questions; they shouldn't be asked, at least they shouldn't be asked in such a forthright way as this. He was confused. His mother's eyes holding him still, unable to move; her gentle, slightly faded face almost stern the way she watched him.

But the thought of Mr. Hartwell for a stepfather and Chester for a stepbrother appalled Patrick. "I can't tell you that," he said feebly. "I just can't!" His eyes grew moist and he was terrified that his mother might see tears.

Her face changed. "Anyway, we've got plenty of time to think about all this. By the way," she said suddenly, "when am I going to meet that girl you mentioned? Jean Tomkins, her name is?"

He was again confused, thinking he had somehow underestimated his mother. "Soon, Mom, soon."

Patrick sloughed off any further questions. "I'm just too sleepy to talk about it any more."

It was 8 a.m. and a mid-August sun warm on his shoulders. Running south on Division Street, beside the railway tracks and past the passenger station, toward the cooperage mills and Bay of Quinte beyond.

For several acres of shoreline, the town garbage dump dominated the bay. For generations past, the village people and, later, townspeople of Trenton had dumped their waste

119

at the water's edge. Dig down far enough, and you'd be liable to uncover some strange things. When the settlement of Trent Port began in the late eighteenth century, at the end of the American Revolution, the immigrants were largely United Empire Loyalists, the losing side in the war.

Their goods and chattels had ended up in the garbage dump when no longer usable. Broken flintlock rifles and corroded British coinage sometimes found their way there. Ragged breeches and worn-out dresses, broken harnesses, splintered wicker baby carriages, all were among the discards; and bones, beef and pork bones, from pioneer repasts; even a few yellowed remnants of wolves and bears that had wandered too close to the early settlement.

In ancient Sumer and Babylon, the kitchen middens provided much information about the long-gone dwellers of the ruins. Archaeologists found such middens invaluable. And if anyone were to take the risk to health and welfare of unearthing the Trenton garbage dump, it would provide an extensive history of the community, a visible record of the past, complete with stinks of assorted virulence and varieties of unpleasantness. Of course, no one was likely to do that, unless the passage of thousands of years makes the descendants of Trenton people curious about their ancestors.

Here on the garbage dump, rats reigned supreme, swarming under and over piles of stinking refuse, breeding in many thousands. A few stray cats and dogs were also among the summer visitors, searching for anything edible. And one or two human derelicts lived in the vicinity, surviving on town charity and assiduous garbage picking as best they might.

Patrick had run into Joe Barr at the dump, and, sometimes on Trenton Streets, apparently lost. Joe was the town idiot. A shambling creature who walked with shoulders bent forward and never looked up unless spoken to. Joe's face was always unshaven, jaw hanging loose, a dribble of saliva running down the sides of his mouth. His age was uncertain, perhaps thirty, perhaps thirty-five. He lived somewhere in the garbage dump.

The Bay of Quinte shoreline southwest of the dump was marshy and the water was shallow for a hundred yards or so. Willows there were, a couple of hundred years old, with thick trunks like fat old men. Patrick leaned against one of them, looking out into the bay.

Five or six miles south he could see the dim shore of Prince Edward County. Beyond a wooded headland, farther southwest, were Twelve O'clock Point and the Murray Canal. Quinte had been named after a mission-station called Kente in western Prince Edward. For many years, settlement of Trent Port and the Quinte area had been slow. But the ex-Europeans gradually replaced the Indians, aided, of course, by cheap booze and the white man's diseases.

It was a quiet history. There were no tales of wars with Indian maidens captured by enemies of Kente, carried off to weeping exile in far-off places. Before the Murray Canal was built near the end of the nineteenth century, Prince Edward had been a peninsula, reaching south into Lake Ontario. After it was built, the county became a man-made island. The present-day village of Carrying Place commemorates the old Indian portage route from Quinte to Lake Ontario, and from the opposite direction.

A well-worn trail over the portage had existed for thousands of years, from bay to lake and vice versa. Along that trail, wearing moccasins or with bare callused feet, young Indians had padded, balancing bark canoes on their shoulders. Their goods and chattels were carried by the Indian women, sometimes with infants also strapped to their shoulders. Glaciers in the last Ice Age – the same ones that had ferried the Glen Miller Rock to its present resting place – had carved out rivers and lakes, gouged out the bottom of the fifty-mile-long Bay of Quinte, etching the present configurations of Canadian landscape at the same time.

Patrick knew something of this from Mr. Hartwell's 1910 Encyclopaedia Britannica. While running near Quinte, a picture of melting glaciers twelve thousand years ago flashed in his mind. Blue ice, a mile thick, covering everything. The land itself compressed downward from that enormous weight, as if a heavy iron plate five thousand miles wide had been used by a celestial giant.

It was enough to make one religious, thinking of those marvellous events for which there were no living witnesses. A god in the sky jumped into his mind. Not Mr. Hartwell's god, no fire-and-brimstone deity, but an engineer god who loved to build things; a god with such a marvellous memory he kept blueprints of the world in his head for millions of years.

Then the god said, "Now's the time. I'm gonna do it!" And he started out for empty space with a handful of mud, which he intended to knead and multiply and make fruitful. But Mrs. God stopped him at the door. "You have to eat breakfast first," she said, and smiled at him.

Patrick started to jog back home, legs and arms moving easily in a rhythm that was like a song. Sometimes he increased or slowed his pace, to make his body match the soundless sound. It was as if the earth was saying something to him through his feet. He didn't know what the earth was saying, but he understood. And pondered that paradox a moment. When a craftsman makes a violin, he carves wood into the shape of his desire, until it becomes an odd-shaped box that reflects and echoes his own mind.

And Patrick's body had become carved and shaped by his mind; and the mind itself had changed from the effort that had formed his different body. It didn't have the Greek ideal of symmetry; his elbows and knees were too knobby for that. But the chest surmounted a lean torso, tanned walnut brown. His legs were a little too muscular to match the rest of him. His shoulders were wide and prominent, shaped so that a spot of light seemed to rest on the rounded part of them above his upper arms.

His face was ordinary until you looked at his eyes. They were hazel, between green and blue, but seemed to hold both colours in abeyance as if the use of either was directed by circumstances. And his character had changed. By reason of school and teachers; because of Kevin living above the small cemetery next door. Knowing Jean Tomkins. From running. And being alive.

Patrick had gained confidence, was no longer quite so self-conscious, so aware of what other people were thinking about him. And he had lost something as well. Very little of the child was left in his face; nothing chubby or tentative about him. At sixteen, he was on the edge of manhood.

Running with a fluid stride that made anything less than five miles an easy workout, he heard something hoarse and strident. Noise of shouting; youths and older children, no sound of girls' voices. They were a short distance away, voices mixed together like tangled barbed wire. And separate sounds, much closer. Panting. Then, rounding a corner, the frantic idiot face of someone Patrick knew – Joe Barr.

The mocking voices were loud now: "Crazy Joe, Crazy Joe, Crazy Joe!"

They almost ran into each other, Joe Barr and Patrick, stopping face to face; Joe panting, his chest heaving. Patrick had seen the same thing happen before, boys running after Joe, harassing the idiot, yelling and calling him names, sometimes throwing stones. A white scar like a small angel danced at the corner of Joe's mouth. Patrick wondered if the reason for it had been a stone.

Without thinking, he grabbed Joe's arm, pulling him into shrubbery beside the road. A moment later the parade of tormentors straggled past, faces red from exertion. And disappeared among some trees, baffled voices becoming distant.

Patrick and Joe stared at each other, only a few inches away. But *was* Joe actually an idiot? They were so close, he could see a new alarm on Joe's face, the quarter-inch black hair that sprouted from his chin and nostrils. And the black eyes – *were* they idiot eyes? True, there was something of a mongoloid look about him, a thickening of the eyelids and heaviness of cheeks. A bit of drool leaked from his mouth.

But an idiot?

"Joe," Patrick said, and waited.

Both their expressions were blank. Then deep lines that curved from the corners of Joe's mouth to his nose seemed to move. Patrick thought, knew, there was intelligence in Joe Barr. He waited expectantly.

"Aw," Joe said. Then, "Aw, aw, aw!" like a human crow. His eyes were black marbles in bristly face; he wanted an answer from Patrick in return.

"Aw," Patrick replied. And tentatively, "Aw?"

It seemed to mean something. There was kindness in Joe's face. Here was communication, here was a friend?

"Aw," Patrick said again, this time eliciting an expression of disappointment on Joe's face. Could he be a deaf mute?

On the dirt road beside the leafy retreat, Joe's tormentors were trailing back to town, disappointed. Patrick pulled at Joe's arm, pushing him lower among the green leaves.

"Aw," Patrick said after a few moments.

Joe grinned unmistakably. If he was an idiot, he was only 30 or 40 per cent idiot.

Patrick had no idea where the man came from. Living on food given him by the Salvation Army and church ladies or thrown away by housewives, Joe had haunted his childhood ever since he could remember. A scarecrow figure stalking the garbage dump, heavy stick in one hand to keep his balance, making a noise to himself that varied from

124

"aw" to "hay" to "hee," not saying anything at all if he could avoid it.

"Crazy Joe," Patrick said, wondering if the word "crazy" meant anything to him.

Joe's face darkened. He grasped Patrick's wrist very tightly. With his other hand he turned Patrick's face directly in front of him. And stared deep and hard into Patrick's eyes, leaving him a little shaken.

But it was all right. Joe knew he didn't mean it. Joe knew. It was a knowledge that made Patrick feel good, lifted his spirits, which hadn't been down anyway.

Joe grabbed both of Patrick's wrists, dragging him out from the bushes, down the road toward the garbage dump. Then off an undecided dirt track onto the nuisance ground. And seemed to know where he was going: zigzagging around smelly heaps of rotting vegetables; the fly-covered body of a dead brown dog, its teeth exposed in a dying snarl; broken six-bushel crates and wooden baskets; decayed remains of town breakfasts, lunches, and suppers; rusty tin cans and bashed-in pails filled with rainwater, insects swimming around in some of them; mouldy clothes; piles of branches pruned from trees, heaped up so they looked like beaver dams.

A world of itself. There were pyramids, oblongs, rectangles, and shapeless clouds of garbage. Black and brown rats scuttled almost under the invaders' feet, squeaking at them in high-pitched voices. One of them popped up ten feet away, near the body of a dead cat, whiskers twitching, staring at them. Joe threw a tin can at it and grinned. "Aw," he said, "aw." His grip on Patrick's wrist never slackened.

At one point, they encountered a smell so strong as to be a physical thing. A wall of smell, a bombardment of the nose. It stopped even Joe briefly, making his nose twitch as they detoured around the stink.

He pulled at Joe's arm, and they paused at a relatively clear place. There was garbage in all directions – east, west, north, south. Mountains and peninsulas of it, islands and headlands of garbage; turbid lakes of liquid garbage smearing their feet. Looking up, Patrick saw the blue and circular sky, billowing cumulus clouds, a crown of purity floating over the garbage. He gasped in relief to see the sky; an escape from earth on which his eyes could rest.

Joe was looking up, too, watching him. His face had a strange expression, as if he wanted to speak but couldn't. His lips moved, his chin trembled. It seemed that he could make hoarse vowel sounds – *a,e,i,o,u* – but couldn't handle consonants. And Patrick would have sworn that Joe felt the same as himself about the blue sky. He pointed up at the ceiling of the earth, and said, "Blue – blue, blue, blue!"

Joe's fingers tightened on his wrist again, dragging him ahead.

Patrick was not frightened, and wondered at himself. Most of the town kids, unless there was a mob of them, were afraid of Joe. And they despised him at the same time. The idiot – if he was an idiot – acted differently from other people, didn't speak recognizable words, smelled a little, wore ragged clothes, had no job. And probably wasn't even aware of the Great War being fought in Europe. Thinking about that, Patrick knew the war didn't enter his own mind very often. Only when he glimpsed an expression of grief on someone's face, or marching khaki on Trenton streets, or looked at the town newspaper and noticed a list of the dead and missing in action.

In the middle of the garbage sea they came to a one-room "cabin." It was small and appeared to measure about eight by ten feet. Unless you were standing directly in front of it, the place was invisible, camouflaged by garbage that looked exactly like the cabin. Patrick stopped to look at it. Joe waved his hand at the place like a proud showman.

The cabin was "put together," rather than constructed, with wooden boards, all sizes of them. Narrow boards were nailed over cracks and seams. None of them were painted, unless they had arrived at the dump painted. No bright colours. Reaching two feet up from the bottom, flattened tin cans were nailed to the walls. Against the rats, Patrick supposed. And junk was piled against the cans, making them invisible without close examination. The roof was flat, with perhaps a six-inch pitch for proper drainage; the salvaged roofing was a coat of many colours, a bleached and faded rainbow.

Joe urged him through the low and almost undetectable doorway. They entered darkness, with only here and there chinks of light from holes in the walls, like small pieces of silver. Joe lit a coal-oil lamp, grinning at him, waving his hand toward shadowy furnishings. "Aw," Joe said, meaning sit down, Patrick thought. He lowered himself gingerly into a sagging chesterfield chair that was losing its stuffing. Joe patted the back of the chair caressingly.

The cabin interior was dark, even with the coal-oil lamp. Two kitchen chairs, one with a broken leg, and small table occupied the room's centre. A narrow cot at the wall with something shapeless at its head. And a kitchen stove about the size of a baby carriage. The stovepipe ran sideways along the ceiling, enclosed by the lid of a steel drum where it exited through the wall instead of roof.

Patrick had a vision of Joe huddled around the stove on cold winter nights, snow piled up outside, the Bay of Quinte frozen, temperature about thirty below zero. Joe shivering, keeping the fire blazing, for once not caring if someone should see a scarlet tongue of flame lifting above the garbage where no flame should be.

Joe extracted a shapeless something from his cot, placing it gently in Patrick's arms. It was a brown teddy bear, quite a large one, about eighteen inches long. Its velour fur was worn; it had shoe-button eyes, rather like Joe's own. Someone had sewn up a hole in its side where the bear had lost some of its sawdust innards. Joe patted the teddy bear as it

127

rested in Patrick's arms, patted it continually and lovingly, with an imploring look at Patrick.

It was embarrassing for him, at first – the whole situation. And rather pitiful, he thought. All those slogans you heard about every human being deserving a chance at the good life and square or round meals every day.... And this particular human being ends up in the garbage without anybody at all making a fuss about it. A man living in the midst of garbage, probably eating it, too, an existence like that of an animal burrowing in the earth.

Apart from the Salvation Army, Patrick didn't know if there were any charities in Trenton. But his mother had talked about the Ladies' Aid, which sounded from its name as if it might be helpful. And Mr. Hartwell, the Reverend Mister Hartwell? Joe was certainly not employable, but something ought to be done for him. The police, would they help? A cold thought entered his brain as he realized something: the police would be more likely to throw the town idiot in jail. And it would be dangerous to ask Mr. Hartwell for help; the same thing might happen.

Joe dragged over a kitchen chair and sat beside him, caressing the wounded teddy bear. His expression asked for understanding, Patrick thought. Or did it ask that he, too, should love and admire the teddy bear? He pointed at the bear. "What's his name, what's the teddy bear's name?" And smiled at Joe.

He felt acutely uncomfortable handing the bear back to its owner. Joe had a dangerous reputation among Trenton children, but that wasn't the reason for his discomfort. He was in a place and situation where he had to act and speak instinctively. There weren't many previous guidelines for what he should do and say.

"What's the teddy bear's name?"

Astonishingly there was intelligence in Joe's eyes. His mouth writhed and twisted sideways. He drew in several big gulps of air; his chest heaved, his eyes bulged. He

128

hugged the brown creature in his arms and swivelled around with it. Then, with an aching gesture of renunciation, he thrust the teddy bear at Patrick.

A word like "you" almost came out of Joe's mouth, a one-syllable word that might have meant, "I like you," or "This is my most precious thing, something of great value, and I give it to you freely."

Patrick held the soiled teddy bear gingerly, thinking: This situation amounted to having power over another person. Or maybe it was what Mr. Hartwell was always talking about, maybe it was love? He squirmed in the chair, and handed the bear back to Joe.

# TWO

# Red McPherson

# 8

PATRICK WENT TO VISIT HIS GRANDFATHER. The days were shorter now in the beginning of September. At the doorway next to a dry-goods store he climbed two flights of dark wooden stairs, then had to find his way down a dark fetid-smelling corridor. Once, he remembered, there had been a light bulb hanging from the ceiling, but it had created shadows as much as light. Now the corridor was a coal mine, a midnight closet. For ten paces he ran his hands along the walls, then stretched an arm ahead to keep from bumping something. And wondered about rats.

There was no sound inside after he knocked on his grandfather's door. He hammered more vigorously, pounding on the wood. And heard a hoarse voice mutter, "Tain't locked, tain't locked. Get in here, whoever you be."

Portugee was in bed, back propped against the wall, with pillows. He glared at Patrick from sunken eyes, "Well, ya took yer time."

"I'm back at school now, and there's homework." And he realized how feeble that sounded while speaking, but was irritated at the excuse being so transparent. Really, there was lots of time, in the evenings and on weekends, and even between stints of running.

"I'll get in more often," he promised.

"Don't matter none," the old man said, turning his head away. Neither spoke for a while, and the silence became uncomfortable.

Portugee lay ensconced in a narrow bed, no wider than a couch. A dark woollen blanket covered him like a black bear's pelt, his face white with a week's beard, the skin

133

flabby and unhealthy-looking. On his cheeks some places looked as if tree limbs had once grown there, and been cut off years ago, but healed badly, leaving knotted scars. His ferocious aspect was muted; even the gravelly voice was softer.

Portugee was sick, Patrick realized. "You've got the flu?" he said.

"A sneakin little cold, but it keeps me snifflin. How 'bout you getting another roll of bum wad from in there?" He pointed at the closet-sized bathroom with a ghastly grin.

Patrick found a roll of toilet paper in the stinking narrow place where you could scarcely turn around without bumping into things.

Portugee blew his nose like the sound of a riverboat announcing arrival.

"Have you seen a doctor?" Patrick said.

"How in hell could I see a doctor?" his grandfather snarled. "It's just the sniffles anyway."

"Have you seen anyone? Visitors, I mean?"

"No poker this week, so nobody come. . . ." The pale eyes darted blue fire at him from under bushy eyebrows. "Ain't seen you for a spell neither." Vitality drained out of his voice, he said, "Well, sit ye down now that you've decided to favour me." He fell back on the bed, a lamp beside it glimmering on white hairs of his beard.

Patrick walked down the long room, shaped like a one-lane bowling alley, standing beside the poker table with its green cloth cover. Two unopened decks of cards stood guard on the windowsill. He peered out on the street, watching pedestrians – soldiers in khaki, housewives hurrying home to prepare supper, a stray dog with a beaten look – and felt depressed.

Patrick was fidgeting, and turned back to his grandfather. "I have to go. Would you like me to call on Dr. Johnson, ask him to look in on you?"

"Won't have no truck with doctors," the old man growled. "How 'bout you stayin with me a spell?"

"I have to get home. Mother wants – "

"Mother wants," the gravelly voice mocked, "mother wants."

Patrick was acutely uncomfortable. "I really want to stay," he stammered.

"He really wants to stay," the parrot voice repeated.

Patrick flushed angrily. "Don't you give me any credit at all? There are things I have to do, can't you understand?"

Portugee's voice grew gentle, "Of course I do. It's just that I like to see you sometimes myself. It's just that I. . . . Makes no difference anyway."

Then the harsh sound was back. "Run along with you, boy. We can talk some other time, other time. . . ." His head fell back on the pillow. "Run along, boy."

On his way home Patrick thought about the flu epidemic that had sent people to bed all over town for the last few weeks. Some deaths had been reported. And beyond Trenton in nearby towns, flu was said to be prevalent. Mrs. McMaster on the next street was sick with it, as were several other people he knew about. A worm of unease began to chew at his mind. Could Portugee have the flu, despite his passing it off as the sniffles? His grandfather was ninety, but had never before seemed subject to the illnesses and broken bones of mortal men, being one of the Olympians himself. But this time it might be different.

He described Portugee's symptoms to his mother at the supper table. "His face was puffy, and he had a sort of cough."

"You go back there when we've finished eating," Mrs. Cameron said. "I'll heat up some chicken broth for him."

She looked seriously amused. "The old pirate! I never remember him being sick before. It's as if when he got mad at anyone, the heat inside him killed all the germs dead. They never dared raise their heads again."

135

Moving cautiously down the dark corridor above the dry-goods store, Patrick lit a kitchen match. It was awkward, holding a pot of chicken broth in one hand and a lighted match in the other.

At the door he said, "Grandfather, Grandfather!" No answer. And thought, I'm the only one who calls him that. He switched names. "Portugee, Portugee!" It sounded rather like a battle cry.

After a moment, without invitation from inside, he tried the door. It opened readily. Inside, things felt different, perhaps because of a continued silence. Beside Portugee's cot, the bed lamp lighted a small space: the old man humped up in bed with his eyes open. Dirty dishes in the sink, a great pile of them. A buzzing housefly circled the lamp elliptically, never stopping. Except for that, silence.

Patrick was cold, almost shivering. Not from air in the room, although it wasn't very warm. He looked at the blanket and grey bed sheets spread over his grandfather's huge body. No movement could be seen, no slight rise and fall denoting breathing. His own breath withheld a moment, then expelled with a *chuff* of sound. He walked away from the bed, walls of the long room feeling very close, closing in on him.

Portugee was dead, he had no doubt. Standing at the window, watching the darkening streets, Patrick realized something about his own life had changed. Incongruously, John Carter, Edgar Rice Burroughs's hero in *A Princess of Mars*, popped into his head. John Carter, the fighting man of Mars, standing on a dawn-lit mountain in Arizona and feeling himself irresistibly drawn toward the red planet hovering on this world's horizon. A great cold, then airlessness, and Captain John Carter with Portugee's face was standing among the Martian canals, ready for new adventures. Portugee on Mars, seeking his own lost princess among the giant green men of the red planet. . . .

Patrick shook his head and shrugged himself away from fantasy. He went back to the bed, staring down at his grandfather's body. Because now it was a "body," a "corpse." But perhaps the old man wasn't really dead? He had the feeling that this was wrong somehow, not the way things should be done: a son, twice removed, standing here calmly wondering whether an old man was dead. As well, desolation, lostness, one of his compass points removed, one of the brackets that supported his existence collapsed. Aloneness.

Fear as well. He had never before discovered anyone recently dead, newly departed from life, the dead person very different from himself. Become alien. About to rot if something didn't halt the process. Whatever the dead man had been thinking about before death was still imprinted on his brain, a message no undertaker could read or brain surgeon decipher. "He was thinking about me," Patrick said aloud, "because I hadn't come to visit him for a long time."

Without knowing he was doing it, he reached a hand under the bedclothes, searching for his grandfather's hand, the wrist, the pulse. The hand he found was warm, but the skin was like a snake's skin, the little tendons underneath gone slack. No movement, no leaping blood.

And no "Whatcha, boy?" to greet him, from yesterday or the day before, ever since he could remember.

Patrick's knees collapsed. Sinking down on the greasy hardwood floor, he leaned his head against Portugee and the dead body, and his grandfather who was both of them.

After five minutes, he went to the sink, splashing cold water on his face above the dirty dishes. And felt slightly better.

At the police station, a fat man with several chins was on duty at the desk. Patrick said to him, "My grandfather –" The last word stuck in his throat, somewhere between death and life.

137

Dryer's Funeral Chapel was on King Street, not far from the church. It had once been the residence of an executive with the Gilmour Lumber Company; the builder's aim had been to distinguish between grand and grandiose. There were pillars in front with Ionic capitals, which leaned toward the grandiose in a small lumber town. The front door had frosted sidelights and transom, sheltered by a classical porch, and was merely grand. The gable roof was olive-coloured slate, with a narrow orange band across the centre, like a tiger with only one stripe.

William Dryer, in order to make room for the main chapel, had torn out the partitions between dining room and living room, replacing them with massive oak columns. The date for this remodelling, called mutilation by some, was 1910. Dryer had never heard of the Ionic order of architecture, but thought the Ionic columns of the porch were *nice*, and spared them. A carved oak and Italian marble fireplace was not spared. It had been covered over with plain oak boards.

Mr. Dryer greeted Mrs. Cameron and Patrick at the door with a damp handshake. His greeting was perhaps a little obsequious, since she was paying for the funeral. A bald man of indeterminate age between forty and sixty, his smile was in perfect and practised good taste, with the practice showing slightly.

"The viewing is in the Loved Ones' Shrine," he said, gesturing toward the oaken columns. "Then you may sign the Book of Remembrance."

Patrick was wearing his new blue serge suit; he felt hot and uncomfortable. He thought there was an odd smell about the place, like chloroform mixed with perfume. It forced him to breathe shallowly and made his stomach twitch.

They stood beside the varnished pine casket, looking down on the last remains of Marshall Portugal Cameron. He had been shaved since Patrick had last seen him. The undertaker had been responsible for these ministrations, Patrick surmised. And Portugee's own iron-black suit with soup stains on the vest had undoubtedly been cleaned. His face was very pale, the knotted marks on his cheeks vestigial. Patrick thought Mr. Dryer must have covered them with some cosmetic powder.

The worst of it was that Portugee didn't seem real any more. He was gussied up for people to look at: his hair combed, his features manipulated into an almost pious expression. Despite the terror he had felt at seeing Portugee dead that first time, he would now have preferred that savage look of death clamped on his grandfather's face.

Startled to think of it, he bent down and peered closely at the masked face of someone he had once known and loved. The arranged features were those of a stranger. Then a dirty white beard sprouted suddenly on the ninety-year-old epidermis, the closed eyes appeared to open, and one of them winked at him unmistakably.

Patrick shook his head vigorously and grinned at his grandfather. "Whatcha, kid?" he said.

Mrs. Cameron grabbed his arm. "Patrick," she said admonishingly, "did I hear you say something nasty?"

"No, Mom. What thing?"

"Nothing, nothing. It's just that that old man is nearly as much alive as anyone here in this room. I thought I heard you speak to him, and he to you . . ."

"Maybe we should get some fresh air, Mom. Are you feeling . . ."

"I'm all right," she said abruptly, and took his arm. "Some of your relatives from Prince Edward just came in. We've got to say hello to them."

These were the Harrigans, who farmed near Wellington, Patrick remembered. His mother was not overly fond of

139

them. "They're snooty," she'd informed him. Cousins, but not kissing cousins; how far removed, he didn't know.

Mrs. Cameron marched him over to them ceremoniously. "Stephen Harrigan," she said. "My son, Patrick."

The coolness between them created a distinct lowering of temperature. But it was only hinted at, and didn't come out in the open.

Stephen Harrigan was a fresh-complexioned man of fifty, with a nose so imperially Roman it was a balcony to his face. His eyes had stared into the sun so often their lids hung down like shutters, showing only slits of faded yellow-brown.

"Patrick," Mr. Harrigan said in acknowledgement.

"And Mamie," his mother went on.

Patrick nodded, since that was all that was required of him. And Mamie, toward whom he was well disposed because he liked her name, smiled at him. His original fear had been that she might attempt to kiss him. Some women of his mother's circle, generally elderly, had that habit. He tried to discourage them.

Then it seemed that all of Trenton crowded into the chapel. Jean Tomkins and her parents; Billy Coons and Jack Corson; two of Patrick's high school teachers, Miss Gothard of geography and Mr. McIver of Latin; Kevin Morris and his parents (Kevin and Patrick eyed each other, both with a look of reassessment); Ada Kemp, hatchet face even sharper with sympathy for Mrs. Cameron; and Mr. Yourex, the blacksmith, tall and gaunt as an emaciated horse.

Patrick and his mother dutifully greeted all of them, Jean last of all. Patrick's and Jean's fingers touched.

Mr. Hartwell also came to pay his respects to the dead, or perhaps it was Mrs. Cameron he respected. Her manner turned very formal as she greeted him, a trace of colour on her cheeks. Using his ecclesiastical title of "Reverend," she urged him into small knots of people, making sure they heard everything he said by occasionally repeating it. This treatment seemed not to displease him. Patrick was disturbed. Chester's grating whine was distilled in his ears from Mr. Hartwell's own voice. He shuddered.

There was a noise at the door. Patrick heard Mr. Dryer say, "You aren't allowed inside. This here's a solemn occasion, only relatives and loved ones. . . ." His voice degenerated into a sputter of saliva in which words drowned.

"Nonsense," a soft tenor voice interrupted Mr. Dryer. A voice clear as a tuning fork, "Nonsense." It wasn't just the tenor voice; there were five other people. All very old, or so they seemed to Patrick. Six old men, two of them wearing red-and-black checked windbreakers; the others in heavy sweaters or worn leather jackets. All were shabby, nondescript as a fallen leaf. But the room changed on their entrance, though Patrick could not have said how it was different.

The group leader was a very tall old man, with the remains of red hair clutching his skull. He clomped over to Patrick's mother, seized her hand, and kissed it with a smacking sound. "Is that you, Elly, behind the veil? Remember me? Red McPherson from Bancroft. You look just as – "

"No, I don't. I haven't looked like that since the day before last year. Red McPherson?" Her eyes sparkled. "I remember a Cyril McPherson Portugee brought to visit. He got inebriated," she went on primly, "and smashed some of my dishes."

Patrick looked at his mother amazedly. This was a dimension of her he hadn't suspected.

She raised her voice, "Are you that same Cyril?"

McPherson looked around him uncomfortably. "I'm Cyril, but I don't come if you call that name. How about trying me with Red."

"This is Patrick," Mrs. Cameron said placidly.

141

Besides the scanty fringe of red hair, Red McPherson had a couple of front teeth missing and pendulous dewlaps. He looked directly at Patrick. "Portugee's grandson," he mused, as if to himself. "There must be something in him. There sure must be. Patrick!" Red McPherson said in an attention-getting tone.

"Yes, Mr. McPherson?"

"Yes, Mr. McPherson," the old man mocked in the same way Portugee had. And considering, "But what else should you call me, you know no more of me than my name."

He clapped a hand over his eyes and peeked out behind it slyly. "You, I know you. You're Portugee's grandson. There's a look of him about you, I'll say that. Let me have your hand."

"Wha-at?" Patrick stammered. "What do you mean?"

"It's clear enough, ain't it? I want to shake the hand of Portugee Cameron's grandson."

There was something unsettling about the old man and his retinue of geriatrics. All of them stood around with their eyes on Patrick, making him feel younger than he had for some time. McPherson waved his hand at the others, shifting a heavy cane to his left hand, "All right, boys, go pay your respects to Portugee. It's nearly the last time you'll see him."

He turned back to Patrick. "Your hand!"

It was a command, not a request. Patrick reached out his hand rather tentatively, wondering what trick might be in store for him. But Red McPherson's hand was like any other, except for the slight remains of calluses and a missing little finger. He managed a grin, but his face felt stiff.

"You knew my grandfather a long time?"

"Yes, a very long time. We worked in the shanties together."

"The shanties?"

"The lumber camps. North on the Trent River and Moira to Renfrew and past there. The other boys, too, on the Skootamatta, Madawaska, and York rivers . . . "

"You just went into the woods and chopped down trees?" Patrick said. "I mean, didn't you work for somebody?"

"Sure we did, the Gilmour Lumber Company. There was other outfits as well, but mostly Gilmours'. You ever hear of it?"

In the mythological past of Trenton, Patrick knew about the Gilmours. "Grandfather worked for them, too?" he said.

"Sure, and them Gilmours're just about responsible for you bein here, too, this very day. And for Trenton bein a prosperous town. They sent slews'n scads of men into the woods. And hundreds more worked in the sawmill. Their plant was right where the dynamite works is today, beside the river."

Red veins in McPherson's face flared a deeper red while he talked. He leaned on his stick more heavily, seeming to grow frail before Patrick's eyes.

"Tell ya what," he said, "you come over and see us tonight. We're stayin at Portugee's place, me an' the boys, them as hasn't got no other place. Come if you like." The faded eyes flashed. "I mean, come if you have a mind to."

McPherson went over to the casket, standing a moment with his friends looking down at the dead man. Then all six left, William Dryer stepping aside hastily to make room.

Patrick looked inquiringly at his mother, "What do you think?"

"Of course you'll go," she said.

They were playing cards at Portugee's green table. Five of them. A light bulb with glass shade dangling above, throwing things beyond the table into shadow.

Watching them, McPherson said, "Rent's paid here, so we might as well use the place."

Patrick nodded. Unoccupied rooms were valuable. Trenton was jammed to its boundaries and beyond by workers at British Chemical, construction men, delegations from Ottawa, local business and farmers supplying the munitions factory. The town had no unemployment problems; everyone was prosperous. Hotels and rooming houses were packed full. Some newly arrived workers had even been forced to sleep in the open until accommodation could be found for them.

Patrick and McPherson watched the game from outside that circle of light. The cardplayers paid no attention to anything outside the circle, eyes fixed hypnotically on the flashing coloured cards. On the table, small heaps of wooden kitchen matches constituted money or its equivalent.

"That there's blackjack," McPherson said a little scornfully. "Game's for idiots with nothin better to do with their brains and time."

A cardplayer with tobacco stains at the corners of his mouth looked up. "What you doin with your time?"

"Waitin till you play out this hand so you can clomb outa that chair and say hello to Portugee's grandson. That too much to ask?"

McPherson looked at Patrick significantly. "They're all stuck back in the shanties. They come outa the woods, they got no manners, don't know how to use a knife and fork or say please. They trip over their own feet and forget how to use the toilet . . . "

At the end of the little speech his voice had grown taunting, eyes sparkling from the fun he was having with his diatribe. The old men paid no attention whatever.

All of them at the card table had a single identity for Patrick. Their personal differences had melted together, their faces blurred, blank of any expression. "Hit me," one of them said. The dealer flipped a card toward him with a finger snap that Patrick admired. Another said, "I'll stand with these." The heap of matches on green baize, pretending to be money swelled and diminished.

"What've ya got?" said the man with tobacco-stained mouth.

Patrick noticed then that at least three of them were chewing tobacco. Their cheeks bulged with it. A silver spittoon near the window was brown and gooey with it. At intervals, a sound like a whistling *slurr-up* denoted ejection of excess saliva.

McPherson said, "Make a poultice of chaw tobacco when ya got a cold, it'll either kill or cure ya."

A winner was eventually declared among the blackjack players; the cards were turned face up, but no one changed expression or appeared elated.

"Idiot's game, like I said," McPherson announced again. I guess you've never seen it played before. Idea is to make the card numbers in your hand add up to twenty-one. Or if it ain't twenty-one, then closer to it than anybody else in the game. Face cards count ten and aces either one or eleven. Deal the first two cards to each player face down, the next up if the next one is wanted. And now you know how to play blackjack."

McPherson grinned, leaning on the cane that supported his bad leg, the grin changing from something derisive to an attractive smile. When he smiled ten years dropped from his face, and Patrick forgot how old he was. "No, I don't know how to play. But I know what 'hit me' means anyway."

The six old men were all standing and smiling at him now. They were shrunken with age, faded with time, but there was a feeling of good fellowship about them. Patrick felt accepted by them. But he sensed a sadness in their faces, an awareness of the end and the beginning. A quick leap in his mind added up their total ages as being about five hundred years. And four times five hundred, then you'd be back before Christ was born.

"This here's Reward Rensaleer," McPherson said, and Patrick realized this was to be his formal introduction to the past. "Anyone with a moniker like that, he's gotta be a Dutchman," McPherson went on. "But where and how that 'Reward' got into it beats me. I'm damn sure his mother didn't think so."

The two old men knew each other so well that insults changed to compliments; their intonations and slight inflections conveyed more than the actual meanings of words. It was a language between them whose import was entirely under the surface. A lengthening vowel or short-ened consonant spoke to their insides, a private language.

Then McPherson abandoned such niceties entirely, "Ree-ward, ya dish-faced Dutch donkey," he snorted, "shake hands with Portugee's grandson, all there is left of Portugee here on earth."

The melodramatic words made Patrick gasp mentally. He shook hands with Reward, wary of these emotional deeps and shallows he appeared to be entering. The Dutchman was small, stoop-shouldered, and with a slightly hooked nose. From the tip of it a bright drop of mucus hung; it glittered like a diamond earring.

"Portugee's grandson," he said, and Patrick could see tears in the old man's eyes.

McPherson produced a bottle of rye whisky and dirty glasses from the sideboard. He distributed them among the ancient recipients with a little swoop of the hand, a cere-mony of hello and farewell. Patrick felt honoured to be there (what would Mom say to see him drinking? he won-dered), and to take part in it.

He took the glass, noticing a fly speck, holding it for McPherson to pour, and felt tears surging behind his eyes and blinked them back. Now that Portugee was dead, his feelings for his grandfather could be acknowledged for what they were and remain unchanged, part of his life, ordinary as a doorknob, marvellous as a door key.

Patrick thought: After Red McPherson says, "To Portugee," will they dash their glasses onto the floor and break them?

They didn't. McPherson said instead, "To Patrick Cameron."

But he couldn't drink to himself, could he?

"It's all right, go ahead and drink; we want you to."

Patrick's first taste of eighty-proof whisky distilled some alarming feelings, left him stuck between embarrassment and 80 per cent enjoyment.

It was cold fire. After he had finished another drink, it was red peppers and original sin. What will Mom think?

McPherson introduced the others. "Sideways Smith. He's from Madoc, near Stoco Lake."

Smith was gaunt as a leafless tree, the lines on his face running crookedly upward – for which opposite reason Patrick surmised the nickname Sideways. When they shook hands he wondered how anyone could call someone Sideways?

Smith seemed to know his thoughts and said, "I'm glad they gave me that name. When people say it, they have a smile that doesn't always show, or it ends too soon to show more than a trace." He grinned, and the lines on his face jumbled. "That way I know what the rest of the world is thinking about.

"Patrick, I owe something to your grandfather. It wasn't anything you can take outa your pockets or pay back. But I wouldn't do that anyway. . . ." And to Patrick's consternation, tears came into the old man's eyes.

147

"This here's Phil Wright," McPherson said hurriedly. "Short for Philemon. He's up near Palmer Rapids, just so you'll know where not to go. Best damn raftsman on the river."

Phil Wright looked it. He was over seventy and short, but his barrel chest retained the remnants of enormous strength. His face was dark, hair only slightly grey, an Indian look about his eyes. When they shook hands, Patrick noticed that he, too, had a finger missing. Try as he might to avoid it, his eyes strayed to that maimed hand.

Wright noticed. "The Gilmour saws," he said. "But I was lucky. There's some lost a hand, an arm, or more'n that."

McPherson said, "Phil knew David Gilmour in the seventies and eighties."

"He was a fancy man, that Gilmour," Wright said reminiscing, "dressed like a dude, and talked like one, too. Played polo in New York, I hear tell. Thought he was better'n anyone else . . . " Wright's cracked lips grinned. "Maybe he was, too. Depends on what you think a man is. Leastways, he had the money that said he was better, whatever money says."

"Dmitri Jones," McPherson went on. "Dmitri was Welsh afore he came to Canada. His mother couldn't stand the thought of them bein Welsh an' claimed he was Russian."

"How did the Russians feel?" Phil Wright said.

Jones gave them a Dmitri look. And Patrick wondered if the milky look in one eye meant cataracts.

"And Farker Newman," McPherson said. "He's got a farm near Tweed, runs a farm."

"My son runs it," Newman corrected, his gold teeth glittering. "Pleased to meet ya."

The old men were beginning to blur in Patrick's mind, or perhaps it was the unaccustomed booze. McPherson waved his arm at them. "You boys can get back to your game while I talk to Portugee's grandson."

They smiled a little shyly and seemed ill at ease. Patrick guessed there was more emotion strewn around here than they were used to ordinarily. And guessed, too, that words were alien to them if the words expressed more than concrete things. But faces said more than words anyway. He wondered what his own face said to them.

"Come an' sit down," McPherson said. "I ain't much of a hand for cards anyway."

"What do you do then?" Patrick said. "I mean, how do you spend your time?"

A quizzical look from McPherson. "Maybe I waste it. Some say readin is a waste of time. I like to read. When the others were playin poker in the shanties, on Sundays or whenever I got the chance, after salt pork an' beans an' tea, I had my nose in a book – "

*A Princess of Mars* floated into Patrick's mind. "What kinda books?"

McPherson looked defensive. "You won't laugh?"

"No."

"Dickens."

"Charles Dickens?"

McPherson was slightly irritated. "Ain't no other Dickens I know of." He blushed and corrected himself, "There *isn't* no other. Sure, Charles Dickens. Think you're the only one reads books?"

John Carter, gentleman of Virginia and swordsman of Mars, faded a little in Patrick's mind. "I didn't mean it that way."

"Sure. *David Copperfield?*"

"Yeah, I read it," Patrick said, memory of those eight hundred pages overwhelming him. "When I first learned to read; not long after that anyway. My mother paid me a nickel a book to read Dickens."

"No!"

"Yes. I wanted to read him anyway, so I suggested it to her. And I thought it was a good idea, a way to get some pocket money."

"And was it?"

"They were so long," Patrick remembered. "And some words I didn't understand. I just had to guess at them. . . . Then I read the one about the French Revolution."

"*A Tale of Two Cities.* London and Paris."

"Madame Defarge."

"Knitting."

"I guess she was."

"And the cart that took them to the guillotine – "

"While she was knitting. . . ."

They grinned at each other, and there was no condescension in Red McPherson's grin. "You're wondering about your grandfather, what he was really like. It turns out he was something different than you thought, than you knew about."

"I guess so. It seemed to me he'd always be there, he'd live forever."

"Yes. Things do seem that way, then they change. You go on and you go on, everything the same; you almost fall asleep from seeing the same things every day. But there's a jolt, someone dies.

"What happens then, everything is thrown out of kilter. One thing changes, and because of that everything else changes. You know?" And McPherson's somewhat watery blue eyes looked in the direction of nothing.

"I felt like you say," Patrick said awkwardly. "I mean, when he died."

McPherson looked at him keenly. "Things rearrange themselves. I could tell you about that, the way I feel about it anyway. You got time?"

Rye whisky spoke in Patrick's veins and alarm bells sounded: What would his mother say if he stayed here with the six old men long past bedtime, while the lost village of Trent Port slept, and the modern town, remembering nothing of its past, dozed in wartime stupor?

"I guess so," he said.

"I spose you got some of this in your history class at school," McPherson went on. "If you didn't, I got a bone to pick with them puling teachers of yours, teaching English history and not ours."

The old man was rocking back and forth in his chair with some passion, the cardplayers glancing at him in concern at the sudden storm. "Take it easy," Phil Wright said soothingly.

"This ain't England," McPherson said with emphasis. "And never think it is. It may have been England settled it; and the English sure did that along with Scotch, Irish, Dutch, German, and everyone else. Most of that in the last hundred years or so. And after they settled it, you know what happened?"

McPherson's glance impaled him on the thought, and he said again, "You know what happened?"

Patrick shook his head, submissive, carried along by the urgency in the old man's eyes.

"What happened? They changed – the people who came here did. They weren't English, Irish, Dutch, or any other damn thing, not any more."

McPherson's eyes watered; he scrubbed his hands across them and flicked the back of his wrist at the floor. "Patrick, you gotta wonder what all this has got to do with your grandfather, with Portugee Cameron."

Patrick nodded, both interested and slightly uncomfortable. "People changed," he prompted.

"Sure they did. You know what happens in a new country?" And, challengingly, "The old country that supplied settlers for the new country strips the place of stuff they can use. Whatever it is, iron ore, furs when furs was wanted, gold, like in Australia, timber, like in Canada. . . .

151

"And I seen it happening." His voice grew plaintive. "I'm not sayin it's wrong, it's just the way things are. But while all this was goin on, things were happening. Other things."

"People changed?" Patrick said helplessly.

"They sure did. Them settlers who got sent to the new country, they started feelin at home. And they said, Home is here. They said, Now is here. They got to like the place. But all the time they kept grumbling and grousing, how awful it was, how terrible it was, how it was like bein no place at all. And you know what, after a while no place at all got to be just fine. You see what I'm gettin at, Patrick?"

"Here's no place?"

"Yep, this is no place and nowhere, and to hell with them that don't like it."

The eyes blazed, and Patrick was intimidated.

"Here's Upper Canada, but where is Portugee Cameron? Remember what I said about the old country stripping the new country of whatever it could use – furs, gold, fish, timber, whatever? Well, that's what happened here for the last hundred years. For a long time the old country's got a right to do that. They spend their money and men and dreams and they say, This place is mine. They say that to anyone, any other country that thinks it can grab something that ain't theirs.

"But you know, Patrick, there comes a time, there comes a time when the old country grabs everything in sight that's valuable, when it ain't right. And when things ain't right, you know that, you feel it inside you. And in between those two times, between when it's right to grab and when it ain't right, that's when things change. When there's revolutions, when there's war . . ."

Patrick's mind felt numb. "Portugee?" He inserted the name like a hangnail for Red McPherson to notice.

"Early Canada was fur, then mining and timber. Portugee was part of that. You take a look at the maps of Upper and Lower Canada, the towns and villages, rivers and lakes, names of places, you see the names of people who settled the country –"

McPherson stopped to pour himself another generous slug of whisky. He motioned to Patrick with the bottle. "No? Well, maybe you shouldn't. Where was I in this history lesson? The cambuse shanties? You heard of them, maybe? No? Well, the cambuse is the cook-house part of the shanties. And the pine forests – you ever stand in a pine grove and hear the wind talkin, trees talkin to each other, and the wind, the wind whispering . . ."

McPherson was drunk, Patrick thought, no doubt of it. But all this pouring out was something he didn't want to end. "Go on," he said.

"What happened in the new country – the old country wanted its furs, its minerals, wanted its timber for ships to help fight faraway wars. And the new country said, I need the money for those things to help make myself what I'm going to be. The new country said, Thank you very much for all the help you've been up to now. Then the two of them looked each other straight in the eye and both said, I'm me and who're you to complain? But both of 'em knew by that time who they were.

"You ever stand in a pine grove, Patrick?"

"No."

"It's like you feel yourself changing into a tree. There's a brown forest floor under your feet from the pine needles, and there's wind higher up, a sound of the sky. Yep, for just an instant or two, you feel like a tree. And the trees them-selves, they was made into ships, sailing ships for all the seas. Sometimes I wondered, did the trees ever feel what it was like to be a ship?"

He stopped, his blue gaze bathing Patrick. "You think I'm talkin foolish? It's the booze talkin? Well, maybe that's so. Anyway – you want to hear about Portugee?"

"Yes," Patrick said quietly.

"It'd be like around 1860, back quite a ways. Maybe before that, it's hard to remember. I was in the shanties for the first time, just a young feller. Feelin my oats, knew everything. Told everybody I knew everything, too. Couldn't keep my mouth shut. And Portugee was there, but we didn't have much to say to each other. He was quiet, the way some big men are, some small men, too, come to that.

"Anyway, the timber we cut in winter was floated down the creeks and rivers to where the Gilmours wanted it to go. After the spring breakup, timber piled up waitin for spring. And when the water was wide and deep enough, they made rafts and cribs and lived on 'em till they got where they were goin. But that's another thing.

"It's when we were havin a drive down the river, hundreds and thousands of sticks of timber. And you know, sometimes they got stuck. What happens sometimes, in the rapids, timber runs into shoals, gets stuck, can't go no farther. It's like a rat's nest the size of a house, the size of ten houses sometimes.

"The sticks behind keep comin, they keep runnin underneath what's already there. It piles up, mounts up, and pretty soon there ain't a log can get loose. This was at Palmer Rapids where we was, quite a piece north.

"A jam to end jams, not like the stuff you put on your toast either. But there's always a key log in those jams, one stick that come it gets loose, all the others will get loose, too."

He stopped, pointing a big finger at Patrick. "You know what I'm talkin about?"

"I think so. Go on, please."

"Please, is it now?" the old man's voice was satiric. "That ain't Portugee talkin, but no matter a that. It was the Madawaska River we was at. Them logs was backed up for half a mile, seemed like. One of them had caught on a rock ledge. It had to be got out to free up the rest of them. I said I'd do it.

"I looked at that jam and kinda shivered. It was thirty – forty feet high, way higher'n us on shore. We just stood there and thought, Migawd. It was a rat's nest, the grand-daddy of jams. And it groaned when the water went through the logs, it creaked and groaned. It said, I'm just waitin for one of you boys to come out here. When you do, I'll grind your bones to powder."

Patrick could *see* the jam. The logs crowded into his mind, groaning threats at loggers along the shore. He felt the way he once had, sitting atop the town bridge, won-dering if he had the nerve to jump into black water below, rocking back and forth in agonized indecision.

"It was April," McPherson went on, "snow still on the ground."

He glanced at the poker players. "Sideways Smith was there, too."

Smith raised his head, hearing his name spoken. All the poker players were listening, cards in hand, eyes looking nowhere.

"I'da backed outa what I said, but when you're young – and I was maybe eighteen – pride gets stuck in your throat."

He swallowed, and, watching, Patrick could see a bony Adam's apple fly up his throat and down like a disappear-ing yo-yo.

"What they did," McPherson said matter-of-factly, "was fasten a rope around me fore I clomb out on that jam, so they could haul me back if the jam shifted sudden like. I went, holdin on to my axe – I'd just run a stone over it, so it was sharp. Scamperin over logs, and they was slippery."

He glanced at Patrick. "You wonder why you do things like that. And think, what a damn fool!"

"Go on, Mr. McPherson."

"The name is Red, and don't you forget it."

"I'm sorry, Red," Patrick said meekly.

"Anyways, there I was on top of them logs, holdin on with one hand and axe in t'other. I clomb down where I could see what the trouble was. All the boys on shore looked respectful like. That kinda tickled me. Portugee was there, too – he was the foreman. And I find that key log – it just *looked* like it was – and chop away at it. I chop away, and just as the last chips fall, the jam shifts. It moves. Or maybe it just thought of movin. Anyway, I knew.

"My foot slips and I feel something grabbin it. Everything happens at once. I'm caught between two logs, my foot is. And I'm stuck there, maybe sixty feet from shore, caught fast in that terrible tangle. The rope around my waist, it wasn't no help. And the jam was shiftin and groanin – "

"What'd you do?"

"Couldn't do nothin. I was fair caught. 'Course I yelled. My foot was hurtin something fierce. Figured I was a goner. Them logs were gonna tumble all over and bust me up some. . . . "

He glanced at Patrick, at that moment seeming younger than he had been, as if the memory awakened something in his blood.

"Go on," Patrick said.

McPherson was in no hurry. Reliving that old moment called for savouring it, lingering over ancient details, half melodrama and half reality.

"There was fire in my foot, burnin at the rest of me, too. The water kept tricklin down under, under. I was fair caught. But I blanked out sort of, and next thing I heard the boys yellin, 'Twist that rope round a log!' So I did. Pulled the slack hard fast while they held the other end.

"And there was Portugee, a kinda angel he looked to me. He'd got there by hangin on to the rope with one hand, peavey in t'other. Them logs shiftin and growlin, I figured neither of us was gonna get out of it. The shore was maybe fifty feet off. I was trapped – "

"What did you do?" Patrick said.

"Didn't do nothin. What could I? It was Portugee. He run his peavey twixt those logs where my foot was, pried 'em apart, dropped the peavey, picked me up like I was a baby, and just danced back over them logs. Just danced back."

"What about the rope?" Patrick said. "What's a peavey?"

"Oh, the rope," McPherson said airily. "Portugee got back too fast to need it. The peavey – long pole with a kinda steel hook on it. Use it on the drives in spring. Any more questions?"

Patrick noticed now that the blackjack players had laid down their cards, faces rapt with memory of the shanties.

"Saved my life, Portugee did. Sideways can tell ya."

McPherson pretended to think Patrick doubted his story.

"It's God's truth," Sideways Smith said, his voice slurred.

And Patrick noticed that all the old men looked a little sloshed, dizzy with remembrance and booze. It occurred to him that they had all left the safekeeping of relatives to come here: daughters and in-laws, some of them coddled and cossetted, the disappearing edge of two generations before. The booze they were drinking, the blackjack game, the bold face they were presenting – it was probably all an act, a show they were putting on for Portugee's grandson. They were playing out the role of big bad loggers, enjoying it, dramatizing themselves like ancient western gunfighters whose arthritic hands made them slow on the draw.

"What were you doin at that log jam, Sideways?"

Sideways Smith's slightly weary face perked up.

"I was prayin, I was prayin real hard. Just hopin Portugee wouldn't stumble, and the jam wouldn't let go when they was comin back to shore. If the logs'd let go, we wouldn't see either of 'em for a spell. That water was cold, ice just gone out.

157

"But the thing was, even if they'd got wet, Red here hadn't done his laundry the week before. His clothes was smellin some. If he'd drowned, the river would've made sure his clothes was clean when they laid him out."

All this was said with a straight face, a serious matter discussed with suitable gravity. Patrick felt bewildered, wondering how he was supposed to act. And all six old men were glancing at him expectantly.

"Would that have meant a cheaper funeral?"

They roared, all of them.

At the chapel door, Mr. Dryer's face changed just enough to have it called a smile when he greeted Patrick and his mother. But it could have been indigestion. And the Harrigans were there. And everyone else Patrick knew, all wearing black.

He had the feeling that night was about to fall, shadows descending, even though it was only two o'clock on a Saturday afternoon in September. The long arctic night was impending, Mrs. Cameron's Redeemer frowning behind the scenes.

Portugee's coffin was surrounded and nearly overwhelmed by flowers. They smelled a little different from garden flowers or the daisies from which you plucked petals and said, *she loves me, she loves me not,* with every petal. They smelled like chloroform or like a hospital.

As they stood looking at Portugee, the Reverend Eustace Hartwell materialized before them.

"Dear lady," he said, "it must be terrible for you!"

Mrs. Cameron looked at him with asperity. "Why would you think that? I never liked the old buffalo very much, and him dying doesn't make him any sweeter for me."

"Mom!" Patrick said reprovingly.

"I know, I know," she said wearily. "But you never had to look after him, Patrick: cook for him, pick up after him, listen to that nasty dirty tongue he had sometimes."

She looked at the minister sharply. "Mr. Hartwell, what will you say about him?"

Hartwell stammered. "Is there something you want me to say? What do you have in mind?"

Mrs. Cameron was thoughtful.

"There's no way all those things I've felt about him so long could get into words now."

She turned toward her son, but Patrick was at the door greeting his six old men – the lame, the halt, and the blind, she characterized them privately.

"Patrick thinks Portugee is a hero," she said to Hartwell. "And so do his friends. Maybe it's true. Besides, it's not the time and the place for me to say what I think. Let it pass."

And her face had a sadness, as much for herself as for the dead old man in his coffin among the flowers.

Mr. Hartwell cleared his throat, marching to a lectern on the raised dais in front. "Onward Christian Soldiers" was implicit in his bearing; God's sergeant-major.

"Dear friends," he said.

The six old men stared at him from the front row.

Mr. Hartwell felt apprehensive for no reason he could think of. "A loved one has left us, and is gathered unto the bosom of the most high –" The idea of Portugee Cameron in the Lord's bosom seemed a little hard on the Lord, and he decided to vary the accustomed ritual. Then Red McPherson was confronting him on the dais.

"Step down there, sonny!"

"Wha-a," Mr. Hartwell faltered. Then, more strongly, "This is an outrage –"

"No it isn't," McPherson said quietly. "We're all Portugee's friends here. And I want to speak about him for the last time; his friends want me to speak for them. You can go on after I'm finished."

159

The church's dignity and his own were in danger, Mr. Hartwell felt. But McPherson's eyes were dangerous to both.

"Yes," he said weakly.

"Step down."

Mr. Hartwell did, replaced at the lectern by the tall old man with a fringe of orange hair, surveying the sixty or so people in the audience.

"Marshall Portugal Cameron," he began, as if Portugee were listening. "Your friends come here to tell you goodbye. We're none of us blood relations like some folks here. But then, I'm not sure that relations are such a great thing anyway – you make your own relations, the ones that stand by you when you need them, the ones you remember. . . . "

He waved his hand at his friends in the audience. "All of us owed Portugee something. Not money. Just for what he was. And what he was, was something bigger than people you meet on the street. But you can't put your finger on it, you only know it's there. Some men, you say they're brave, they have character; they know a lot of things or they know hardly anything. But just a few are like Portugee – you can't say hardly nothin about them, because you just *feel* what they are."

When McPherson paused, Patrick hunched around in the hard chair and sneaked a look at people in the audience. They had that glazed look, which means waiting for something to end. Mr. Hartwell, briefly deprived of his job as a speaker of polite nothings for society – that had aroused a momentary interest, a spark of wakefulness. Now they were on the verge of sleep.

"Wake up!" McPherson shouted suddenly, in a high voice that whistled through the gap where a couple of teeth were missing. "Wake up!"

Everyone looked startled at this breach of protocol and departure from custom. Mr. Hartwell rose from his seat, attempting to reassert some authority.

160

"Siddown, sonny!" McPherson said harshly. "Ye'll get your chance when I'm done. I'm not done yet."

Mr. Hartwell sat down.

"There's six of us come here," McPherson went on. "We come here on accounta Portugee Cameron, what he was like, what he meant to us . . ."

And the old men, sitting together on the front row of seats, nodded in unison, like turtles sitting on a river bank.

"Yessir," Sideways Smith muttered. Dmitri Jones blinked away a tear and nodded vigorously.

"All of us worked for the Gilmours." McPherson pointed his finger at the audience. "You know who Gilmour was?"

A few people nodded, all of them now wide awake in their attention.

"For those who don't know, I'll tell ya –"

He stopped, again pointing his finger at them emphatically. And Patrick noticed Mr. Dryer stir from his guard post at the door.

"The Gilmour Lumber Company sat itself down where that British dynamite plant sits right now. It ain't there no more, of course. But you can see traces, least I could when I went out there. And the Gilmours, they was what built this town. They made Trenton.

"God help us all, they made Trenton!

"Some of us worked in the cambuse shanties in the bush, some of us in the river sawmill. There was hundreds worked for the Gilmours, sometimes thousands; over the years, many thousands. They *was* Trenton."

He paused impressively. "I worked for 'em at the mill when I got too old for the shanties."

He held up his hand to show the place where a finger had been. "Yah, I lost a finger. Some lost more'n that.

"There was David – he was the last of them, the Gilmours. He built a dam across the Trent River by weasellin money outa the town council. David, he was like most rich

161

people – much wants more. Then he used the dam for his own profit. And every single time afterwards that water leaped over the top of that dam, it said, *Gilmour, Gilmour, Gilmour*.

"That plant built this town way back in the last century. And I spose you're wonderin what all this has to do with Portugee. Well, they're gone, the Gilmours, all gone. They came from the old country to make money, and they left when there was no more to be made. They're gone. And the woods is mostly gone as well, the pine woods."

A haze of memory in McPherson's eyes, he stopped for a moment. Then, "The pine woods. Trees higher'n any place in this town, higher'n the post office, higher'n. . . ."

The voice trailed off; Patrick stiffened where he sat. Red McPherson looked terrible. His face had gone white, he seemed to waver above the lectern. Mrs. Cameron nudged Mr. Hartwell, sitting beside her.

"Go up there and help him to a seat," she whispered.

McPherson staggered visibly as he flopped down beside the other old men. But there was something puzzling: McPherson's eyes were clear and alert, there was even a little twinkle in them.


Patrick mentioned the oddness to Jean next day.

"McPherson looked like he was going to faint, and yet he had this funny expression. It made me wonder if it was all an act that he was putting on – but I can't think of a reason for it."

"He's awfully old," Jean said. "You don't suppose –"

"What?"

"No, it couldn't be. At least I don't think so."

"Jean, will you tell me what you're thinking about!"

"Maybe he couldn't think of anything else to say. So he pretended to be faint and need help back to his seat. He'd said just about everything, hadn't he?"

Patrick was shocked. "He wouldn't do that" – and chewing at the thought a little – "would he?" Then, "Sure he would, if he felt like it."

They looked at each other, as if discovering something about the other person.

"Old people can get away with just about anything," Jean said. "So can babies. And he can always deny it if anyone suspects."

She giggled, and a tide of red came up from the neck of her blouse like an invading army. It touched her chin and cheeks while Patrick watched, fascinated by the crimson transformation: like watching white marble quickly become dark sandstone.

"Why are you looking at me like that?" she said.

"I'm just wondering if you do that with me, pretend to one thing while you're feeling something quite different."

She stared at him challengingly, then reverted to someone much younger than she was. "Wouldn't you like to know? But I am fond of you, Patrick." And thoughtfully, "At least, I suppose so."

She ducked away from his reaching hands. "Wait, wait! Do you want to go swimming? You can rescue me from drowning."

Patrick looked at her amazedly.

On the lawn afterwards, with sunlit water whispering nearby, he kept his eyes on the girl's face. They were both sixteen, and it scared him a little to think of it. To be that age was to be still a child in the opinion of adults. He noticed the way they looked at him, indulgently, making allowances or not making them, guessing at his age if they didn't already know, dismissing him as a factor in their own lives.

But apart from experience and certain matters requiring judgement, Patrick couldn't think of any important way he differed from grown-ups. He watched Jean, whose eyes were closed lying in the sun. She seemed asleep, but he wasn't sure of that either. That amazing blue glowed through her eyelids. Then she was looking at him. For a moment, all he knew was a great flood of blue. It poured and poured over him.

# 9

THE SIX OLD MEN STAYED ON in Trenton. McPherson appropriated the bed in Portugee's upstairs apartment. Sideways Smith and Phil Wright spread newspapers on the floor, and located an old mattress. The other three disappeared on the downtown streets.

It was a holiday of sorts for Wright. He lived with his younger sister, Laura. When her husband died, living with her had been an easy arrangement. The only time her temper became uncertain was when he didn't show up or was late for meals, for which he readily admitted his culpability. But really, that was a small penalty for companionship and the familiar face of someone you'd known all your life. Then Portugee dying – a friendliness removed, all memories of him becoming fixed and unchanging.

The rent on this bowling-alley-shaped room was paid until the end of September. That meant three more days here, he supposed, then back to Laura. All the days of this last summer had fled into each other quickly. Wright was seventy-three now, and much of his time was spent remembering the past. In a rowboat on the river, thinking of the tall pines near Palmer Rapids. The moment when axe blade and crosscut saw had taken a tree's life – and you could tell when that happened – the pine tree like a man so tall he reached the sky, the last moment before he fell. . . .

A whisper on the wind. The foreknowledge of an ending. Then a ground rush of air all around, as if a sudden hurricane contained inside a thousand-foot circumference wailed in his ears as the pine tree cried its death. And then the dismembering of what had become a corpse. What had been something alive was become wood, a substance you could burn in a stove.

In the beverage room of the Gilbert House, Wright sat alone and sipped beer; then gulped some of it quickly, remembering the chug-a-lug time when a whole quart had descended his gullet without stopping. That had been on a wager with Sideways Smith. The smile on his face made a thin young man with acne at the next table catch his sleeve, at what he thought was friendliness. Wright frowned at him. The man turned away hastily from the dark nineteenth-century face.

Among the other faces in his mind was Portugee's. The woods, the cambuse shanties. Being fifteen again, working in the woods. Come to think of it, a year younger than Portugee's grandson. A kid, but used to taking care of himself, able to do a man's work, the long muscles of his back developed from swinging an axe. The memory of somehow offending another man, he didn't remember how, a huge man with a full black beard.

And falling. Pain, snow, and dizziness. Black beard standing over him, leg drawn back about to put the boots to him. Then a quiet voice, a voice so soft you strained your ears to listen and didn't know why. The voice said, "Back off." That's all, just two words. A voice so different from all the loud noises around, like a breeze or river sound.

It was Portugee, of course. And he tried to recapture that one moment again. But the deliberate effort to do so made his thoughts blank out. He couldn't remember. Instead of Portugee's face, a feeling of the man himself overwhelmed him.

He lifted his glass – "To absent friends" – and gulped his beer and smiled.

The acne'd neighbour turned hopefully in beverage-room friendship. Too late. Wright used the washroom and left, strolling down Dundas Street, the town's main drag, in late-afternoon sunshine. The day shift at British Chemical

166

was nearly over. A few soldiers in uniform were at loose ends on the street. Housewives were on their way back home with groceries. And Philemon Wright, sometime logger and ex-farmer, was wondering what to do with himself: Back to Tweed tomorrow, or stay another day at Portugee's old apartment?

He passed Weller's Theatre, noticing a lettered card in front that said, Stage Show: Admission $1.50. That was a lot of money, he reflected, when a workman's wage was 35 cents an hour. But the town was crazy with prosperity, hotels and rooming houses were full up, merchants happy despite shortages, full employment. Money was coming out of people's ears. It was only the elderly who had a hard time. Wright saw his reflection in a store window, and stopped to look at himself.

A dark-haired man who might pass for a dozen years younger than his true age; some people even said he looked as if he had Indian blood. And very heavily built. Laura fed him well; even so, he didn't weigh much more than during the Gilmour days.

He leaned forward and peered at himself in the window, chuckling at his own vanity. The same face and muscles, yet not the same. In the old time, he could swing an axe like an oiled machine, arms working in the two basic movements: a hard but easy swing forward with steel biting wood; the return swing backward with a feathery wave of axe at the sky. And sweat breaking on his forehead despite zero weather.

There were moments when it had become a dream, the movements of a grotesque dancer in the forest, a semaphore whose meaning he had never deciphered. Another memory of Portugee, at a log jam on the Black River. Some narrow rapids; a log boom above them in slower water; logs released downriver a few at a time.

Men with pike poles guiding the logs. And bad luck, a stick lodged against rocks. Dozens of logs piling up behind the first one, disaster in slow motion. Two minutes later, the jam stretched from shore to shore. Like a house, like sixteen beavers building a dam.

Watching himself, his reflected face in the store window seemed to grow younger. Hands closed into fists, tension entered him like a familiar stranger, his dark eyes shone with the moment.

Someone yelled an obscenity. Its meaning was: Stop sending down logs from the boom upriver. Wait. WAIT! And the jam so tight it was a big wooden basket, a pine castle for the Gilmours to live in like medieval lords.

The key log not identified.

"Get out there!" someone yelled. "All hands and the cook. Get those pike poles to work on that crooked log stickin up in the air. . . ."

It was Portugee, boss foreman, face red from all the shouting. "Peaveys and pikes, get 'em in there. Wait for the word now – Haayyay ho, Heave! Heyyay – heave!"

From sixty years ago, Phil Wright heard a man's voice whispering in his ears, while he stared into the store window, hypnotized by memory.

Portugee's soft voice said, "Phil!"

He thought the jam must have let go, and leaped back from the roar of water and logs and danger of dying on the Black River – only a pair of worn-out logger's boots to mark the burial spot.

"Phil Wright," the voice said again. "You nearly knocked me head over heels, and me carryin a dozen eggs. Turn around. Don't you remember me?"

It was like there were two of you at one time. One standing on a street in Trenton in 1918, and a war going on with Germany; the other Phil Wright was working in the shanties on the Black River for the Gilmours in 1860. He shook his head vigorously, to clear his mind, hands clenched hard.

"Julie," he said. "Julie Morgan – "

168

"Now that you remember me," the voice that wasn't Portugee's said, "are you going to help pick up the groceries you knocked out of my arms?"

She smiled, a woman you wouldn't want to say was middle-aged because the smile wasn't. Brown hair, a small dimple in her right cheek that came and went as she spoke, and a look he remembered. Of trust? No, just a waiting look. Amazingly slim, he thought she was, after so many years.

"Julie, how do you stay the way you were? You look like a girl. Come to think of it, you are a girl."

"I work," she said quickly. "Now help me pick up this stuff you knocked down like the great lummox you are."

He glanced at her sideways while they tried to repair a brown paper grocery bag that was unrepairable.

"No use," he said, "just pile me up with it. Eggs, meat, potatoes, bread, what else?"

"You've got most of it. Now head for King Street, and I'll tell you where to stop. You do remember where King Street is, don't you?"

"The church?"

"The place you never went to," she twinkled at him. "The Reverend Hartwell runs it now."

"I've met the man. Can't say I thought a great deal of him on short acquaintance."

"No, you were never one for sitting still long, or liking anyone but me you met for the first time in a place of worship."

"It wasn't inside the church," he protested. "I saw you coming out and ran after you."

"So you did," she said calmly. "Now let's get these things home before the meat goes bad."

They went, he with his arms tumbled up with groceries, she with a thoughtful look. They stopped at a small frame house, west of the church, set back from the street among some trees.

169

"This is it," she said. "Just drop things on the kitchen table. And wait here. I've got to change; these are my working clothes. How about a beer while you're waiting? It's not very cold. I wasn't here for the iceman this week."

"Doesn't matter," he said.

He slumped on a kitchen chair, the Julie of forty years ago dancing into his mind. The year? Migawd, it could have been about 1878. Wandering the town streets on Sunday, walking off a hangover, when this vision of an angel appeared from the church, followed by a lot of non-angels. He'd followed her, too, up King Street, she all in white from church-going and a black hymn book in hand; he in black-and-red checked shirt and logging boots. He wasn't dressed much differently now, except for the boots.

Amazingly, she hadn't rebuffed him when she turned to see who was nearly breathing down her neck. He'd stammered a little speaking to her. Trying to be suave and sophisticated? No, trying to pick up an angel in a muddy little colonial town no one had ever heard of.

Julie had looked at his week-old beard and said, "You'd better shave that off. Then I can see what's underneath. Go home and shave." It was a command.

Later, they met by the river, just north of the covered bridge that resembled an elongated farmer's barn and trembled under the hammering feet of horses. There had been more trees and fewer houses than there were now in this modern town.

Phil Wright hadn't been quite so awkward with the opposite gender as he seemed to Julie. Growing up on a farm had made him familiar with mating animals, and he hadn't escaped his own sexual initiation much earlier. But the girl, Julie Morgan, left him nearly speechless at age thirty-nine.

There'd been a "romance" between them that summer, but he was inhibited by his own age: fifteen years older than the girl. And now, when she came back to the kitchen at age fifty-eight, wearing another white dress and with carpet slippers on her feet – he felt as if time had reversed itself back into 1878.

"I'm sorry," she said, pointing at the slippers. "My feet hurt. Being on them all day doesn't help."

"Doing what?"

"Cleaning rooms at the Gilbert House, making beds." And ironically, "It's a job. One has to make a living somehow. What about you?"

"Oh, I'm retired," he said airily. "A piece north of here. Living on the interest from my gilt-edge investments."

A silence then; and it went on and on, just like noise.

"I should be going," he said.

"For God's sake, why? I haven't seen you in donkey's years."

She stared at him, amazed.

"Where's your husband?" he blurted.

"Is that the reason? I haven't got one any more. He died. And if you think I couldn't speak to an old friend, an old *boyfriend*, and have a beer with him in my kitchen even if Arthur wasn't dead, then maybe you had better go."

The look she gave him was defiant.

"I'm sorry."

"I've never understood that feeling you had and still have about me. Of guilt, maybe. Is it guilt, Phil?"

Acutely embarrassed, he swung his legs back and forth under the kitchen table.

"I guess so. You were always so young, and life in the woods was – I don't know," he finished miserably.

She took his hand, leading him into the living room. Pulling him down onto a couch beside her, she said, "Hold me."

Folding his arms around her, something stirred in him. He thought he should go back to Sideways Smith and McPherson. Then forgot about it.

"Remember beside the river, and those other times?" he said.

And sunshine from the going-down sun touched his red-and-black shoulders with late warmth.

"Another time, but here is now," she said.

"I know," and held her closer.

Patrick went to see Red McPherson the next Sunday. The old man was in Portugee's bed with the flu. He was sniffling and kept on sniffling.

"My head feels like a squeeze box. Promise me you won't get that Hartwell guy to preach over me at the funeral."

The effort of saying it exhausted him; his head fell back on a grey-looking pillow.

"A doctor?" Patrick said.

McPherson groaned and blew his nose on some wadded toilet paper. "You gotta ride it out," he said. "Wake up in the night sweating, then cold when I throw the cover off. Wait till you feel so bad it can't get worse. When it gets worse you begin to feel better." He looked at Patrick malevolently.

"At least it hasn't made you lose your tongue. What about some tea?"

"Can you make it?"

"You can tell me."

"Can ya boil water, kid?"

Patrick flushed. "I am trying to help," he said mildly.

"I know, I know."

McPherson pried himself up on the narrow bed, pointing toward the sinkful of unwashed dishes.

"Over there. Find the kettle and boil some water. Find the tea and the teapot; spoonful of tea in the pot and pour water over it . . ."

The instructions became more explicit as Patrick searched around the sink, then plugged in a battered hot plate. But finally tea was achieved – a kind of minor triumph, Patrick felt. McPherson gulped it hot with noises of satisfaction, an *ah* sound between sniffs.

"That's the stuff, boy. Puts lead in your pecker."

For one instant, Patrick thought it was Portugee speaking. But he felt annoyed.

"You told me to call you Red, which I have trouble doing. How about Patrick in return? That's my name, you know."

"I apologize," McPherson said.

His watery eyes blinked, and he was almost courtly as he bobbed his head toward Patrick.

"I been used to bein in the bush, and callin the men there boys. Then I got old after a while" – his voice defiant – "I mean, people looked at me different, and I thought they must be lookin at someone else. But, of course, it was me. They didn't know – what was in my head, that was the same. They didn't know."

He stared at Patrick threateningly and sniffed. "How 'bout a drink of rum?"

"Well . . ."

"Tea's fine, but rum's better – that's what I say. Get the bottle." He pointed at the card table near the front window.

Patrick obeyed, in some amazement at himself. And noticed that the bottle had a pirate with a moustache on the label. It was half empty.

"Glasses," McPherson ordered.

Patrick found a couple of dirty water glasses in the sink, holding them so the old man could see.

"Don't wash 'em. Them's the glasses the boys used afore Portugee went to earth."

The booze blazed a fiery trail to Patrick's stomach. He thought of his mother's oatmeal porridge that morning –

sticky as grey flypaper – and wondered if the stuck-together front and back of his stomach would be dissolved apart by the rum. He gasped.

McPherson sneezed.

"It ain't the booze," he said. "I'm sick with the flu. A lot of other people are, too. I hear there's an epidemic – in Boston, New York, all over."

He fell back on the pillow, waving one hand languidly.

"Got something to tell you. Sideways is in the hoose-gow – "

"Wha–at?" Patrick stammered. "What's hoosegow?"

"The jail, the jug, durance vile, if you want it laid out for you."

Patrick was somewhat stunned, as if someone had kept hitting him on the head with the things that had been happening lately – hitting him gently, not hard enough to do any permanent damage.

"What'd he do?"

"Got drunk. Then wandered down to the police station. He stuck his head inside the door, put both thumbs in his ears, waggled his fingers at the cops. He went 'wah-wah-wah' at the toughest cop in Trenton."

Thoughtfully, "He'd do that in the shanties sometimes when he got tired of beans and pork. Phil Wright would pick him up and dunk him head first in a snowbank when it happened."

"How do you know all this?"

"That Sideways got dunked in a snowbank? You forget, I was there."

"Don't play games. How do you know he's in jail?"

"I've got a friend in the cops. He came and told me."

"That's terrible at his age. Can't we get him out? Do something?"

"Not very likely. The chief is mad, from what I hear. That Sideways, he flies off in different directions than other people."

McPherson was remembering. "There was one St. Patrick's Day – in March, I guess it was – that he got a lot of people mad at him – "

Patrick felt a little hesitant in asking what happened on St. Patrick's Day because of his own name. He raised his eyebrows when he saw McPherson watching him closely.

"Well?"

"At night, you know, we'd be sharpenin axes and gettin things ready for next day. Sometimes there was stud poker or blackjack, if you wasn't too damn tired. And the cook would have a big iron pot of oatmeal porridge hangin over the fire. You could swing it back and forth when the fire was hot or when it was low. It stayed warm all night when we hit the sack – "

Patrick thought McPherson was still playing games: "What's all this got to do with St. Patrick's Day?"

"Hang on to your drawers," McPherson told him. "I'm comin to that. Well, seems like Sideways got at that porridge and doctored it some. In the night mebbe, when we was asleep. Everybody made quite a ruckus in the morning."

The old man's head peered up from the blankets like a perky sparrow. "How 'bout reachin me another drink?"

"What happened to the porridge?" Patrick said, pouring a small shot into McPherson's dirty glass.

"Sideways had gotten hold of some vegetable dye or watercolours. When we come to look at the porridge in the morning, it was green so bright it was like nobody ever saw green before. Sideways didn't mind. He had a big dollop of that green stuff on his tin plate, sprinkled it with sugar, and sat there eatin like nothin had happened."

"Did Phil Wright dunk him in the snow?"

"Well, ya see, we couldn't prove he did it. Nobody was watchin him in the middle of the night . . ."

Patrick's mind's eye journeyed back into the past, where a tableau of angry-faced men in heavy windbreakers and homespun pants surrounded another man. This much younger man was Sideways Smith, calmly eating green porridge. He felt his own face move in a grin, and thought, I'd never do a thing like that. And then, How can I be so sure?

Aloud he said, "How did it happen? I mean that he's still in town?"

"Well, the three of us, Phil Wright, Sideways, and me, we decided to stay for a while. The other three took off for home. We got the rent money together for another month."

"How'd you do that?"

McPherson looked embarrassed. "There's people we know, and we kinda put the arm on them. And we hit up some of the guys comin outa the Gilbert House at closing time. They'd just got their pay cheques like, from the fireworks plant over the river – "

"You mean you panhandled?"

McPherson reached for the toilet paper judiciously and blew his nose with a sound between sniff and honk.

"Nothin like that. Anyway, Sideways is in jail. We gotta get him out."

"You said the chief was mad at him."

"That's so, but I figure you could talk to the man. It's Sunday, and maybe his heart could be softened on the Lord's day."

"Where's Phil Wright? What about him speaking to the chief?"

"Oh, he ran into an old girlfriend. Keepin him kinda busy."

The voice grew gentle, "I'm afraid it's gotta be you."

McPherson looked at him critically. "You wasn't plannin on goin to church anyway, I guess. Those clothes you're wearin, you've got other stuff, haven't you? Better go home and change into them before you talk to the chief."

Patrick was uncomfortable wearing the stiff blue serge suit his mother had picked out for him last fall. It was tight around the chest and shoulders already. And the shirt collar felt like iron. Passing a store window, he stopped to look at himself. Fairly tall, fairly heavy, mature enough to pass for maybe eighteen or nineteen. He stuck out his tongue at himself and tried to laugh away his nervousness.

In the market square the police station looked like a railway terminal; its wide-roof overhang protected farmer vendors from rain and snow. Patrick thought it resembled a stone fort; there were bars on some of the lower floor windows. The place was also a jail for overnight drunks and rowdies.

Patrick was ushered into the chief's office by a young constable who winked at him. Then he stood uncomfortably before a huge desk, shifting from one foot to the other before the man looked at him.

Chief Murray was fifty years old, a man of vast size. Even sitting down, in blue uniform with metal buttons, he was overwhelming. In the tiny office you couldn't look at anything else. On the side of a mountain, there was nothing but the mountain.

Patrick introduced himself, and said, "It's about Sideways Smith –"

The chief's voice was high, almost girlish. "That old boozer," he said. "You a friend of his?"

"Well, sort of," Patrick said, and launched into the whole story of his grandfather and the six old men at Portugee's funeral.

While he was speaking, it seemed the chief's eyes lost focus, and Patrick felt himself receding. And finally, that he had become bodiless, but his spirit was circling around the police station in a wide orbit that made him dizzy. He cleared his throat to make himself return.

"I'm sorta looking after them," he explained.

"That Sideways fella, he'll take a lot of lookin after." And judiciously, "You're making yourself responsible?"

177

"That's right," he said.

And Patrick felt things were going well. The vastness behind the desk had not erupted and overwhelmed him with scorn. In fact, the big face with an aureole of grey hair looked kindly, like a cement wall that meant no harm unless it fell on someone.

"I won't ask how old you are." The vastness grinned. "But do your best to keep the old man out of trouble. I meant to let him go this morning anyway. He's slept it off by now."

"Th-thank you," Patrick stammered.

"I knew your grandfather," the chief said, rising to his feet and extending his hand. "You look like him."

"Well, thanks."

It seemed there was a continuing warmth emanating from his grandfather, some aspect of the old man still alive.

Outside, where churchgoers in their Sunday best were going by on their way to King Street church, Sideways Smith looked at him reproachfully.

"I was asleep," he said. "You coulda waited a little longer. . . ."


Patrick talked about it with Jean. "I'm the old men's keeper," he explained. "I guess I sort of inherited the job."

"Who did you inherit from?" the girl asked. "I didn't know they had keepers."

"Well, not their parents anyway. I mean, their sons and daughters, whoever was looking after them before. It seems they've decided to stay in town a while. They've dug up a couple of spare cots from somewhere, and settled right in – "

"You've become a father," she twinkled at him. "And rather earlier than most."

"Yeah, I know it's funny."

They were walking the gravel road toward Glen Miller. The Trent River there was a quarter-mile wide – a quarter-mile of sparkle and sun glimmer, a pavement of light.

They veered off the road at a path winding westward through the woods. And climbing a hundred-foot ridge, past a field of poison ivy with the plant's triple leaves turning a mid-September red, they crossed a small creek that made lisping sounds in its shallows. In its deeper water, a hint of shimmering movement.

"Maybe brook trout," Patrick said.

All around them leaves were turning into autumn colours. Some of the maple trees had only tinges of red, as if they hadn't wholly committed themselves to the scarlet changes. A few scattered oaks were a heavy shade of maroon. Sunlight shining through leaves dappled the ground with moving yellow and crimson patches as the wind blew.

Patrick gestured toward the leaves. "A celebration?"

"I think so. Everyone comes to the party, and everyone goes away together."

They stopped at the Glen Miller Rock.

"I looked it up in the encyclopaedia," Patrick said. He took her arm, pointing at the summit, "Wanta climb?"

Touching her skirt and blouse, Jean said, "I'm not dressed for it. Why don't you – "

Patrick was staring up at the broad blue sky, clouds drifting above them.

"You know, the ice was a mile thick where we're standing now."

"Well, that's interesting," Jean said.

"And this rock was a hitchhiker inside the glacier, coming from the Lord knows where."

He stared upward with a trance-like look. "Look up there and you can almost imagine what it was like twelve thousand years ago. Billions of tons of glacier moving south, everything underneath sealed with ice. And that

179

hitchhiker rock just over our heads loosening up in the melting ice, waiting to fall right where it is now. . . . Can you imagine what it was like when the ice melted?" he demanded. "Rivers on top of the glacier, rivers pouring out underneath, new lakes being born all around here. . . . And that rock, where did it come from?"

He gestured vaguely toward the north. "Maybe the Murray Hills, or maybe a thousand miles farther north. I don't know enough geology to say."

His expression became rebellious. "But I will know; I intend to find out."

"Being a professor, chalk dust in his hair, wearing glasses, muttering about something to himself no one else can hear. Is that what you intend to be?" Jean said.

Patrick grinned. "Not exactly. All geologists aren't profs. Some go into the north and make maps of rock formations, others study the earth's crust and strata, the reason it is like it is. But I didn't mean that. I do intend to find out something about everything, and everything is interesting. Don't you think so, Jean?"

He took her arm. They found a place where the wind had collected leaves like coloured foam. On their backs, they stared up at a sky of ponderous, slowly drifting clouds.

"Look," he said, and took her hand. "That one cloud with the notch in its bottom, it must be about the same height as the hitchhiking rock was. Now close your eyes."

He waited a moment, watching a tendril of blonde hair fall over her cheek and the very white face that was not a complete stranger to the sun. Very white and very tall, he mused to himself. And again, something without thought stirred in him.

"Pretend," he said. "Pretend the glacier is directly over our heads, we're lying in a dry place between under-ice rivers. It's like we're inside a big green cave, and the green light is touching your face right now. The rock is beginning to loosen, making grating noises up there, so far away, so far away. . . ."

His voice was hypnotic, slurring over the vowels in words, smoothing them into sounds like the small stones in the brook had made earlier.

"A mile up there in the sky inside the moving glacier, embedded in melting ice, there's a rock the size of a house. And it's about to fall, right where we are now. It will burrow into the earth from the speed of its own fall, a stone comet.

"And there will be a moment when we can see what's happening. A dark shadow will cross in front of our eyes; there will be no sun or moon; only the night."

He leaned close to her ear and whispered softly, "Jean, it's coming. Look up and see it, the rock falling, falling!"

"Stop it, Patrick," she scolded, sitting up abruptly.

The landscape wavered in her vision, then coloured leaves returned to focus in her blue gaze. She pressed a forefinger against his nose. "Were you trying to hypnotize me? If so, you nearly succeeded."

On their feet again, he took the scolding hand, pressing it to his mouth with a low sweeping bow.

"Now where did you see that done before?" she wanted to know. "I guess in the movies. You keep it up, the way you've been acting, and every time we see each other I'll have to get acquainted all over again."

"And won't it be fun, someone new every time?"

He picked up an armful of leaves and let them cascade over her head. She found her own leaves for the same purpose. They ran down the path to the brook, each laughing at the other's silliness, their strangeness grown familiar. And yet they saw something different whenever their eyes met.

Stopping for breath at the Glen Miller Road, the girl's expression was oddly changed. "Launcelot," she said, "my Launcelot . . ."

Patrick smiled and took her hand.

181

✧ ✧ ✧

Phil Wright and Sideways Smith looked worried. They had their chairs pulled close to the sick man's bed when Patrick called next day. McPherson seemed a bit unsettled as well, faded eyes following Dr. Johnson's expression.

"Hem," the doctor said portentously.

Wright and Smith both started. "How's he doin, Doc?" they said anxiously.

Dr. Johnson folded the stethoscope he'd been using – Phil Wright thought it was like water-witching a well – and said, "Pretty good. No need for flowers a while yet."

McPherson grabbed both sides of the mattress, pulling himself semi-upright. "Thanks a helluva lot," he growled. "What does 'pretty good' mean?"

"You're no spring chicken, you know," Dr. Johnson said.

"Never claimed I was."

"You have to rest; in fact, you must rest."

"I am resting, resting all the time," McPherson said querulously.

"Well, you need more."

Dr. Johnson leaned back on the kitchen chair, his expression judicious and magisterial, Patrick thought. A fat man, about forty, roly-poly almost, a doctor-dumpling; his clothes so tight he might overflow if one strained button should pop. But a good doctor, people said, his face like an occidental Buddha, hands locked across his large belly.

"Not just rest, sleep, too."

"How can we help, Doc?" Phil Wright wanted to know.

"You might begin by cleaning up this place. And wash the floor. It's so greasy I almost skidded from the door to the windows."

McPherson groaned. "What's that got to do with me bein sick?"

182

"Cleanliness is next to godliness," Dr. Johnson said sternly, but his eyes chuckled.

"How long's all this goin on? I just have the sniffles, not the plague."

Dr. Johnson's manner changed. "Now you listen to me," he said severely, "there's an epidemic in this town, and it ain't the sniffles – *isn't* the sniffles," he corrected. "And maybe it is the plague, even if we don't call influenza the Black Death."

Smith and Wright looked a little alarmed; Patrick was, too.

"This town's got near six thousand people," Johnson went on, "and I'd say maybe one-third of them have the flu. The same number, more or less, over in Belleville. And thousands more in Toronto. The same down in the U.S. of A. Many thousands."

"I'd like to help," Patrick said.

Dr. Johnson's voice was gentler. "You can," he said. "McPherson should stay in bed and stay warm. No wandering around this place in bare feet; no booze either. And you have to understand: there's really no cure for influenza except bed rest and time. Lots of liquids, fruit juice, maybe an egg and some toast."

"Is that all?" McPherson said.

"A bowel movement in the morning. Every morning. That's very important, a bowel movement."

Dr. Johnson's eyes grew distant, as if all the bowel movements of the world were flushing through his brain.

"What you just said – an epidemic?" McPherson wanted to know.

"I could name you names," Johnson said. "Mrs. McMaster on Ford Street. Right close to you, Patrick. Four more on King Street. Six on Division. A lot more across the river. More, more, more. I've got a couple in bed at my place, two youngsters. They're getting better, others aren't."

"You member Ludger Chapdelaine?" McPherson said suddenly. "Sideways, you remember him. Guy from Quebec, cook in the shanties at Palmer Rapids? Came with us one time when we went to Belleville for some drinks. Wizened little old man . . ."

"No, I don't," Sideways said.

"Sure you do," McPherson coaxed. "The cops in Belleville threw you in jail for making remarks about their mothers – "

"Well, gentlemen, I have to go," Dr. Johnson said.

"You said epidemic, Doc. Well, Ludger Chapdelaine talked about an epidemic in Quebec, way back in the 1830s. And thousands died there, too."

Dr. Johnson was shocked out of saying what doctors are supposed to say. He said, "My God, cholera?"

"Yeah, cholera."

"I remember that old boy," Phil Wright said.

"I'd wake up early, but Chappie was awake ahead of me every time. We'd drink some tea together and get talkin. He was in his late sixties then. Told me about it, said he'd been to an island in the river where they kept people when they were sick – "

"Grosse Isle, the quarantine sheds in the St. Lawrence," Johnson murmured.

"You know about it?"

"Just a little. It's in the history books."

"Well, it seems they stopped the ships there, downriver from Quebec City. Immigrants from the old country had to get off and be looked at by doctors. They'd been cooped up tween decks for weeks at a time on the trip across the Atlantic. In dirt and garbage and stink. And they got sick, those people did. Chappie had a job deliverin groceries to that island, what's its name?"

"Grosse Isle," Johnson said again.

"Yeah, the island. Takin food there, he got to know some of the people; told 'em what things were like in Quebec and

Montreal and Upper Canada. Said he liked the people. Then, when they'd become sorta friends, they'd get sick. I mean, even while he was talkin with them, he'd see their faces change. The cholera . . . ''

McPherson's voice was getting hoarse, but his own illness was forgotten as he remembered Ludger Chapdelaine and how the cholera came to Canada.

"They'd vomit, and seem to need water all the time," McPherson went on. They'd drink water, and vomit some more; and they had diarrhea; they stank. He'd be talkin to them, Ludger said he was, then they didn't seem to hear him no more – ''

McPherson looked around at Johnson and the others.

"You sure you want to hear all this?"

"Go on," Johnson said.

"I'm not sure when it was," McPherson said. "Chappie didn't mention the year, but 1832 would be about right. He said the sick people had to sleep on the docks, on the street, anywhere – if they had no money. Or even if they did. The poor people, some of them died the same day they got sick. He said it was like seein ghosts; everybody got old before they died. Eyes pushed back in their heads, lips blue, and they had wrinkled faces; some of them weren't right in the head. They wandered around that island not knowing where they were or where they were going, old men and old women, who got that way in less than a day. . . . ''

McPherson was sitting up in bed, his voice a hypnotic wheeze. Sideways Smith, Phil Wright, Dr. Johnson, and Patrick – none of them could look away, all had a vision of the cholera ghost in the same room with them.

"Some of them would stagger round that island, that Grosse Isle," McPherson went on. "Yeah, and they'd be thirsty, want to drink all the time. When they went down to the shore to drink at the river, they'd fall in the water, some of them, and stay there, too weak to get out. But that wasn't the worst of it – ''

185

Listening to McPherson, Patrick had the weird feeling that all of them in Portugee's old apartment had been infected by the cholera, transmission by voice of an ancient plague. The death cart was rumbling over cobbled streets, a new moon obscured by clouds floating above the doomed planet.

"In Quebec, barrels of tar burning outside houses. People thought it would burn away the plague. People mourning the dead. Sometimes" – he went on impressively – "they weren't dead. The carter that picked up the bodies, he was busy and in a hurry – "

"You mean – what?"

"I'd like some tea," McPherson said. "I'm doin a lot of talkin."

"I admire your memory of this friend, this Ludger Chapdelaine," Dr. Johnson said, rubbing his eyes tiredly. "But I really must go. I have to visit British Chemical later."

"Sometimes they weren't dead," McPherson said again.

And Patrick could see the old man was enjoying himself. He sipped the tea delicately, from a coffee mug Sideways Smith handed him.

"There was a place they took the bodies, and they had to get the dead into the ground quick, on accounta everybody was afraid of 'em, afraid they'd get the cholera from touchin the dead bodies. And sometimes they buried 'em a little too quick, Chappie told me. There was this family – "

"I have to go," Dr. Johnson broke in.

He grabbed his jacket and bustled toward the door, turning there to say, "Bowel movements, lots of liquid, stay in bed." An incantation and formula, even a goodbye.

McPherson was propped up against the pillows, his face on the same level as his audience in their chairs. Blotches of colour in his cheeks from the excitement of remembering Ludger Chapdelaine, the cook's story skipping the generations from McPherson to Dr. Johnson, the words creating

186

shadowy pictures of the burning tar barrels and death carts in Quebec City.

"Old Ludger," McPherson said. "I been thinkin of him lately; seems like now there's so much more time than there was. . . ."

He glanced at Phil Wright and Sideways Smith. "You'd maybe be thinkin some of the same things as me. And Patrick" – the watery eyes enveloped him – "you look at the three of us, us old men, and you see back in time a few years. But when I looked into Ludger Chapdelaine's eyes, I saw clear back to the 1830s. And what I saw was fear."

Patrick arrived home. The dog was a bloody and ragged heap lying in the long grass. Its stomach was split open at the side, showing grey guts and pink tubes escaping from the fur. As he stood silently, his mother brought out a blanket and threw it over Gyp. Without that covering, he felt as if his own feelings were naked, exposed for everyone to see.

"How'd it happen?" he said.

"A car going by. Gyp ran out in front, crossing the road to chase something. The driver stopped. We carried him into the yard."

Mrs. Cameron touched a place on her wrist where a red mark showed. "He bit me when we carried him; didn't hurt much though. And he died right after that.

"I'd better tend to this bite." She laid her hand on his shoulder. "Can you look after things?"

"Did you notice what kind of car it was?"

"Maybe it was a Ford."

Just barely human, a photograph of Henry Ford wavered into Patrick's mind. He didn't have any idea what Henry Ford actually looked like, but conjured up a nasty image of a devil with whip and pitchfork, and knew it was false.

"Yeah, he said, "I'll look after Gyp."

Patrick got a shovel from the woodshed, and started to dig a hole in the backyard under some bushy cedars. It was hard digging in the stony ground. He started to sweat in the late-afternoon sun and stripped off his shirt, hanging it over a tree branch.

When the hole was about three feet deep, he laid the dog's body on dark brown earth. There was a huge old bone Gyp had been gnawing on in his nest under the woodshed. Patrick retrieved it, placing the bone near the dog's muzzle. Then he shovelled earth into the hole, sprinkling it lightly and picking out small stones from the loose earth. He wasn't sure why he was doing this, but it was a way of deferring to the dog's feelings, even if Gyp couldn't feel anything now.

He went into the house, and said he didn't feel much like supper.

Mrs. Cameron said, "Tomorrow you can have a good breakfast before school." She gave him a quick look. "I know, it's an empty feeling. Did you see Jean?"

He nodded and wandered out again. On Corson's dock he watched a perch in the river that had lost its equilibrium. It was struggling, kept swimming around in a circle lying on its side, as if its sense of up and down was gone. When it got tangled in some weeds near the shore his attention wandered.

In his river hideaway behind Redick's Sash and Door Factory, he watched water bugs skating atop the red willow roots, thinking of an adolescent Gyp. The dog had been only a few weeks old when Mrs. Cameron brought him home from the market. A squirming bundle of fur with ingratiating tongue and insatiable curiosity, Gyp chewed at ends of blankets, tablecloths, socks, shoes and laces, laundry, anything. Often his presence was known by a puddle of water on the kitchen linoleum, an unrepentant yapping when propelled into the backyard by Mrs. Cameron's broom.

Fully grown, a warrior dog, somnambulist by day and stalker of neighbouring chicken runs by night. Companion of forest trails and sniffer-out of groundhogs on wandering afternoons of heat and small-boy boredom. Patrick had been eight when Gyp came home from market. And that would make him an elderly dog now; eight years old at his death.

Patrick leaned against fragrant pine boards, a tendril of Red McPherson's tale of lost forests, like body hair on the planet, drifting through his mind. He felt insensate, a log of flesh, the last stop before vegetable. For this moment he remembered nothing, surrounded by a long silence: a silence he could think about afterwards as something apart, separate from the flowing seamless stream of eternity.

But the idea of eternity was something he had never grasped anyway. Something that didn't end?

Now was later than these deathly events that had shaken his own life. Now was separate from the benchmark of Gyp's departure; his grandfather's absence tucked in a fold of memory where it was safe from change. Now was after a very long white streak outlined on the blackness of his mind, a distancing of his now-self and then-self.

He realized he was playing with words, making them jump through hoops in his mind. When that self-conscious thought occurred to him, the white streak in his head joined eternity again and went rushing away. His grandfather dead, Gyp dead, shadows on the river perceptibly darker and changed. It occurred to him that every change is the death of something that's left behind and forgotten. Sadly, he knew Gyp would be forgotten and wondered what else would be lost. . . .

# THREE

# Thanksgiving Day

# 10

OCTOBER 14, THANKSGIVING DAY. The siren at British
Chemical blew at 6:47 p.m. The sound was like a screw-
driver digging into the ears of everyone and everything
that heard. The air was blistered and hurt by the prolonged
screaming.

Animals on the wooded slopes of Mount Pelion heard it,
lifting their muzzles to sniff the air. A fox hunting in the
evening scented a rabbit. It stopped to listen, needle nose
and foxy face alert, the rabbit scent momentarily destroyed
by the sound. A black bear, wandering far south of its
autumn range, also heard and paid little attention. And
farm dogs howled in sympathy in Hastings County, Northumberland and Prince Edward. All the animals knew,
somewhere in their pragmatic minds, that inhuman unnat-
ural sound was a human sound.

On Dundas Street, the Trenton main drag, there were
few pedestrians. On Front, Alfred, Scott, Barbara, College, and Marmora streets, there were even fewer. For most
people it was a day of rest, a holiday. They were eating
Thanksgiving dinner, or about to, momentarily shocked
by the siren, in the midst of washing their hands, using the
toilet, or chatting with friends on this social occasion.

But they knew, at least most of them did. When they
heard the siren, an apprehensive expression appeared on
their faces, touched with fear often, and leaving a question
still hanging in their minds. The old fear, whose focus was
British Chemical; fear added to and increased by the Halifax explosion of 1917; fear that invaded the blood, joining
systole and diastole, racing outward and inward with the
pumping of the heart.

They began to straggle out onto downtown streets, the people. While the siren screamed, they had a blank look on their faces. When it stopped, they began to gabble to each other. They said, "What's happened?" They said, "I knew it would happen" – and that negated the first question.

They began to think about who it was they loved better than themselves, or nearly as well. And some started to think about their money, those who had any. If their money was in the bank, it ought to be okay; if it was hidden in some secret place around the house or backyard, they had better repossess it and make sure it was ready to serve them in case of need.

This was what they had feared, imagined, or even thought they had known. British Chemical would blow the town of Trenton off the face of the earth. T.N.T., the three-headed monster, was the end of the world. Squash and pumpkin would wither green and orange and black in the fields; Mars and Jupiter, planets of fire, would careen close and collide with earth. Spring wheat would die in the furrows; tides of the sea reach heights of one hundred feet and towering waves submerge the land. It was Apocalypse. And a short time later when the explosions began, it was also Exodus. But not limited to the Children of Israel in this latter day of terror, *anno Domini*, 1918. People began to leave Trenton. Those who could, those who were able, those who had help or could hire help. On foot, on horseback, by horse-drawn wagon and buggy, by automobile; and some even by canoe and rowboat downriver, under the iron bridge and out onto the Bay of Quinte, to offshore islands and nearby Prince Edward County.

When the siren screamed, Patrick had been talking to Jean and her mother in the cottage by the river. Supper was nearly ready on the big kitchen stove.

"Your father should be here any minute," Mrs. Tomkins had said to Jean. "He told me 6:45. I'm afraid he's a little late."

And the siren screamed.

They were silent at first, faces empty of expression; the noise drowning that little humming one hears sometimes inside the inner ear. It was a noise to set the teeth on edge, destroying privacy of the body's internal sounds.

Patrick went to the window, looking southeast. It required a distinct effort for him to speak.

"There's a glow in the sky," he said.

All of them stared from the window, seeing the fiery glow like a leftover patch of sunset on the wrong horizon.

"Eagle will be there," Mrs. Tomkins said. "He'll be at the plant still. That fire must've started before he left."

The girl took Patrick's arm and said to her mother, "Why not try to phone?"

Mrs. Tomkins's distracted look cleared. She grabbed the box telephone's handle, winding it frantically. The thing buzzed in her ear.

"British Chemical?" she said hopefully. Then, irritated, "No, no, I want the British Chemical Company in Trenton."

The telephone made a mechanical noise, like a metal frog. Mrs. Tomkins turned to Jean and Patrick, "It's Eva Curtis at the company switchboard." She listened intently. "Mr. James E. Tomkins, do you know where he is?"

Hanging up the receiver after a few moments, she said, "The lines are very busy, but Miss Curtis is staying on the job. The fire started on Honeysuckle Hill and the nitrator building is burning, it sounded like. It seems they did something wrong in the mix, and the acid kept getting hotter and hotter. Then it boiled over and started the fire."

"How bad is it?" Patrick said. "Did she say anything more?"

"Pretty bad, but the fire engine and men are fighting it. Maybe soon they'll – "

Her face lost colour, the words trailing off.

"Where's father?" Jean said urgently.

"They don't know where anybody is," Mrs. Tomkins said, her mouth working convulsively. "They don't know. We just have to wait."

While they stood there uncertainly, a flash like sheet lightning ignited the southeastern horizon; a sombre reddish glow replaced the room's own light. The cottage rocked on its foundations, appearing briefly to lift, then settled back, trembling.

The cottage windows shattered. Glass landed on the linoleum floor with a rattling sound like dried peas. The sound tore at their eardrums, driving thought from their minds. They held on to each other like people in a hurricane, arms wound tightly around each other's bodies, fingers clutching.

Patrick lifted his head after a moment. He tried to loosen his fingers from Jean and her mother, and theirs from him, hands trembling violently. Jean was shaking, her mouth open, lips moving as if she were speaking. But no words came out.

Finally she stuttered, "I–I–I . . ."

Patrick took her in his arms again, rocking back and forth while he held her.

"It's all over," he said, looking at Mrs. Tomkins, who now seemed fairly self-possessed.

She seized a broom, beginning to sweep shards of glass away from the room's centre. She gave Patrick a shaky smile and brushed glass off a chair seat.

"Make her sit down. There's some tea on the stove."

The lights went out. The three of them stood where they were for several seconds, feeling stunned. Then their eyes adjusted to evening darkness and faint light of moon and stars from broken windows.

"I've got some candles somewhere," Mrs. Tomkins said.

She fumbled in the kitchen cupboard and produced white wax candles.

"I don't know what's going to happen at the plant," she said, "but we'll just have to wait here. Eagle will be coming, I know he will – " Her voice broke, with a catch in her throat. "Patrick, what about your mother?"

And Jean laughed. It was a strange sound with a kind of chicken's cluck included, except that it went up and down the scale in near hysteria.

Patrick grabbed her again. Mrs. Tomkins wrapped her arms around both of them, whispering, "There, there," as if her daughter had reverted to being an infant again. They made a dark huddle together in the midst of broken glass, candlelight flicking back and forth in the breeze coming through empty window frames.

There had been so little time between the explosion, lights going out, glass spewing onto the floor, then outside darkness entering the cottage. His brain seemed to be nowhere, suspended in the void and unable to function, his last thought still hovering unfinished in his brain.

He sent his mind back before all this happened, tried to think of the last thing that had been important – his mother, McPherson, the vanished Gyp, Joe Barr, Kevin Morris, Jean. . . . And shook himself to clear his head. Kevin Morris and Jean the last on his impromptu list? Besides, how could you make any sense of what's in your mind when the world is about to end? And *was* the world about to end?

"Let's go outside," he said.

They stood by the river in faint starlight, calmer now, for it was impossible to sustain the desperate feelings that came from the explosion, the shattered windows and darkness.

"Patrick, Jean and I will wait here," Mrs. Tomkins said, "until Eagle comes. He won't leave us alone."

There was faith and a curious dignity in her voice. "But you, Patrick, you'll have to look after your mother."

It was incredible, he thought, to be living through this strangeness. From being more or less a nonentity, Jean's almost unnoticeable mother, Mrs. Tomkins, had become someone he admired. She was a person of . . . of . . . . And he failed to complete the sentence in his mind.

She took his hand. "Say goodbye to Jean. You understand that we do have to stay here. Eagle knows where we are, and he'll come. You have to find out what's happening to your own people."

She went back into the candle-lit cottage. Patrick held on to Jean's hand, thinking about Eagle Tomkins – in whom he had failed to notice reasons for evoking such qualities of loyalty. He squeezed the hand hard, staring at the ghostly white face shimmering, moth-like, close to his own.

The girl's face was working itself into little grimaces that formed on her cheeks, her chin and forehead, in separate regional geographies of turbulence. It scared him. He realized he hadn't really known this girl and her mother at all until the present moment.

"Jean," he whispered urgently in her ear, shaking her shoulders, holding her back from him. "Jean!"

Her name had the effect of making her eyes focus on him, coming back from wherever she had been with a small time lag between there and here. Her eyes, blank concentric circles with nothing at the centre, then himself appearing there – but he couldn't see himself. And shook her again, but gently. "I have to go."

"I know," she said. "But you'll come back. I want you to. Promise me you'll come back!"

It was eerie, standing in the star-shine with a girl he hadn't met until last spring; now with little strands of what he felt for her trembling in his mind, joining in a strong cable of love. Or was it love, a thing so hard to imagine it was almost mythical.

"Jean," he said.

She buried her face in his shoulder, gasping incoherent syllables.

"What, Jean? What?"

"Promise me you'll come back," she said clearly. "Lovers always return to each other. They cross rivers and mountains and deserts . . ."

It was shocking to him, the conception of himself in her mind. He saw himself in sun helmet – with a canteen nearly empty of water dangling on his shoulder – sweating, and staggering over a mountain pass, crossing a thousand-mile desert. He saw himself swimming with weak and faltering strokes across a mile-wide river. Filled with crocodiles? Jean cheering him on from the distant shore. And he sank, drowning in those fathomless blue eyes.

"I'll come back," he said, marvelling at the many different compartments in his own mind.

On the road home, Patrick fell into the loping medium-length stride in which he was most comfortable, jacket flapping in the self-created breeze. The river glittered darkly nearby, lights of Hart's Corners and Trenton ahead. More ominously, a red glow tinged the southeastern sky, licking at the horizon.

British Chemical was burning; the further implications of that fact numbed his brain. He remembered what the telephone operator, Eva Curtis, had said to Jean's mother: the fire began on Honeysuckle Hill. Honeysuckle, scarlet-flowered shrubbery beside his mother's house, a delicate magnetic lure for bees, whose name now joined T.N.T., the three-headed monster in his mind. The gentle and violent united, opposites become meaningless.

He rounded a bend in the road that matched the river's gentle curve, and the sky turned livid. Not just light, but light that had become more than itself. It pulsed and glowed. A wide carpet of light climbed the sky, stayed there for perceptible moments 5,000 feet above the earth; nodules of gold and silver leaped and subsided on the carpet's undersurface, fire storms playing here and there, blisters and boils in a disease of light.

Noise followed light, hammering the senses. It knocked him flat on the road, a blow that struck Patrick on every part of his body, wind that was noise and sound that was God. He was afraid, but so shocked he didn't know he was afraid. His head had struck the road hard enough to make him dizzy; his arms and legs twisted feebly in the air, as if detached from his body.

"Stop it!" Patrick told his arms and legs.

They seemed to obey, became quiet, but with an uncontrollable twitch animating them every few seconds.

He climbed to his feet, noticing the dark shape of Mayhew's gristmill just ahead. And began to jog forward again, wavering back and forth to both sides of the road. Reaching a culvert where water drained from the millpond, he staggered to the stream and threw cold water over his face. Handfuls of water. It soaked the front of his shirt, and ran down his chest.

One shoulder was hurt from his fall on the road. The left shoulder. He rubbed it, beginning to shiver from the cold water. On the road above, he heard the clop-clop of horses' feet, wanting to call out to them that he was hurt. But part of his mind drew away and said, Maybe I'm not hurt very much. He worked the shoulder back and forth gingerly. Not bad. He'd survive. And heard someone running above on the road, feet going *sluff-sluff-sluff*. . . .

On the last mile south he regained his composure, shutting the fire across the river out of his mind – shutting out everything but his mother, McPherson, and the other two old men, Joe Barr on the garbage flats near Quinte. . . . And Mrs. McMaster in bed recovering from the flu; and Maclean, the pump-maker, had flu as well. So did Mr.

Yourex, the blacksmith. Half the town was in bed, the other half scared to death of death.

He chuckled, and choked the chuckle backward in his throat.

When he reached the overhead railway bridge, light from the burning munitions plant vaulted the river, turning houses on both sides of the road into unfamiliar shapes. Houses were distorted by shadows, leaping into prominence when the flames leaped, sinking back into shadow villages and hamlets of rumour when fire lessened.

Looking back over his shoulder, flames behind still lighted his way ahead. They glittered on broken windows of houses, reflecting red on remaining fragments of glass. The river itself appeared on fire, every small wave a separate flame.

He noticed a smell overtaking him, a yellow smell, unpleasant but mixed with sweetness. In the air – a breathing heaviness. And remembered chemistry classes at Trenton High, the rotten-egg awfulness you couldn't escape. Remembered sulphur and molasses his mother dosed him with every spring, a healthful nastiness. The sulphur mountain beside British Chemical, the yellow hill with its burning fumaroles.

He stopped, turning his head upward. Sniffing. The whole sky was filled with it. Sulphur. He couldn't actually see the stuff floating over the river, but knew it was there. A brimstone smell, the devil's own chemistry lesson. Illustrations from Dante's *Inferno* flashed in his mind, miasma of hell – and he kept on running.

Windows were shattered all along Front Street. Streetlights were broken, too, so that Patrick ran in darkness except for the burning sky.

People were coming out of their houses, standing on porches and front lawns, gazing fixedly across the river. One man grabbed at his arm, "Where you goin?" – sounding as if his mouth was full of flour. Patrick shook him off.

Further along, little groups were gathered in the road, men, women, and children as well. A young woman stopped him by moving directly into his path at the last moment, holding him and peering into his face from six inches away. She said, "Who – who?" and Patrick's skin prickled. Light from across the river gave her a crazed look when she tried to pull him off the road. He saw that she was only a girl, no older than himself.

"Come and talk to me," she said almost rationally. "I'm scared."

The girl followed him for half a block, calling after him – until he poured a little more of himself into his legs and pumping arms. Despite anxiety for his mother and McPherson, exultation at these extra reserves of energy was like a drug. He raised himself on his toes for a few strides and seemed, literally, to be treading on air. Then let himself down an inch's fraction, allowing his heels to touch ground, changing gears for the last hundred yards. Slowing . . . hardly winded.

Then anxiety returned. The house was empty. He found his mother in the backyard, talking to Mrs. Morris, Kevin hovering nearby. She was relieved to see her son.

"Patrick, we're going to Prince Edward County. We've got to go. It isn't safe here in town!"

"That's right, it isn't," Mrs. Morris said excitedly. "There's T.N.T. and gunpowder, all sorts of stuff waiting to explode. Somebody on the street told me the fire was close to boxcars loaded with it . . ." her voice trailed off, dark face agitated.

"I know you're not especially fond of your cousins, Patrick," Mrs. Cameron said.

"Neither are you, Mom."

She looked embarrassed. "Nothing I've ever said would lead you to think that," she said with some asperity. "They're blood relations. They'll receive us well." But she looked doubtful. "I know they will."

"Sure, Mom," Patrick said. "Just the same, if there was any other place to go – you've got friends near Wooler." He stopped, thinking about it. "But that's right past where the trouble is." He avoided the word *danger*, skipping over it quickly. "Sure, the Harrigans. And the firefighters will likely get the fire out soon anyway."

"We don't know that," Kevin said in that tone of voice Patrick didn't like.

But when his eyes met Kevin's, their hurry-up look seemed to say, "Let's humour our mothers; you and I don't have to believe what they believe. We'll make up our own minds, eh?" And Kevin smiled at him.

"John's getting the car out," Mrs. Morris said, "but he can't find the crank. I used it for a doorstop and forgot to put it back in the toolbox."

They heard a shout from the Morris garage, a chug-chug sound, then a couple of swear words. Mrs. Morris looked at her neighbour apologetically.

"I'll be fine, Mom. You go," Patrick said. "There's Mrs. McMaster, she's got the flu. There's Red McPherson and Joe Barr. I need to look after them."

"You're more important to me than those people," Mrs. Cameron said. "I've only got one son and I don't want to see him blown sky-high." She made the words sound offhand and casual, but there was no doubt she meant them.

Kevin said, "There's people I want to see about, too." And turned to Patrick, "Maybe we can work together on this. We both do some running. We can join the folks later, pick up a ride from somebody."

"Or shank's mare if we don't," Patrick said.

They were judging each other, he could see from the look in Kevin's eyes. And it would certainly be much easier to mount any kind of rescue or moving operation with both of them available to push or pull. But that was look-ing at the black side of things, the worst side. Patrick thought: We both know what the other is thinking, and what there is to do.

And said it aloud, "We know, don't we?" His eyes meeting Kevin's.

"Yes, we do," Kevin said. Enough words, the right amount to agree and not exaggerate.

"What are you talking about?" Mrs. Morris wanted to know.

"We're okay here, Mother. And we can't leave people trapped in town, who can't help themselves. Now can we?"

Mrs. Morris said, "I suppose not." But she looked dubious.

"We can get a ride out to the county any time," Patrick said. "People are going. Wagons, autos, some walking. I bet the road to Twelve O'clock Point over the canal is crowded. But there's lots of time for us to leave – "

John Morris honked the car horn.

Mrs. Morris went over to her husband and told him what the boys intended to do.

"Joe Barry and his helper are over there," Mr. Morris said. "Barry is the yard engineer for the railway. He'll move explosives out safely." He shouted to Kevin, "Look, if you want to stay, I think it'll be all right for maybe another hour." Looking at his son sternly: "Not more than that. And I'm sure those people will finish off the fire anyway. But I'd like you and Patrick to see about Mrs. McMaster and Ian. They're old. Then I want you to get out."

"We will, Dad," Kevin said.

"Patrick, you listen to what Mr. Morris is saying," Mrs. Cameron said sharply. "Do what you must, then both of you come to the Harrigans' over the canal bridge. All right, now?"

"I promise," Patrick said.

"We both promise," Kevin added.

The sky flooded with light as he spoke, showing every crack in the red-painted old barn in the backyard.

"We're going now, Patrick. Remember your promise," Mrs. Cameron said, looking anxious.

The Model T started off, and another great sweep of light covered them at the same moment. He could see with clarity the little scar near Kevin's eye where some unnamed kid had thrown a stone before they both went to school. The wound had required a couple of stitches. And Kevin thought that he, Patrick, had thrown the stone, wouldn't listen to any denials. Now the light had removed shadows between them, and they were almost friends.

Patrick closed his eyes into slits, almost blinded by the light. Kevin touched his shoulder. "You okay, kid?" And the grin, which could be interpreted any way you liked.

"Yah, I'm okay, son. Let's go."

Then the world exploded, throwing them violently sideways onto the ground. They scrambled to their feet after a moment, too shocked to speak. Their heads empty of all thought. Only fear.

# 11

IN OCTOBER, FORESTS FOR MILES around Trenton, red and yellow leaves had not made a final decision to relinquish their trees. Now the decision was suddenly made for them. They were swept away in all directions from the blast's epicentre, like a flight of crimson and yellow birds flying before the wind. The nearly leafless trees moaned and whispered from the great wind's passing, straining at their anchors in the earth.

When silence returned, sparrows, crows, and blue jays were stripped of cover; even small burrowing animals felt the blast, grains of earth and tiny stones falling on furry backs in underground tunnels.

At British Chemical, nitric acid had been drained from tanks into the Trent River, to prevent it joining the burning mess. And a yellow cloud of sulphur, blown into the sky by repeated explosions, drifted slowly down on river water. The rapids below No. 1 dam acted like washing-machine paddles to mix it into poison. On the fish it acted as a stimulant. They made sudden darting wriggling movements; some rose to the surface, swimming sideways in circles, little puddles of colour. And they died.

They were running along the railway tracks, feet rasping on the cinders. Joe Barry was bent over to avoid inhaling any more smoke than necessary. His eyes stung from the mixture of sulphur-nitric-acid-guncotton ingredients of the devil's brew at British Chemical. A metal button on the right shoulder of his overalls kept coming undone. When he stopped to refasten it, his eyes ran tears from the smoke.

Ted Ferguson had to stop and wait for him. "You sure you know where we parked that yard engine? I can't see a damn thing in the smoke." His voice grew querulous. "Why don't we just go home and say we did? Joe, we're off-duty. You had no call to roust me out afore we had supper."

Barry glared at him. "There ain't no time to argue about that. You can put in for overtime when we get that stuff outa here."

He grabbed the other man's shoulder, spinning him around and pushing him forward. "Now run, dammit!"

And they ran, bent low in the grey woolly smother, dodging and twisting to avoid obstacles seen at the last moment. Ferguson stopped suddenly, his mind registering a late meaning from what had been said before.

"What stuff?" he wanted to know. "What stuff do we hafta get outa here?"

Barry pushed him ahead. "You put your mind to it, you'll figure it out," he said. "Now get a move on."

Tongues of fire were licking through the smoke. No. 1 dam and the Trent River were lost in it. Remains of the sulphur mountain had melted in the heat, bubbling nauseously with noises like the interior of a disturbed stomach. Even the thirty-foot-tall wooden conveyor trestles connecting guncotton shops with T.N.T. and nitric acid buildings – these were nibbled and chewed by fire.

It was a disease, Barry thought. Fire was a disease, and it had no cure but water. Then he gasped, a stitch in his side from the unaccustomed running, and bit his tongue to make one pain forget the other. "This damn war. . . ."

The siding was just beyond Bunker Hill, but it looked different with snakes of smoke coiling and plunging in the heated air. Then the yard engine bulked up, a friendly black angel standing quiet in the smother. They climbed into it.

"We're here, Ted," he said to Ferguson, "and that's half the battle."

And under his breath, "Hi, Myrtle, remember me?" He patted the black steel caressingly. "Sure you do, sure you remember." And aloud to Ferguson, "Let's see if there's enough steam left to move this old lady." His breathing whistled slightly as he studied the gauge. "Sure there is, I know there is," he said confidently, reassuringly to Ferguson, and maybe to himself as well. He smoothed his face of any expression but confidence.

"We can make it!"

He closed a switch, pulled a familiar lever. The yard engine gave a steel tremor, its murmuring heart awakening after dozing sleep.

"Yowee!" Barry yelled. "Bunker Hill here we come."

The iron feet grated against steel rails of the roadbed on the lips of a whisper of steam. Joe Barry thought of engine, wheels and rails like that, even though he knew both were cold steel. Iron against iron, the old–lady–monster pretending to be a young newly born dragon, eating fire and devouring horizons.

Ferguson noticed the engineer's slight grin, and wondered: How could anyone grin at a time like this, when they were liable to burn, fry or explode, and die like broiled hamburg steak?

The yard engine achieved, after initial hesitations, the speed of a slow walk: an old lady strolling in the park. Barry leaned his head from the cab, straining to see anything ahead; but hearing interfered with seeing. Gusts of air swept around them, gales and hurricanes of smoke and heated gases. Fire roared, cracked, rumbled, spoke a fire-language; they were swaddled and buffeted by noise.

Somewhere ahead they heard the *crump* sound of a small explosion. Like someone blowing up a brown paper grocery bag and hitting it with their fist. Ferguson's mind made some connections: Maybe that was the guncotton line? Barry had said, "You'll figure it out." What was there to figure out?

A three-headed monster peered into his mind. "T.-N.-T.," he stammered fearfully. "That's what's in them boxcars. T.N.T.!"

Ferguson's jaw quivered from saying the forbidden three-letter word. "You didn't tell me," he accused the engineer. "You didn't tell me!"

"Stop blatherin," Barry said disgustedly. "You think this place makes teddy bears for Santa Claus? Or maybe Tinkertoys and horehound candy? Come off it!"

Ferguson trembled violently. "We could get killed. The town could blow to hell and gone, and us with it. Remember what happened to Halifax . . ."

"Ain't nothin gonna happen to us," Barry said soothingly. "Worst thing ever happened to me – " he stopped, thinking the worst thing was when they assigned apprentice brakie and switchman Ted Ferguson to the fatherly ministrations of engineer Joe Barry.

"Lotsa worse things," he said. "Nothing's gonna happen – it's the luck of the Irish. . . ." he finished lamely.

They bumped against something on the tracks – like a body? – and shuddered to a stop.

"Get out there and hook us up," Barry said gently. "We've got two boxcars to move out from Bunker Hill. Now listen to me, Ted, you've done it hundreds of times before . . ." And saw that Ferguson was shaking, his teeth nearly chattering. The man was useless.

Wrapping a bandanna around his face, he jumped down from the engine and secured the coupling. Back in the cab, he said, "There, nothing to it."

The yard engine and two boxcars crept backward slowly, almost stopping at the switches. "Pressure low, low," Barry muttered, coaxing and wheedling under his breath. "Not much farther, old lady."

They moved south inch by inch, seemingly, and emerged from smoke into ordinary evening darkness and the tunnel of their own headlights. And lights on the river sparkled reassuringly. The first house they saw drifted past as if it were moving and not themselves; its curtains bellied outward through broken windows.

The wheel's song changed to a hoarse rumble over the railway bridge. Barry nodded his head approvingly while they cruised south down Division Street, turtle-slow, and saw no one at all on the streets.

"We're gonna make it, Myrtle, I know we are," Barry said softly. He motioned from the cab window. "That's the town hall and market square; you seen them before. Mayor Ireland's not there today. And that's the police station, but I don't see the chief."

He glanced at Ferguson, "Ted, you see our esteemed police chief out there past the level crossing?"

The brakeman coughed the last bit of rotten-egg smell from his lungs. "You talkin to me or God?" he wheezed. "Well, thank you very much: I had enough of this place. I'm gonna put in for a job in the yards at Toronto or Kingston. I sure had enough of it here. . . ."

"You do that, Ted," Barry said dreamily. "I'll give you any help I can."

Over on the left side they glimpsed the Bay of Quinte, its waves tipped with light. Two miles away from British Chemical, the sky remained brilliant from fires burning on Bunker Hill to the northeast. The yard engine and two boxcars loaded with T.N.T. drifted along, throwing vague shadows of themselves beside the tracks. A dog barked in the street. Barry could see the C.N.R. roundhouse coming slowly to meet them, like a ship at sea with its lights blazing. . . .

Bill Pickell said, "I was fishing." He sounded as if he didn't believe his own statement. Reaching out a hand toward his

210

wife on the flatbed of the moving wagon, he touched her large belly that held their unborn child. Wind raced past them in the darkness – or else they raced past the wind – their horse's feet thudding against an invisible roadway.

"Do you believe this, Margaret?" he said unbelievingly.

"Oh, Bill," she whispered, "it doesn't matter whether I believe anything: it's happening. Hang on to me, please. I need something to hang on to. I need – "

She moaned, and bit back the rest of it, feeling his arms close around her.

"She okay?" Wes Hyatt yelled from the spring seat ahead, holding the reins in both hands. "I can hardly see you back there. Is Margaret all right?"

"She's in labour, Wes. Any chance you takin it a bit easier?" Pickell said. "We're jigglin pretty hard sometimes. And Sis, how 'bout you comin back here. I forgot to bring enough blankets . . ."

I forgot every damn thing, he accused himself, taking his sister's arm when her silhouette appeared behind the seat.

"Easy-daisy, Sis," he murmured. "I've got you so you can't fall. Now I'm going up to sit with Wesley. Okay?"

They rocked on through the night, points of light from the river showing between trees, dark woods to the west, moon and stars behind clouds.

"Them cousins of yours," Wes Hyatt said. "You sure they're gonna welcome somebody showing up in the middle of the night about to have a baby, even if you are kin to them?"

"Sure they will," and Pickell's voice was sputtering. "We did things for them, we did. . . . Besides, they're Christians, and it's their Christian duty to help people."

Hyatt's satiric look was lost in the night. He said, "Yah" – in a peculiar tone, then added, "*Sure* they're Christians."

It stopped Pickell with words halfway between his brain and mouth, and he reverted to the astonishing thing he had been thinking about.

"I was fishing," he said in wonderment like a child. "I was on the riverbank. There's a big ol' bass I hooked last summer, and it got away, took my tackle and all. A whopper it was. . . . I was gonna taxiderm it maybe. . . . I'm standing there and it took my worm, least I think it did.

"Then someone yelled from across the river, 'Fire! Fire!' They saw me by the river and screamed at me the world was gonna blow up – " He glanced at Hyatt oddly, "Wes, you think the world's gonna blow up?"

"The world'll be okay," Hyatt said soothingly. "It's Margaret we have to worry about right now." And the horses settled into a metronomic rhythm, hypnotic in its regularity.

The Murray Hills bulked all around them. Hills with gentle undulations, overlooking farms hidden in small valleys and tucked away like earth's afterthoughts. By day, maple, oak, poplar, beech, the clever deciduous trees which slept and survived winter by shedding their leaves, and withdrawing their innermost selves from the cold – all these were robed for the season. Vivid shades of red, orange, maroon, and yellow.

"I wish we could see them," Wes Hyatt said. "I wish we could see the colours."

The sky lit up at his words with sudden brilliant light; the crimson Murray Hills fondled in an unhealthy glare. A moment later, an odd *CRUMP* – like a potato falling on soft ground of the inner ear – and an appalling wind swept around the wagon, again stripping leaves from trees and whistling in bare branches of naked oak, maple, poplar, beech; threatening evergreen pine, cedar, and spruce with a similar fate.

The horse stopped, shaking and trembling, as the light died away. Hyatt leaped from his seat, seized the bridle, and whispered in a hairy ear, "Emily, just stand here and be quiet, let your blood settle, and stop tumbling around on that racetrack you got inside you. Remember me? I'm the

212

guy gives you a lump of sugar, maybe an apple in the morning, currycombs you, and washes you. Remember now?"

The horse stood there, its trembling gradually lessening. Then it gave its head a shake, which Hyatt thought meant calmness.

Bill Pickell had jumped from the wagon. "You hear that, you hear? The world's gonna blow up in our faces, the world – "

"Shaddup, Bill," Hyatt said wearily.

Slowly and with careful explicitness he said, "You are about to become a father, Mr. Pickell. The situation calls for quietness and not alarming your wife any more than she's already alarmed." He lowered his voice to the whisper of a whisper, "It means, would you please shaddup, get back on the wagon, and let's go."

Again the wagon moved ahead, the horse tentative and uncertain now. Hyatt talked to it soothingly, with a confidence in his voice he didn't feel. The road kept changing and dark perspectives altered; he felt his body leaning forward involuntarily, the wagon's motion ahead causing slack in the harness. And remembered the long two-mile hill on the approaches to Wooler; a hill the kids tobogganed down in winter, screaming in delicious terror at their increasing speed.

"The door came right off its hinges," Pickell said eerily.

"What?"

"The door, after I came back from the river – I was holding the door knob in my hand. There was a helluvan explosion, the door blew off; the door knob came off in my hand. I didn't know what to do with it, just stood there holding it – "

Hyatt pulled back on the reins to slow their descent into Wooler. A thin *yippity-yip* sounded from the wagon's flat-bed behind them; it brought Bill Pickell back from holding on to the doorknob into now.

"She okay, Sis?"

"No, she's not okay. I think she's liable to have that baby right now, right here – "

Hyatt stopped the horse. "No houses around," he said, "no lights anywhere."

Pickell said, "Far's I know, there's no doctor in Wooler. Sis, whaddaya think?"

"What're we going for then?" she said. "It's kinda crazy – "

Silence in the night; no frog or cricket said anything. The pregnant woman moaned, her legs drawn up and splayed outward.

"What'll we do?" Pickell said. "Wes –?"

"Turn around and go back." Hyatt sounded surly. "I dunno why we came this far anyways. Never saw Christians I thought was much good . . . never did."

"Sis, what's your vote?" And Pickell had pulled himself together, voice sounding calm in the quiet night.

"Turn around then. Maybe there's a doctor left somewhere in Trenton."

Wes Hyatt swung the wagon around on the road, its wheels grating on gravel.

Margaret Pickell screamed.

"Go back there and give her something to bite on," Hyatt said to Bill Pickell. "Tear something off your shirt and bunch it up. She'll break off her teeth if you don't."

He winced as another scream shuddered on the wind. A dog barked, hearing it; he wondered if the dog was male or female, had felt the same pain itself.

They raced back toward Trenton. And now Hyatt began to wonder about the fire and explosions at British Chemical, as if there'd been a delay in his full perception of danger. How do we know what's happening there, he thought to himself.

Darkness streamed past, the wagon careening from side to side. And Bill Pickell crawled back to the spring seat in front, holding on to the vehicle's wooden sides precariously.

"I don't know how long it'll be, maybe soon."

Pickell's lips were trembling, a trickle of saliva at one corner of his mouth. "Wes, you think she's gonna be all right?"

"Of course she will," Hyatt said reassuringly. And under his breath, "How in hell would I know?"

From charcoal darkness, the sky became an enormous white bed sheet above their heads, a leprous white that pulsed and glowed three-dimensionally. Shortly after this false morning, sound came; a hard, black muscle of air pushed them sideways on the wagon. Margaret Pickell screamed again, the sound uniting with the explosion, as if earth itself had experienced an earth-agony.

But terror had become commonplace. They slumped inside their skins, leaned against their bones like marionettes become flaccid from this repetition of the unbearable. The pregnant woman seemed too exhausted to speak, and sighed with a long exhalation of breath. Ahead of them, lights glimmered; a glow and sulphur smell from the river.

"This place is Hart's Corners," Pickell announced. "And Mayhew's Mill," he added a moment later.

"But I don't see any house lights around. Sis?" He leaned backward. "You see anything?"

"A barn," she told him, a note of desperation in her voice. "We've got to stop. There just isn't any more time."

The two men felt their way into the barn, reaching ahead of them to touch things. It was cavernous, empty except for musty hay in one corner. Hyatt struck a match, its flame glinting on dirty glass. A storm lantern hung on the wall. He shook it back and forth, rewarded by the slosh of oil inside. Lighted, the lantern revealed stable doors, cracked harness hanging from a nail, and nothing else.

215

"Cattle stalls, but no stock," Hyatt said. "Mangers, and no feed."

"Let's bring her into the barn," Bill Pickell said. "No time to go any farther. It's near midnight – "

"You realize we're almost back where we started from?" Hyatt said drily. "Hart's Corners is near part of Trenton, where we're at. Close to the T.N.T. This town's liable to go sky-high any minute, and us with it."

"Can't help that," Pickell said shortly.

They cradled the pregnant woman into the barn with hands locked together, her body convulsed with seismic tremors; the coloured sky flickering outside.

Pickell stripped off shirt and sweater for a bed on the hay; Wes Hyatt contributed his checked windbreaker. And Pickell had a strange feeling, as if he had set into motion large forces because of his wife's pregnancy, forces far beyond his knowledge or control. It was a thought that gave some dignity to all this smelly disarray of war and death, and the planet moving through empty space; a new life to which he had made a small contribution.

He straightened his shoulders, reaching for Margaret's hand. The hand was like iron, and clenched into a claw.

"Get the hell outa here!" his sister told him urgently.

Outside, he felt hard-done-by, bereft of love on Thanksgiving Day. Yes, it really was Thanksgiving Day. Wes Hyatt clapped him on the shoulder, hard.

"Bill, you're gonna have a son and heir." Then a female thought occurred to him, but he brushed it aside. "Where's them cigars?"

Roy Morrow had worked all day and into early evening, getting in the grain harvest at his farm sixteen miles north of Trenton. He was stowing his threshing machine in the barn, when the darkness stopped being darkness; the sky

216

glowed rose-pink and red, a blinding white. Everything started to shake, including the horses. They trembled and rolled their eyes when he approached them. The farmhouse shuddered.

Morrow's wife ran from the back door and stood with her husband. They were speechless. In bed they lay awake, listening to explosions that kept coming at intervals. Just when they decided things were being brought under control, the room filled with noise; walls, ceiling, and floor hammered noise at them.

Near dawn, and long sleepless, they were able to distinguish different sounds which, they speculated, depended on the source and type of explosion. Some were like a man learning to speak for the first time in his life; one syllable long, drawn out to become a short explosive sentence. The sound of a fat man eating soup with a large spoon, spilling half of it, and going *ur-r-p*. Pants ripping. Somebody farting in the big room of the world. The ear made its own adjustments and parallels, in order that the brain might rationalize and comfort itself.

It was bright morning when they fell asleep.

In Trenton, a man named Alan Dempsey was thrown out of bed by the explosion. It was after midnight. He scrambled to his feet and looked at the bed distrustfully. From his upstairs window shadows could be seen moving back and forth in the yard. The road changed colour to red and orange, reverted back to its own grey dirt colour, then sank into darkness. Dempsey finally yawned and went back to bed.

The Gauthier family had the flu, but not with the epidemic's full virulence. All of them stayed in the kitchen where a

217

woodstove provided more heat than elsewhere. Winnifred Gauthier and her father went into the garden to watch changing lights in the sky produced by fires at British Chemical on the evening of October 14. They heard a shrill whistle whining toward them out of the night. Something landed where the garden potatoes had been with a *chunk* sound in the earth. A small asteroid? Some eastern king's spare crown? A jagged fragment of metal from the munitions factory. Winnifred's father touched it gingerly, and pulled his hand back quickly. "Hot," he said.

Gordon Coughlin and his family were having Thanksgiving dinner at home in the dining room. They were waiting for Mr. Coughlin to carve the turkey, everyone watching him. The chandelier over their heads glittered with light, which also flashed off the carving knife and cutlery. They waited. Then everything shook: walls of the room, table, dishes, chairs, cutlery, people; everything. A loud *CRUMP* followed, as if all the furniture upstairs had tumbled over. Overhead, the glass chandelier swayed and fell, landing atop the Thanksgiving turkey, emitting little tinkling sounds. Coughlin stared at his shaking hands.

Billy Coons and Jack Corson were fishing for mudcats near the B.W. Powers coal sheds. They had eaten an early supper in order to get onto the river at dusk when mudcats were most likely to be biting. Drop your hook, baited with angleworms picked off wet lawns the night before; let the hook sink down into the river bottom ooze, leave it there a few minutes, then give it a gentle yank. If you were lucky, a devil's face with waving black horns would be leaping at you in the boat. Very good eating, too. Billy Coons claimed mudcats looked like Maclean the pump-maker, or maybe Maclean's convict brother, if he had such a brother.

The fish weren't biting. They shoved the skiff farther out into the river, letting it drift downstream, trolling as they went. Jack Corson stretched out luxuriously on the bottom of the boat, wrapped in a blanket, letting his fingers trail in the water.

"What happened to Patrick? Did you ask him to come?"

"He's got a girl," Billy Coons said.

"So what?"

"Well, you know. . . . Don't you?"

"Yah, I guess so. What's he doin with her? How far'd he get?"

"Patrick isn't likely to tell me that. Maybe you wanta ask him . . ."

"Nah, I don't. Billy, pass me one of them beer you sneaked from your old man."

They sucked contentedly on the brew, letting fish bite or not bite as the fish preferred. The boat drifted downriver, turning sideways and picking up speed at concrete abutments of the town bridge where the current ran swiftly.

They were dozing, almost asleep, when the sky turned inside out; night reversed itself and became day again. When the first explosion came, river waves were flattened as if a large hand from the sky had pressed down.

"British Chemical," Billy Coons said shakily. "Mom always said it would blow – "

"Yeah," Corson said wonderingly, light and shadows chasing over his face.

Coming to fuller awareness of danger, he grabbed the oars, starting to yank on them wildly.

"Let's get outa here."

Behind them the sky became a furnace; there was a crackling sound borne to them on the cool breeze. Half a mile south of the town bridge Jack Corson dipped his oars into the water too deeply. The left oar leaped from its oarlock, escaping his grasp, and plopped into the dark Bay of Quinte.

"Oh Christ!" Billy Coons said.

"I could swim for it."

"No you couldn't. I can't even see the bridge from here."

"Well then, we can paddle to shore with the other oar."

"No we can't! The boat would just go around in circles!"

They sat silently, the sky northeast of them growing brighter.

"How about yelling, both of us at once?" Jack Corson said.

They stood up and yelled, but the sound seemed to encounter a barrier in the air and their own words came back to them faintly. As if they were the only audience for their voices, an echo returned full circle.

More explosions lit the sky as the boat drifted southeasterly on the Bay of Quinte. At midnight, holding on to the gunwales tiredly with aching muscles, they scraped on a gravelly bottom in the darkness. An island. And stumbled ashore with their blankets.

"What about your mom and dad?" Billy Coons said.

"What about yours?"

Their eyes groped into the darkness, light from the burning munitions factory providing small illumination at a ten-mile distance.

"To hell with it," Billy Coons said. "I can't see the shore. And it's too far to swim."

"I'm kinda sleepy anyway," Jack Corson said, yawning.

Among tangled shrubbery they found a hollow place on the island where the terrain suddenly dipped. Wrapping themselves in blankets, they curled around each other for warmth, and went to sleep.

Ralph Bonter, a Trenton jeweller, was in Toronto at the time of the British Chemical fires and explosions. When he tried to buy his train ticket home next day at Union Station, he was told the whole town had blown up the night before. Trenton, it was said, no longer existed.

Most of the store windows on Front and Dundas streets were broken at the first explosion. And the streetlights – many of them shattered early, others freakishly didn't. One near the bridge signalled another at the railway crossing. Silence. Enough light left for a pedestrian to notice the glitter of broken glass. But there were no pedestrians.

In semi-darkness, a tinkle of glass. A small shard had fallen from its window frame. No one heard. But the silence was incomplete. It was like the silence when you hear a ringing in the ears, with your mind a blank. The silence of fear. If nothing happens, if you don't fall asleep, if no one speaks, if no footsteps pass by on the street, no vehicle on the road – you begin to wonder what alien world is this you have come to. . . .

An old man with a lantern appeared. He swung the lantern back and forth, revealing a white-bearded face with each upward swing. The old man had seemed to arise from the earth near Lottie Jones, Florist, then shuffled east toward the bridge.

He wore a long black coat that twisted around his legs as he marched toward the river. His lips moved under the beard, but no sound came. Other people were suddenly milling together on the street when he reached Simmons's Drugstore; two or three with their own lanterns; one man with a long white candle that he shielded from the wind. They crowded around the old man in the black coat, who looked like an Old Testament prophet.

The face behind the beard was a little mad. The old man lifted both arms toward people gathered around him; his coat spread out like the black wings of a bird.

"The end of the world is at hand!" he screamed at the crowd. "The Four Horsemen of the Apocalypse are here; the Destroying Angel with fiery sword in hand has arrived in Trenton, that accursed town. The Jezebels will die; the Whore of Babylon will be cast down from a high place. And their blood will be licked up from the streets by dogs. Trenton has sinned."

He climbed onto a bushel crate, waving black wings at the crowd.

"Tell us what we must do to be saved," a voice whispered sibilantly.

"Tell us, tell us!" a woman in the crowd yelled.

"Tell us, tell us!" they screamed at the prophet.

"You must be washed in the blood of the Lamb," he told them, voice hissing like a snake.

"Washed in the blood of the Lamb!" chanted the crowd.

"But first, Sodom and Gomorrah must be destroyed. And there shall be no more sin in the land of Israel. You must be washed in the blood of the Lamb!"

"He's crazy; plumb loco," said someone in the crowd.

"No, no, he's a man of God. He speaks in tongues and is bodied forth in the word of the Lord."

"What'n hell does that mean?"

"He's crazy," the same man insisted.

A wave of movement went over the crowd, people near the front staggering.

"Who you pushin?" a woman shouted indignantly.

Another woman screamed, "Get away from me, get away. I can see what you want, get away . . ."

"You sonofabitch! I'll fix you . . ."

The crowd surged forward like a heavy liquid, a human wave. The prophet disappeared from view, then came up like flotsam, waving his arms as if summoning the vengeful Lord. One fight was going on at the edge of the crowd, another at the centre. Rings of onlookers encircled the combatants, watching them avidly. A fever seemed to overtake a few of the men; they swung their fists like clubs at faces closest to them.

"Migawd, what's got into them?" Sideways Smith said from the upper window where he and Phil Wright were watching.

"Get that scrawny neck of yours back from the glass," Wright told him, holding up a piece of glass from the shattered window.

"There useta be some goin's-on in the shanties," Sideways said, "but that there preacher takes the frosted bicuspid fruitcake. In fact, he is the fruitcake."

"What's goin on out there?" McPherson demanded from the other end of the room.

Phil Wright rushed over and pushed him back down into the chair. "You know what the doc said about flu."

"I wanta know what's happenin," McPherson said rebelliously.

"Just some preacher tryin to get the crowd heated up," Wright told him. "No call for you to get agitated. Guy thinks he's John the Baptist at a baked beans soirée."

When Patrick came into the room, McPherson was again struggling to get up. He subsided, grumbling: "When hell's busting loose, they won't let me outa this chair. What's the news, Patrick?"

"I don't know much more'n you do," Patrick said, while the three old men watched him anxiously. Light from a big coal-oil lamp flickered in their faces.

"There's been some explosions. There may be more. Some say the whole town's gonna be blown off the map. People are leaving, getting out, going in all directions long as it's out."

The old men were less impressive to Patrick by this time, hesitating and uncertain in manner and speech. The years, which had seemingly been held in abeyance by Portugee's funeral and their arrival in Trenton, darkened their faces, bent their shoulders, and whispered in their speech.

"What about us?" Smith said, almost timidly. "Where are the people goin?"

"Everywhere," Patrick said. "Some walking, some in cars, in wagons, on horseback, every way you can think of. To Belleville, on the York Road to Brighton, north to Frankford" – thinking of Jean and her mother – "south over the Murray Canal to Prince Edward, Wellington, and Picton. . . . Anywhere, anyhow – but away."

He rubbed his eyes, feeling tired and distracted by the rush of events; everything seemed to have happened all at once. Horses and motor cars had been crashing through his veins; flashing lights in the depths of his brain. They stopped now, and he breathed heavily.

"People are climbing Mount Pelion to get away. There's a hollow place at the top they think protects them from the explosions."

Patrick at the ancients dubiously. "But the mountain is about six hundred feet high, maybe more. It's a pretty good climb. Maybe Phil could get up there."

Patrick glanced at Smith judiciously. "I'm supposed to look after Mr. Smith here. Police Chief Murray more or less placed him in my charge . . ."

"I ain't in nobody's charge," Sideways sputtered indignantly. "You can just forget about that right now."

Then, his irritation forgotten, "What are we gonna do?"

"I could maybe get you up there," Patrick said. "Up the mountain. Me and Kevin Morris, he's helping me. But it's liable to be chilly that high in the open air at night. It's no place for someone getting over the flu." He glanced at McPherson.

224

The fire was red geraniums, thought Corporal Ernest Cunnell, standing at the guardhouse door. It bloomed, it died, it revived and sprang up again. Then it was like yellow tulips, then pale red roses, iris's blue tongues in his mother's garden. The flowers had become mobile and leaped from their roots into the air: he was hypnotized. He shook himself violently to clear his head and come awake.

Two other guards rushed past him. He grabbed a sleeve. "Where the hell you goin? Aren't you on duty?"

"Duty nothin," one of them gasped. "This place is goin sky-high any minute."

Both men disappeared in the smoky haze, running toward the river.

Past Bunker Hill, Cunnell caught glimpses of men running in the smoke and flames, mouths open, gasping for air. Hayden, the company foreman, was dashing around like a cat with its tail cut off. The fire alarm shrieked warning and cried for help, a red cry, a scarlet appeal. Everybody heard, but very few did anything.

General manager John Barclay did do something. He noticed the wooden overhead trestles had caught fire. The trestles conveyed sulphuric and nitric acids in pipelines to other areas of the huge munitions complex. Fire was creeping along them like a powder train, ready to trigger an explosion wherever the fuse went.

"Stop!" Barclay shouted to a man running past.

"Hell with you, bub," the man said, and kept on running.

But a few others recognized the plant manager's smoke-stained face. They used fire axes to attack the trestles, but flames drove them back. Another explosion deafened them briefly; they stood helplessly watching the trestles burn. Three more men made the attempt, soaking themselves with water from fire hoses. They crawled around the gun-cotton lines, fell to with axes, coughing painfully in the smoke.

225

"It's falling!" someone shrieked. And they ran.

Another explosion.

Anyone unprotected by buildings was smashed flat on the ground. Timber, fragments of steel, chunks of broken concrete, even earth itself sailed into the sky above the earth. It fell on plant property from its mile-high apogee; it fell in the river; it fell on Trenton's east side; and it fell west beyond the river. An appalling carpet of fire soared up from British Chemical, hung there like the Children of Israel's pillar of fire in the desert. Unwanted by the sky, it subsided, fell, replaced by ribbons and tendrils of flame criss-crossing with snaky bodies in the lower heavens.

TELEGRAM: To Commanding Officer, Military District #3, Kingston, Ontario:
"Please render all possible assistance to sufferers from explosion in Trenton."
　　　　　Signed, Adjutant-General, Ottawa, Canada

At the company switchboard, Eva Curtis stayed on duty. Her hands made motions of semaphore; her voice conveyed meaning. She said hello and thank you, while broken glass kept falling from jagged window frames. It tinkled, small shards of it, and wind gusted through from the vast places outside.

Eva Curtis said, "Yes, sir. The fire is bad, but we hope soon to get it under control." She said, "It's Mr. Barclay, the general manager, you want? I don't know. He's very busy. I'm sorry, I don't think I can reach him for you. Would you try later, please."

She went to the door, feet crunching over glass. Near Bunker Hill, fire raised a great wall of light, with a crimson head on top that snored and gulped air like a slobbering monster. Above and below No. 1 dam, the tops of waves were tinted red as the tongues of animals. Close to burning buildings, fire varied its language to a deep *urrr* sound, softened its vowels to dreaming consonants, then screeched like demon crows in the newly minted morning before and after creation. The fire sang.

Miss Curtis shuddered and went back to the switchboard.

Trenton houses emptied, as if they had been lifted, turned sideways, and shaken vigorously. Buildings emptied and darkened; only here and there might a wavering candle be seen. As if someone, a malign god perhaps, had poured a deadly gas into all human dwelling places. The people fled, faces drained of blood, silent and shaken, or voluble and silly.

Fire sirens at the munitions factory, screaming and sighing, had the same effect as the Pied Piper of Hamelin Town in reverse. Except that the inhabitants of Trenton were not rats. And the town kids who had chanted, "Ladybug, Ladybug, fly away home/Your house is on fire and your children alone" – were not aware that they, too, had become Mother Ladybug's children.

And the sirens screamed.

# 12

THE ADDRESS WAS BEYOND Trenton's eastern town limits, where Dundas Street became the Belleville road. An October moon sailed overhead. "Old man Ostrum's a bad cripple," Ian McMaster had told Patrick and Kevin. "He can't hear very well either, so you'll have to yell to get him out of there. Emma and me'll get ready while you're gone."

No answer when they pounded on Ostrum's door, the huge old-fashioned brick house like a solid blob in surrounding darkness. When Kevin turned the door handle, it opened easily. "I'm going in," he said. "You wait here for me."

Patrick said, "Okay," but felt a twitch of annoyance at this take-charge attitude, the relegation of himself to second-in-command of nothing much. But he shrugged, and waited on the porch like a good little boy.

"Nobody home," Kevin announced, reappearing in the gloom. "Somebody must've taken him away, maybe to Belleville. Anyway, he's off our hands."

The wafting scent of a skunk was faintly smellable in the cool night air. It brought Joe Barr and the garbage dump rushing into Patrick's mind: the idiot's lantern jaw spewing out a stream of "aws" like black crows in a stormy sky. . . .

"Joe Barr," he said.

"Joe who?" Kevin wanted to know.

Patrick explained, and said, "I think we'd better get him out of there, maybe take him up the mountain. The McMasters are probably still getting ready – "

"Let's not get him out and say we did," Kevin blurted abruptly. "There's people more useful than idiots we could – "

"Kevin!" Patrick said scathingly.

There was a brief silence, and Kevin grinned placatingly. It was an attractive grin, and made it difficult not to like the owner. Patrick mused about that, thinking: Why do I always get myself into this spot, where I'm the one sounds like a snob or a goody-goody and can't look reality in the face? Sure, other people are more useful than Joe, but Joe is Joe and I don't know who those other useful people are. . . .

"I'll race you," Kevin said.

"What?"

"From here to the C.N.R. station. No – maybe a little farther than that; I need space to run. We race from here to the roundhouse; then we walk to where your friend lives. Okay?"

At first Patrick felt like saying Joe Barr wasn't a friend, but changed his mind. He noticed that all expression had left Kevin's face, then the attractive smile reappeared. And who was this stranger living next door, Patrick wondered? Someone he hadn't really known about before, someone whose moods changed as the smile changed, and became deep sincerity and likeability at need?

"Look, Patrick, don't you ever feel like measuring yourself against something besides time, something human? You've been running all summer, you ought to be in top physical condition. Now's your chance to find out how good you are. . . ."

The smile was challenging, slightly irritating to Patrick. It grated against his conception of himself; it even poked innocent fun at the sweating runner learning who he was on the Glen Miller road.

"All right," he said.

It was easy at first. But when they reached the town's outskirts, Kevin was far ahead. His own legs felt heavy and difficult to retrieve after they reached their farthest extent away from him, as if he were throwing some part of himself away continually, then had to haul it back quickly where the rest of him was. Thinking about it made his knees wobble, and that made his elbows slap against his ribs as if he were a scarecrow. He zigzagged down the road to Herman Street, wondering who Herman was and why they named a street after him. . . .

"Who was Herman, who was he, that all his swains commend him?" He heard someone's voice sing out the nonsense words. Then his knees and elbows straightened, his stride became the customary far-reaching lope that required no thought whatever. But why am I nervous, he said to himself? Why did I start to unravel, like a stitch had been dropped in my mother's knitting? And snorted. No, it wasn't Kevin made me that way; it was me.

He opened his stride slightly, so that ahead of him the light grey windbreaker Kevin wore stopped retreating any more than its present hundred-yard distance. Breathing easily now, he decided that the distance from Belleville road to railway roundhouse was about three miles. And tried to remember the feeling of running three miles as fast as he had ever covered that distance before. But time and distance were hard to relate to each other. He glanced sideways to see the housefronts blur as his pace increased still more. Perhaps, just perhaps, Kevin was coming back to him. Then he saw a white face that looked very interested in his progress, staring.

He felt better about things; that face ahead wasn't quite so comfortable about the pursuer behind. A worm of doubt had been planted in Kevin's brain, and was gnawing there. His own thoughts veered to Mrs. Morris, her little digs about Patrick's inability to equal her own son's marvellous intelligence. Did Kevin also feel superior, agreeing with his mother that he was destined for a leadership role in the world? And therefore look down on himself, having decided that he, Patrick, was a failure before he'd even started to run. . . .

To run? The thought brought him back to himself. Grace Church blurred past as he made the turn west, down Dundas Street hill; and saw the two hotels, nearly opposite each other, the Royal and Union. He was fifty feet behind at the button factory east of the bridge, then he choked on his own chuckle, thinking of Mrs. Morris talking to his mother. That chuckle cost him thirty feet.

He regained that distance and more, too, traversing thumping wooden planks of the bridge's pedestrian walkway. Kevin's flailing elbows were only a few feet ahead when once again the thought occurred to him: Does Kevin make me nervous? And Kevin is Kevin to the extent that it doesn't allow me to be me? That seemed a bit ridiculous.

Kevin's head seemed to turn almost to a full 180 degrees, looking backward as he ran, the white face ridged in deep lines, a mask so pale Patrick couldn't take his eyes away from it. Kevin must be worried he couldn't win this race, this piddling little run to nowhere that meant nothing to either of them unless their minds made it important. Unless their minds. . . . And that was the key, Patrick thought. Kevin's mind had made this race very important to himself, which meant that he felt insecure where Patrick was concerned. But why on earth should that be so?

The next time Kevin's head turned to look backward, Patrick grinned as hard as he could, a grin that projected confidence and good fellowship. Did it also convey friendship? Patrick wasn't very sure of that, not yet anyway. In the same instant, a tickle in his brain made him remember a scrap of information Kevin had let drop about running. Patrick had been convalescing from his experiences at British Chemical, Kevin sitting near the bed talking to him. He couldn't remember exactly what was said, some aspect of Kevin's running abilities. He couldn't remember what it was. Failing the words, could he remember the thought? And could the thought help him in some way now?

Glancing north along the river, Patrick could see red and orange pustules of flame colouring the sky, making downtown look weirdly unreal. At this moment the shopping area was deserted. Human beings had disappeared, having left the town or perhaps taken refuge in their cellars. And Patrick wondered about the flu victims – had most of them been able to escape?

After leaving the bridge and passing Simmons's Drugstore, Kevin veered onto the empty roadway. Patrick remained on the sidewalk, his feet immediately encountering slippery shards of glass from store windows shattered by the explosions. Skidding over the broken glass was like first learning to ice-skate: reeling ahead without being able to stop, slithering sideways with body and head wanting to go in different directions, hips jerking violently, arms waving for balance.

And panic. Patrick knew that falling meant mangled arms and legs from the razor-sharp glass. He tried to direct his reeling passage into a doorway, against a utility pole, any non-dangerous place he could stop. And finally wound up in a bundle of arms and legs in the Gilbert Hotel entrance, face down on cold stone.

Staggering off the sidewalk to the road, he saw Kevin a hundred feet ahead looking back at him. There was enough light to see the other boy's expression. It was so much like triumph that Patrick was suddenly sick and felt like vomiting. But he straightened, forced his legs into motion again, and doggedly started to run.

There was a dullness in his head when they turned south at the railway tracks and passed the C.N.R. station. As if he could see only in little snatches of things, when his bobbing head allowed vision. And after the dim lighting of the main street gave way to moonlit cinders beside the steel rails, he was nearly blind for the first few moments. Kevin was just visible ahead of him, the whirring sound of feet on

232

cinders drifting back. And again that other pallid face turned backward, assessing its advantage.

Along the cinders he gained some ground on Kevin, but at such cost to himself as he had never paid when running alone. The space between them lessened; not foot by foot, but rather inch by inch.

Twenty feet ahead, Kevin's shirt flapped in the wind of his passage. Kevin's shirt! How could that be? Then he realized that Kevin must have discarded his grey windbreaker somewhere along the route, in order to run without encumbrance. Intending to go back and retrieve it later? Of course. Which emphasized that this impromptu race was very important to his clever neighbour. The race might even have been planned beforehand, a thought so devious on Kevin's part that Patrick couldn't help snickering.

There seemed to be several conditions or stages of running he passed through. One of them was of heavy laboured progress, during which his strength drained away ounce by ounce with sweat pouring from his body. Another in which he skimmed over the ground, and felt a euphoria in running that birds might feel flying. And yet a third stage, during which he seemed not to be running at all, his mind floating free to think strange thoughts, like how long it would take to reach the outer planets at this rate of speed. All three stages being enhancements of what he had experienced before, when competing only with himself.

Glancing ahead at the upper part of Kevin's body, it seemed they were held together in the same position by invisible ropes, and neither could escape the other. His mouth was wide open now, jaws moving as if he were attempting to eat the cool October evening; the air a compound of smoke from the fire and sweetish garbage odour. And wondered if Kevin's mouth was open, before he glimpsed the black O in a white mask when Kevin again looked backward.

Lights from the cooperage mill near Quinte threw their shadows onto the right of way. Noticing those moving shadows, he realized there was no way he could get ahead of Kevin: they were both running on the same side of the tracks, and there wasn't room to pass. With a hop, skip, and jump that scarcely broke stride, he leaped to the opposite side on the right; and they were running nearly opposite each other.

The black O's in white faces stared across the tracks at each other – then both suddenly disappeared from view. A dark boxcar loomed mountainous between the runners; then another, followed by a silent yard engine with a curl of steam drifting from somewhere on the black shape. No train crew in sight.

Patrick was discouraged. All his natural running abilities and strength of body had failed to overtake Kevin. He broke stride momentarily, feeling defeat overtaking him. And Kevin had increased his lead to fifteen feet at this point, lights from the roundhouse appearing a quarter-mile ahead.

Then, unbidden, the scene at his bedside when he was recovering from his experiences at British Chemical, and Kevin had been visiting him – that scene recreated itself in his mind. They were talking about running. Kevin's voice was rueful when he said, "I have no finishing kick." Which meant that after a long race or even a fairly short one, Kevin couldn't increase speed at the end of a race, couldn't summon extra pounds and ounces of himself to pour into his legs. Perhaps couldn't win when it was important to win; perhaps had run races during school field days and discovered this vital lack in himself, reached somewhere inside in search of it and discovered . . . nothing.

But he, Patrick, how could he be so sure he possessed this "finishing kick" himself? And knew that he had to stay within a dozen feet of Kevin to find out. If he didn't stay that close, nothing would help him, not the finishing kick or anything else. And Kevin at this moment was running away from him, didn't even turn his head to look backward any longer. Kevin was sure of himself now, seemed to know he was winning.

To hell with it, Patrick thought. This may be only a race, but it's as important as anything I can think of right now. Because now is now – no past, no future. And what about that goddam superior look from Kevin all next winter if I lose? Question: How do you like being second best, Patrick? How do you like being third or fourth best, or worst at anything – last, last, last?

Anger roared in his head and down to his legs. Not mild irritation or the so-so condition of being mildly provoked. The genuine article. And it was wood and coal burning hard with the bellows of his lungs pumping; it was light blazing in his brain. And he ran, as he had not known how to do before, as if the earlier part of his race had been practice only. Prelude, preliminary exercise.

Then the anger disappeared, fell away from him. Thought vanished from his mind; his body integrated itself, arms, legs, head, torso, all joined and meshed together as one. As a bird is nothing but bird, an animal completely an animal – he was joined to himself.

It was not that running became any easier, because his feet and legs were still telegraphing they felt terrible; his arms and the muscles of his back were sending urgent messages they'd like a rest. His mind told them: No, you can't have a rest, not for a while longer. First we've got to overcome that thirty-foot lead the other guy has. And he didn't say "Kevin" any longer; that word was much too friendly.

Now the moon which had lighted their steps before was competing with lights from the roundhouse ahead. And the running shadows, which had preceded them and sometimes been outriders beside them, retreated to the rear. And the other guy was nervous, Patrick thought. Kevin's mouth was opening and closing like a gaffed fish when he glanced backward.

Patrick began to encourage himself, talk to his feet and legs, tell his arms and the stiffening vertebrae of his neck that it wasn't much farther, they could do it. And he believed that now, he knew that now. Feeling a lofty contempt for anybody who thought he couldn't win this unimportant little race, this terribly important raging war of a race. He said to the troops, We're gaining, boys! Creeping up on him. Don't let up now. And when he looks behind again, you, Patrick, make sure to keep your mouth closed.

Kevin did look behind, his face a map of torture, ridged and contorted with effort. And they were ten feet apart, with Patrick gaining. Abreast of the first lights they were even, and stayed that way, both so aware of the other they felt joined by a shadowy umbilical cord. Then a sovereign floating feeling, lassitude even, was beginning to overcome Patrick. And they were coasting, drifting sideways and awry from straight ahead, staggering. A cindery sound drifted up to them, like millions of tiny crickets singing from the railway roadbed under their feet.

They stopped where the tracks entered the roundhouse, each turned away from the other. Kevin's mouth was open, gasping, his chest heaving.

Patrick said, "Dead even. Want to go back to Herman Street and do it again?"

Kevin gave him a wan look, "No thanks."

"You okay?"

"Sure!" In an irritated tone: "Are you?"

"Naturally," Patrick said, thinking that was the right word, and chuckling as he said it.

Somewhere in his mind he was recreating that hour-long moment, the endless instant when the two of them were directly abreast, frozen forever in time it seemed, when he knew absolutely. . . . When he knew what? He reached out in himself and gathered together the information and data available from his scattered body parts, added and subtracted the plus-and-minus probabilities in himself. Then asked the question to which he did not know the answer: If I had poured out a little more of myself when we were running even, a little more willpower, an ounce more of guts, would I have been able to pass Kevin and win the race?

His reply to himself was: Perhaps.

They looked at each other, and Patrick knew things had changed; there had been a shifting of values and attitudes between them because of the race. Adjustments in their personal relations would have to be made in accordance with these new circumstances. And thinking suddenly of Kevin's windbreaker, probably abandoned near Grace Church, he smiled.

"What's the joke?" Kevin wanted to know.

"Ourselves. Wasting energy like that. With Joe, then the McMasters to help get somewhere safer . . ."

"Maybe it is funny," Kevin conceded, and grinned. "Let's call a truce for the rest of the night. What do you say?"

Then, at the edge of the garbage dump, Patrick pointed to a place where glue-like yellow ooze and rusty tin cans seemed to separate. "Maybe the path is here. Give it a try anyway."

At the flattened tin can and scrap lumber shack, he knocked. And had the feeling of being watched from a spyhole. Then Joe stood in front of him, eating beans from a tin bowl, lamplight behind him, grinning. The long jaw still owned its quarter-inch beard that seemed perpetual, never getting any longer. Joe's dark, child-like eyes were cordial, his face twisted into a grimace. "Aw," he said. "Aw."

Patrick reached out and took his hand. "There's been a fire," he said. And pointed toward a sky-glow that trembled and dimmed and swelled, lending Bay of Quinte waves a look like gelatin.

"This whole place is liable to blow up," he said, and looked earnestly into Joe Barr's face.

His words had no effect whatever. Joe grinned happily, continuing to spoon beans into his mouth.

"Bang-bang!" Patrick said loudly, waving his arms in the air. "Very dangerous. Bang-bang!"

"Boom-boom," Kevin said with a straight face.

Patrick glanced at him bitterly. "You're a big help!"

Joe proffered his bowl of beans to Patrick, pushing the spoon toward him, delighted with the idea. "Aw," he said invitingly.

Patrick and Kevin both pointed at the sky, then tried to mimic an explosion. They jumped into the air among wet garbage, stricken expressions on their faces.

"Boom!" Kevin shouted.

"Aa-aa," wheezed Patrick, simulating agony.

Joe looked sympathetic, very much concerned. "Aw," he said, patting Patrick on the shoulder.

"I don't think this is getting us anywhere," Kevin said. "How about we take his arms and kinda frog-march him away from here? How would that be?"

But when they grabbed Joe's arms, urging him toward the outward path, he planted his feet stubbornly. With a twitch of shoulders he shrugged both of them a full ten feet away, landing them in especially nauseous wet garbage. There hadn't even been a struggle. They lay there, astounded in the heavy stink, looking at each other with very serious expressions.

Patrick began to laugh, and Kevin did too, the kind of laughter at your own follies and misjudgements that make you forgive other people for not being you. And remembering his nervous fear running south on the river road, Patrick knew that was gone.

On their feet again, Kevin said, "Let's go. I think he wants to be alone."

The idiot, who wasn't an idiot, jaw swaying like a jib sail in changeable winds, waved at them. They waved back.

Kevin said, "Let that be a lesson to me." He grinned. "And to you, too, Patrick."

Stumbling through the islands and archipelagos of garbage, Patrick felt that something wasn't right; ordinary reality and the expectedness of life were being turned upside down, the established order of things becoming disestablished. He sneaked a sideways glance at Kevin, and noticed that Kevin was doing the same to him.

"Wanta give it another try?" Patrick said.

And both of them knew he meant helping somebody else escape being blown up; and both knew it meant much more.

In Belleville, Frankford, Brighton, Wellington, Picton, Cobourg, all the towns and villages in Hastings, Prince Edward and Northumberland counties, people knew for sure the European war was winding down. Newspapers told them so. Mons, Ypres, Flanders, and Passchendaele were among the French places where "our boys" were fighting the good fight in this "war to end wars," in this "struggle to the death" against an evil German kaiser. The output of claptrap, of slogans and catch phrases, was slowing down. Speeches from politicians had noticeably diminished in volume and frequency. Army recruiters no longer harangued young men about "the death of civilization" and "the end of the world as we know it."

Then, on the night of October 14, 1918, British Chemical in Trenton exploded and burned. For townspeople, the war would again become real, more than a story glamorized with foreign place-names. The myth of local young men dying in Europe was not a myth, but factual as the flapping clothesline bearing Monday's washing. And tangible as autumn leaves in deciduous forests on the old Hastings Road to Bancroft and Maynooth. That diseased glow in the sky over Trenton, seen for more than twenty miles, said: "You're next!" The Four Horsemen rode again through back alleys and main drags of nearby towns. The dogs of war revived and snarled at everyone. Old clichés awoke, decided they were not at all outmoded, and were born again in the mouths of politicians.

The phone rang at a house on Bridge Street in Belleville. And at houses in Brighton and Wellington. It rang in other towns and on other streets as well. No one replied when householders said hello. Dogs barked, and in the Belleville near-slum of Stoney Lonesome other dogs replied. Dishes in sideboards and cupboards clinked, glasses trembled on their shelves. All small things moved a little, seemed to be strange and sentient for a moment, then settled back again into their long familiarity.

An aesthete might have found some beauty in the night sky over Trenton. Some did. It was like flowers, all those colours, the spring bridal of flowers. And some people probed their minds for the right words to describe it. Philosophically, it was like the end of the world in all mythologies; it was like seeing the various changing faces of God or the Devil leaning close to earth with an enormous face and cursing. But finally, it was exactly what it was.


The explosions came at irregular intervals, alternating in degree of force and effect. People were thrown to the ground, or the floor, or the street. Some of them moaned and screamed; others prayed – aloud or with lips moving silently, calling on their Redeemer, calling, calling. . . . All thoughts of profit and loss, love and hate – these were replaced by apprehension and fear. By greater or lesser fear, whose fluctuations sometimes permitted other emotions to return in strange normalcy.

Red McPherson, recovering from influenza in Portugee's old apartment, worried about Patrick. He said to Phil Wright, "This war is like a log jam in history. It'll be over soon."

His friend looked at him disgustedly. "You're as high-falutin as you always was. What about Patrick?"

"That's what I mean," McPherson said, standing on the cold floor in his long underwear, wavering like a thin old tree in high winds.

Reflectively, "It's come about somehow that he's responsible for us . . . "

"But we're responsible for him at the same time. Now put some shoes on," Wright commanded. "There's nothing much we can do for Patrick right now, or even for ourselves. Old men our age can't run and jump and fight or make love. . . ." He stopped, thinking about it. "Well, maybe a little."

"He'll come back here when he's through do-goodin," McPherson said.

"Why should he?"

"Because that's what he is, what he's like" – in a disgusted voice.

"Didn't you have any sons or daughters of your own you could make a fuss about? Now that you're teetering at the graveyard edge, near a hundred years old, you cling to your own life by holdin on to a boy's – "

They glared at each other. McPherson shuffled forward until his face peered down at his friend's face from a six-inch distance. "What about you? That old girlfriend – ain't you hangin on to her like a bulldog with rotten teeth?"

"Sure I am. Wouldn't you?"

He slipped his arm around McPherson's shoulders, steering him back toward the chair.

"Leggo me!" McPherson said, covering his legs with a blanket.

"Phil?"

"Yes?"

"What about a drink?"

The bottle of rye was produced from its nest between two pillows. They swigged. Both said "Ah" the way whisky-drinkers do, the sound between a sigh and a gasp of pain.

"You think like he's your son or your grandson," Wright said accusingly.

"It won't last much longer."

"No. . . ."

McPherson raised the bottle again. "Here's to Patrick," and passed it to his friend.

"Philemon, mon," he said, the Scots burr surfacing in his voice, "you got anything else you'd rather be doin?"

"No."

"Then sit with me a spell, would ye . . . an' there's a sight more booze here than on the Gatineau, or on the Chaudière and Palmer Rapids." He chuckled. "We've time for aught we want to do between now and then and the devil . . ."

Phil Wright raised the bottle. "Here's to Gilmour, here's to Tiberius Wright, here's to Gillies and Eddy and Hughson. Here's to us, the wage slaves gone free. Here's to Portugee Cameron . . ."

"Don't get carried away, Phil."

"And Patrick – "

A cold breeze snapped through the blanket they had nailed across the shattered window. Muted noise came on the wind, soft expostulations of life, quiet acceptances and almost silence.

# 13

HALFWAY UP THE MOUNTAIN they stopped, gasping for breath. It wasn't like running, Patrick thought, when the energy drained out of you more slowly. And you had some warning before complete exhaustion.

He shoved his foot against the wheelchair containing Mrs. McMaster, to keep it from getting away on them. And said, "Let's take a break."

Kevin nodded. He was in little better condition, slumped on the grassy hillside. Ian McMaster's rasping breath sounded as if he needed new lungs. Emma McMaster, wrapped in blankets and comforters, hot-water bottle at her feet, seemed barely conscious.

"Ah," she said raggedly, "you boys, I love you both. . . ."

Kevin looked back over the slanting path that wound diagonally up Mount Pelion, as if climbing the mountain straight ahead was too much for man or beast.

He said, "Let's get a horse."

"Mr. McMaster, you good for a little way more?" Patrick wanted to know.

The old man nodded dully, head hanging down.

Behind them, Trenton was a patchwork of darkness, shadows overlaid with shadows. Moonlight and starlight competed with burning sky above the mountain crest, and lost. Below them were no streetlights or house lights; the doomsday explosions had extinguished everything. All that was familiar had become strange. None of the four on the mountain could even predict the next thought or word waiting in their minds, nor what the previously ordinary earth beneath their feet might do.

The sky's red light intensified without warning, glaring into their eyeballs from above the crest of Mount Pelion. The earth shook and trembled. Lying flat on his back in weariness, Patrick noticed the wheelchair moving. It slipped away from them sideways, as if it hadn't yet fully made up its mind to go, then darted away from them on the mountain's switchback descent.

"Kevin!" he yelled and leaped after it. Between them they managed to control the wheeled contraption.

"Thank you, Patrick," Emma McMaster said calmly.

The mountain sprawled right and left, rather than coming to a peak at the top. A shallow valley there sheltered some three hundred people from direct impact of the explosions. They were scattered on the sloping terrain, most of them middle-aged or old, wrapped in blankets and comforters; some with small camp-fires providing warmth and light.

Their faces turned to Patrick apathetically when he looked at them, eyes attracted by movement but completely blank, so tired they were not aware of their surroundings. A few slept, but most were awake, their reactions slowed and dulled.

Patrick remembered a book – Dante's *Inferno* – he had once looked at rather than read. The artist had sketched faces like these, some with open mouths, staring eyes, rational thought absent. More like animals than people. Having gone beyond terror and reached the state of lesser beings, flesh without mind.

Many of these refugees on Mount Pelion probably had the flu, or were recovering from it. An image of the cholera victims on the Quebec waterfront flew into his mind. People with haunted faces, death-tinged and pale, wondering who would be next to die, tar barrels burning in front of their doorways. McPherson's tale of the Grosse Isle immigrants relayed from the past via the logging shanties cook, old Ludger Chapdelaine . . .

244

He shook himself, remembered that here was now, and now was Emma and Ian McMaster.

"What do you think, Kevin?" he said. "Where's a good place to camp?"

The hollow-topped mountain was cross-hatched with the light from camp-fires. Those people nearest to the new arrivals were indifferent and scared at the same time. They were also curious but only vaguely so, a few raising their heads to watch; others were praying. A low murmur of The Lord's Prayer in various stages of saying could be heard in soft complaint to the deity. Everyone had blankets, or some form of covering, including burlap bags. Three or four crude tents had been rigged up, using coats, blankets, and other items of clothing.

After Patrick and Kevin's charges were settled in the lee of a big rock, Emma McMaster said, "We'll be perfectly all right, Patrick. If the town doesn't disappear tonight, you can see we get back down in the morning. And thank you both, Ian and I do."

In some consternation he saw tears shining in her eyes. "We'll come back for you in the morning," he said hastily.

He and Kevin now seemed to have an unspoken agreement, tacit but genuine. How was it that he'd thought Kevin snooty, haughty, and unapproachable? Kevin had been, but not only that. His wonderment showed on his face – or perhaps it did.

Kevin said, "You never know, do you, Patrick?"

They wandered through the clumps and dark clots of refugees from the town below, but only near the camp-fires could they discern faces clearly. At the crowded centre of the "encampment" someone began to sing. A young woman with voice like crystal. She sang "Nearer My God to Thee" with such a belief in the reality of her God that Patrick's own mind wavered in its disbelief. The crystal sound lifted and hung, trembled and vibrated, and, falling, left its absence imprinted on the air around.

245

◇ ◇ ◇

Shortly after midnight, the explosions at British Chemical had ended. The town was nearly emptied of people, except the very old and those whom illness had made captive. And there were a stubborn few who refused to leave their homes, despite broken windows, the strange behaviour of dishes on shelves, and the sky glare from the munitions factory that swelled and diminished.

The disaster had repercussions among domestic pets as well. Patrick noticed several cats in the arms of refugees on Mount Pelion. And dogs howled at the waxing and waning of light. They set up a shrieking chorus that may have been partly canine communication, to the effect that their masters had deserted them and they might escape to the forest. But most of them stayed. In the small hours, a plaintive note in their whinings, a bewilderment and puzzle their brains were incapable of unravelling.

After three more trips up the mountain, Patrick and Kevin decided Trenton would probably remain comparatively intact, despite the doom-criers. At 3 a.m., exhausted after their rescue operations, the road to the Murray Canal and Prince Edward County seemed much too far at that time of night. Patrick had tried several times to reach Jean Tomkins by telephone, without result. And tried also to reach his mother at the Harrigans'.

Kevin said, "If I know my father, he's long abed."

"They'll be worried about us, don't you think?"

"It's all over, that's what I think. For the time being anyway. I'm for bed." Kevin yawned widely. "How about you?"

Three hours later while Patrick was in the midst of sleep – a tiredness in his bones like running to the world's edge – his bedroom world flew apart. A noise like the Last Trump,

246

which could only be imagined since it had never happened. Noise like a pounding at Patrick's head, sound that was a blow. After any new thing that happens for the first time, you try to make a parallel with something already known. And Buster Brown firecrackers flew incongruously into Patrick's mind.

They were made of green cardboard, shaped like a shotgun shell, and about the same size. You lit the fuse, covered them with an empty tin can, and the can vanished into the sky with the sound of a smothered cough. This was Buster Brown, this bedroom explosion, but magnified to a degree that the parallel was ridiculous.

Patrick sat up in bed, checked his arms and legs, found that all his various parts were still attached, and he sighed. A tinkle of glass came from the nearly empty window frame. He sighed again. Disaster and death – he was being warned of them time after time. And growing numb to the warnings, inured to disaster, he went back to sleep.


Mrs. Cameron returned by mid-morning, and fussed him out of bed. She wanted to know why he hadn't joined her at the Harrigans; what the situation was at British Chemical; and had he seen Mr. Hartwell? Patrick tried to answer in the midst of splashing water on his face, snatching at breakfast, muttering no, yes, and maybe to all questions.

Mrs. Cameron reached out for him as he finished breakfast, wrapped him in her arms with a half sob. "I'm glad," she said, "I'm glad – "

Patrick knew what she meant.

He got out his bicycle from the woodshed, an old C.C.M., and anointed the wheel sprockets with oil. It hadn't been used since spring when he'd started running. At Hart's Corners he passed three soldiers with harried expressions walking south. They looked at him as if he were crazy. Across the river at British Chemical there was thick smoke. Ant-like figures were scurrying around, some waving their arms and gesticulating. There was a chimney fire at a farmhouse on the Frankford Road. He saw a man come out of the barn with a pail, running.

Mrs. Tomkins greeted him wordlessly at the cottage, motioning him inside. Jean had been sitting in the kitchen, staring through the window at the river road. Her face had lost its last tinge of colour and had a bleached pallor. They faced each other in silence for several seconds. He reached out his hand to her. The girl ignored it.

"You didn't come," she said.

"I tried to phone," Patrick said, and thought, What's wrong with her?

"You promised," she accused him.

"Jean," he said in despair, "Kevin Morris and I were helping people get away from Trenton. Mrs. McMaster who lives around the corner from us on Ford Street. She had the flu. We pushed her wheelchair up the mountain. And the others were – "

But Jean appeared not to be listening, hearing nothing but an inner voice.

"I know that you had to go. But you had to be here, too. You promised."

"Be reasonable. I came here as soon as I could." And thought, guiltily, that he'd come after having a pretty good sleep. "I was worn out from climbing up and down that mountain . . ."

It occurred to him as he spoke that Mrs. McMaster and Ian were probably still there, crouching over a bonfire in the mountain declivity. And she just getting over the flu, her husband, an elderly man, in last night's chill air. . . . Those others, too, the girl singing "Nearer My God to Thee" with a songbird's voice.

"Be reasonable," he said again. And was nearly overwhelmed by a sense of loss, of life changing from one instant to another.

"I wanted to come back," he said. "I tried. The telephone didn't work right when I phoned. And people kept asking me to do things while the explosions were going on – "

He watched her face while he spoke. The words didn't seem to register on her hearing. The blue eyes were blank, slim patrician nose like those affixed to dummies in store windows wearing beautiful dresses. Jean's mouth was squinched up and severe. He hardly recognized her.

"Leave me," she said.

"Huh?"

"Leave me."

Irritation began to overwhelm him. "Didn't you hear what I said? The telephone wouldn't work and I couldn't get back. I came as soon as I could – "

He stopped abruptly. What he'd said must have seemed like excuses, and he didn't need any of those. She appeared not to be listening to him, paying no attention whatever. She looked straight through him, as if he wasn't there. It made him feel six years old again. . . .

Patrick left, holding his shoulders back, trying to appear indifferent, thinking he was doing a lousy job of it.

On the porch steps Jean's mother drew him aside. "I'm sorry, Patrick. She's like that sometimes, kind of uppity with her nose in the air."

Mrs. Tomkins couldn't have been more than forty, her own face an almost identical white mask with Jean's. But lines were sketched in around the lips and eyes; the blank paper was written on; but her blue eyes had more than a touch of humour in them.

"Eagle phoned," she said. He's all right. But it's Jean I'm worried about. She thinks she's a heroine in somebody's novel. Not that you're any first prize in the Irish Sweepstakes. Still, you are a human being."

Patrick was surprised, but kept himself from showing it. "Thank you, ma'am. I can say the same about you."

Mrs. Tomkins's eyes strayed to the river, its blue waves capped with white. She spoke to herself more than to him, the daughter a distant ghost in her mother's eyes.

"She was reading the *Morte d'Arthur* last year, about the Knights of the Round Table. Sometimes she thinks she's Guinevere. That makes things difficult if you're not Launcelot or Arthur. And, Patrick, you don't look like Launcelot or Arthur."

"Sorry," he said, with a straight face.

Jean's mother ignored the comment. "I think she'll get over it – if we give her time." And now the tone was conspiratorial. "Can you give her some time?"

Patrick hesitated. "She was pretty definite, telling me to go away."

"She'll change," Mrs. Tomkins said. "Again, and again. We all do. Wait a week, then speak to her. Will you do that?"

Patrick thought of the girl's unbending attitude, eyes like marbles, the finality of her voice. He hesitated. "I'll think about it." And realized this was ungenerous after Jean's mother had been so open and vulnerable herself.

"No, you won't," Mrs. Tomkins said, her voice losing its vibrancy. "You won't think about it." And there was an appeal in the words. "It's happened before, you know. She can touch someone else, someone like you. And then it ends, for no reason or any reason.

"You know," and she looked at him intently, "I'm sure you know – I'm afraid for her."

Patrick took Kevin Morris along when he went to see McPherson that evening. When the two of them had manoeuvred Mrs. McMaster's wheelchair down the mountain earlier, she remarked that they acted like old friends in the flush of reacquaintance after long separation.

But to mention that brought their less friendly relations to mind, which both thought should be avoided.

McPherson was more tactful, perhaps sensing how it was between them. His doggy face was relaxed, dewlaps under his chin hung like decorations of a long life. He wore a ragged old bathrobe, lounging in the apartment's only comfortable chair, which Portugee had once reserved for himself.

"Well, boys," he greeted them, "the town seems to have survived. And I hear tell the war is nearly over. What d'ye think of that?"

"Seems like Red McPherson is going to survive as well. I'm more interested in that right now," Patrick said. "And this is Kevin Morris; he lives next door to me."

The old man nodded at Kevin. "Yeah, I'll survive. But the flu left me feeling like a rooster being near pecked to death in a barnyard full of chickens. Either of you care for some hair of the dog?"

He produced a half-empty pint bottle, waving it at them. "No? Well, I don't mind if I do." He swigged a good two ounces, then made the bottle disappear somewhere in the old bathrobe.

"Sit ye down and tell me about yourselves. Some o' them bangs fair shook me outa bed, like the world was farting fire. Minds me of when we had to blow out log jams on the Madawaska."

"Mr. McPherson is an old logger," Patrick said to Kevin by way of explanation.

The "old logger" looked at them reproachfully. "I don't mind so much actually bein old, though it ain't the condition I was born to. But I object to this continual reference to my extreme age, on accounta it seems to accentuate the negative."

Patrick was astonished at what was being done to words in McPherson's mouth; the commonplace sounds were not coming out as expected.

"Huh?" he said, feeling inadequate.

"I was actually a young logger. And when I was forty-five, I started to become an old farmer."

The dewlaps swung and stabilized. McPherson's eyes twinkled at the two boys. He turned to Kevin. "An old man yarnin about the past; if I say it, that's okay. That's where we all came from, the past . . ."

"It doesn't matter how old you are or how young you were, not to me," Kevin said. "But would you explain that young logger, old farmer mention . . . please."

Kevin smiled at the old man with such charm and warmth Patrick felt demeaned that he hadn't suspected these depths of character in his friend.

"It's a kinda story," McPherson said.

Oh migawd, thought Patrick, and withdrew mentally from centre stage in favour of Kevin.

"I'd been in the woods for donkey's years, I guess," McPherson said. "Then I started to think about trees."

"And what did you think?" Kevin wanted to know, without a hint of condescension in his voice.

"It was the pine forests at night that did it. I useta go out there after work, when the poker games was goin on in the shanties. Snow on the ground. Enough light from stars and moon to see my shadow in the woods. Only my shadow. I was listenin all the time I was there. The wind made its way through the upper branches, through the pine needles, and it was a kinda song – "

"What did the song say?" Patrick asked.

"I don't know. Of course it wasn't like a human song. And it was very old, maybe five hundred years, maybe a lot more. . . . And the old ones, you could hear them say their names when the wind came to wake them from daylight sleep. And all the trees in the woods said their names. Their names was music – "

An exalted note came into McPherson's voice. "I useta watch them in the dark and listen. Before the moon went

252

down. Snow around their trunks melted in a circle, and that sound in the branches that came from way back – I think it came from when trees was first trees, when they began to remember what the world was like in the old days – "

A weird little tremor mounted Patrick's backbone and stopped at his brain. He tried to keep his voice ordinary: "And that's when you became a farmer?"

"That's when. I read books when I got the chance. When they first came here from the old country, travellers said there was pine trees two hundred and fifty feet tall; there was trees and the fathers and grandfathers of trees. There was mothers and grandmothers in the old time. And when the seeds of the pine-cone grew, it was two and three years before they grew enough to make new trees. A human woman takes nine months to make a child. *Pinus strobus*, it takes him an' her years – "

"Him and her?" Kevin said.

"Where's yer school botany?" McPherson said, smiling. "There's always man and woman, him *and* her."

Jean would find that pleasing, Patrick thought: the centuries leap back to King Arthur and Guinevere; the Romans gone and Launcelot wandering the forests of ancient Britain to look for her.

"You ever talk about this to your friends?" Kevin asked. "There must've been times – "

"Sure – sharpenin axes, time after tea when you were gettin ready to go back into the bush; and before sleep when the voices in your head began to quiet down – "

McPherson was silent then, a little shrunken in the big chair from illness, his mind casting back to an earlier time. It occurred to Patrick that the old man was a mystic, not the kind with turban and labelled "swami" by followers, but an everyday mystic, one who conjured water magic from a kitchen faucet. Whose mind leaped around things, saw the world differently from the measurers and counters and explainers. A rushing warmth for McPherson flooded Patrick's mind and heart.

He glanced at Kevin, wondering what he was thinking. Anticipating the look, Kevin's eyes met his own, a wavelength established for both. The pause lengthened, became rather uncanny, broken only by Patrick rising to stoke the woodstove.

"You think it's kinda odd?" McPherson said defensively.

"No," Kevin said. But perhaps it actually was a little strange. "I've heard of people who stopped hunting because they didn't want to kill any more animals. Maybe that was partly the idea of killing, and partly the look in a deer's eyes when it died."

"But trees?" McPherson inquired, the question probing Kevin's insides rather than his own. "Trees? *Pinus strobus?*"

"You had a feeling, I guess." And Kevin was uncertain now.

"Yes, I had a feeling. . . . Other lives than mine, you might say. I remember my feelings then, that being here was a gift, *is* a gift, even if I didn't know the name of the giver. As the white pine was a gift to earth. And in the winter, the long winter – "

"Yes?"

"After work, after I'd eaten, going out into the snow, there was a friendliness about the forest. Only bear or wolverine you had to think about sometimes." McPherson's eyes were blank, allowing shadows of the past to flicker into the present.

"It was a shadow, the wolverine. I only saw but two all those years. A kind of flatness in the snow, a shadow that moved when other shadows were still. Once the moon was behind clouds, like a bandage over my eyes. When it cleared again I saw animal eyes. From not more than five feet away. What they were doing was judging me, they were deciding whether to allow me to go away or whether – it was looking into another kind of darkness, those eyes.

There was light inside them. Things were moving, dice being shaken. Then another cloud crossed the moon, and the thing was gone. As if I'd imagined it."

He shrugged, eyes again focusing on his visitors. "That's by the way, of course. I quit the woods after that. I was forty-five years old and had never done anything else. I learned. And after that was the farm. . . ."

Kevin stared at him in wonderment.

McPherson spoke directly to him, "I wanted to explain about myself to Patrick." Again gently.

"We should go," Patrick said to McPherson. "You'll be tired. And where've Phil Wright and Sideways gotten to? Are they planning permanent residence here?"

"Sideways is getting reacquainted with the Trenton police force," McPherson said drily, "in case of future need of friends." He chuckled. "And Phil Wright is considering marriage. He discussed it with me earlier. It seems his prospective bride is much younger. . . ."

Getting into bed after leaving Kevin, and forgiving himself for being amused by Kevin's reaction to McPherson, he was still puzzled. Lying in darkness, he retraced his memory of events for the past month or so, conjuring the faces of people in his head, his mind having photographed something about them, caught them smiling or frowning or thoughtful. With concentrated effort, the shadows would come clear briefly, and features of people he knew stand out from their background.

But his concentration wavered; the faces would not stay with him. There was just a flash of them, then a page in his mind turned and they were gone. Even his mother was transient there. Briefly, he had seen Portugee, even heard the old man's laughter like dry leaves rattling together. And McPherson's red-brown wrinkled face with pendulous dewlaps, which gave him the look of an elderly blood-hound.

And that idea of McPherson's, wanting to make *Pinus strobus* immune to murder by profane loggers, sacred to grow and increase the pine-tree tribe for five hundred years by divine dispensation. McPherson's own fiat and decree. It was biblical, it was earth law. Beasts of the forest and flowers of the field roamed freely in his brain, clamouring for immortality. And before the little white engineers of his mind stopped building bridges to connect large land masses of facts, he happened on a discovery that kept him awake a little longer.

McPherson was different every time he saw him. The old man tailored his speech to his audience. With Phil Wright and Sideways Smith, he talked like a logger in a cambuse shanty at Palmer Rapids or on the Madawaska. With Dr. Johnson, he had been an amateur historian of the cholera epidemic in early nineteenth-century Canada. With Patrick, he had been a gentle replacement for Portugee. With Kevin, a biology instructor.

A tide of affection for Red McPherson overwhelmed him, and he slept.


Through a gap in the window sheet came a stammer of breeze. Patrick woke abruptly, listening for Gyp stirring under the woodshed where the dog sometimes groaned, preparing for dawn. Then he remembered: Gyp was dead. And Portugee was dead. There were no replacements for sorrow and loss. A feeling of desolation poured into his mind. The small bird that was part of himself flew franti-cally among white pillars and grey grottoes of his brain, in an effort to escape the knowledge of loss. . . .

And he thought: I am saying goodbye to another part of myself, a younger self and a more innocent one. And went over all the reasons for regret that Jean had not stayed what she seemed to be. The candid words from her, that absolute calm, broken when a thought was immediately visible as a white shadow crossing the white face.

But why should the girl stay the same? He, Patrick, had not. Why should Jean? And neither had McPherson. Nor Kevin. Nor anybody else if he knew them longer than the long instant of meeting and judging.

There was something attractive about her being Guinevere in a long white gown spangled with sequins, waiting for pure-hearted Launcelot to come along on his horse and knock off the fearsome dragon just as it was about to eat her alive. But only attractive when she was aware of her own playacting at being Guinevere, and not if taken over entirely by the dead queen. The situation was both sad and funny, he thought, though am I playacting at being me, Patrick Cameron, making myself up as I go along? Perhaps, as time passes, both she and I will come closer to knowing who we are. . . .

He looked back at himself, across the long summer of 1918. That other self at the telescope's opposite end was almost a stranger. There was no doubt, no doubt at all, that he had changed. His own appetites and attitudes had changed and developed; the enormous weight of having adults staring at the adolescent that was himself had lifted from his shoulders. Other people thought of him differently now, even speculated about him. He could see it in their faces.

It had been more than legs and body that thinned and grew taut with exercise. The mind was keeping time with the same music that his body already knew. There was a mystery about himself that lured and beckoned, projecting above the apparent surface of himself. And all this last summer, the white-gowned figure of Guinevere as Jean paraded across his mind into the bedroom, with a swagger of hips that reality could not equal.

He smiled and fell asleep again.

257

# 14

THE RIVER THAT SAID *GILMOUR! GILMOUR!* as it leaped over No. 1 dam was swollen and engorged by autumn rains. Tributary creeks and streams poured into it from the north and west and east. Downriver from the dam, inside a calm protected area, were floating bodies. Bloated by internal gases, perch, rock bass, sunfish, small mouth bass, pickerel, and a few wayward pike jostled together in the October sun. As if the dead had clustered together for comfort. Colours dull, they rocked gently up and down with the small waves.

A sudden surge of water made the bodies thud softly together without sound. From the river's upper reaches, a two-foot pike nosed among them. Its shadowy arrow-shaped body was a dark green light among the dead. Then it dashed away quickly for no apparent reason, its killer-face a mask of teeth and appetite. Farther south, at the town bridge, it came upon a small perch; and swallowed it and was gone between one thought and another.

Overhead, Canada geese were flying south. They talked to each other in the sky, about what great aviators they were, what marvellous lovers, and how they're the bravest birds in this world or any other. No one contradicted them. Smaller birds were quiet, having in mind the possible presence of predators.

The yellow clouds of sulphur in the sky and corrosive nitric acid in the river disappeared quickly. But their effects lingered. Small animals and birds died in forests near the town; fish died in the river. Human casualties from the flu epidemic were much larger, as a result of exposure to cold and weather during the first panicky flight.

In November, the earth's northern axis tilted farther away from the sun. Snow fell. At the burned and shattered ruins of British Chemical, traces of the disaster disappeared. White replaced black. Arches and grottoes like those of a children's fairyland transformed the site. Foundations undulated and footings became secretive. Earth was smoothing over and disguising its more unpleasant places with the cosmetics of time.

During the years immediately following the First World War, children played in the ruins. Few of them were aware of the reasons their playground existed. Succeeding generations were entirely unaware of how close their town had come to disappearing from the face of the earth. If they had known, it's unlikely that any subsequent event would have been different.

Al Purdy was born in 1918, in Wooler, Ontario. He wrote his first poem at the age of thirteen and published his first collection of poetry, *The Enchanted Echo*, in 1944. In a writing career that spanned over fifty years, he published over thirty books of poetry; a novel; two volumes of memoirs, most recently *Reaching for the Beaufort Sea*; and four books of correspondence, including *Margaret Laurence – Al Purdy: A Friendship in Letters*. His final collection of poetry, *Beyond Remembering: The Collected Poems of Al Purdy*, will be released posthumously in the fall of 2000. Purdy also wrote radio and television plays for the CBC, served as writer-in-residence at a number of Canadian universities, and edited several anthologies of poetry.

As a teenager during the Great Depression, Purdy rode the rails across Canada. In the Second World War he served in the RCAF, and after the war he worked at a wide variety of jobs until the early 1960s, when he was able to support himself as a writer, editor, and poet.

Moving to Roblin Lake in Ameliasburg, Ontario, in the late 1950s provided Purdy with a base from which he travelled and wrote. Later, he divided his time between North Saanich, British Columbia, and the Roblin Lake cottage.

Purdy won numerous awards for his poetry, including the Canadian Authors Association Award, two Governor General's Awards (for *The Cariboo Horses* in 1965 and *The Collected Poems of Al Purdy, 1956-1986* in 1986), and, most recently, the Voice of the Land Award, a special award created by the League of Canadian Poets specifically to honour Purdy's unique contribution to Canada. He was appointed to the Order of Canada in 1982 and to the Order of Ontario in 1987. Al Purdy died in North Saanich, B.C., on April 21, 2000.